D1012996

Giant
SHORT & SHIVERY

Giant
SHORT & SHIVERY

Retold by
Robert D. San Souci

Illustrated by Katherine Coville
and Jacqueline Rogers

BARNES
&NOBLE
BOOKS
NEW YORK

Short & Shivery
Text copyright © 1987 by Robert D. Sans Souci
Illustrations © 1987 by Doubleday
A division of Bantam Doubleday Dell Publishing Group, Inc.

More Short & Shivery
Text copyright © 1994 by Robert D Sans Souci
Illustrations © by Katherine Coville and Jacqueline Rogers

This edition published by Barnes & Noble, Inc.,
by arrangement with Bantam Doubleday Dell Books for Young Readers,
a division of Bantam Doubleday Dell Publishing Group Inc., New York, New York, USA

All rights reserved. No part of this book may be used or
reproduced in any manner whatsoever without the written permission of the Publisher.

1998 Barnes & Noble Books

ISBN 0-7607-1145-3

Printed and bound in the United States of America

98 99 00 01 02 M 9 8 7 6 5 4 3 2 1

SHORT
& SHIVERY

THIRTY CHILLING TALES

Retold by ROBERT D. SAN SOUCI

Illustrated by Katherine Coville

ACKNOWLEDGMENTS

Grateful acknowledgment is made to the following for permission to adapt their copyrighted material.

"The Witch Cat" is based in part upon the tale of the same name in *Ghosts of the Carolinas* by Nancy Roberts, copyright 1962, 1967, and used with the kind permission of Bright Mountain Books, Asheville, North Carolina.

"The Ghostly Little Girl" is based on a story by Randall A. Reinstedt that appeared in Mr. Reinstedt's *Ghostly Tales & Mysterious Happenings of Old Monterey,* copyright 1977, used with the permission of Ghost Town Publications, Carmel, California.

"The Skeleton's Dance" is based, with the permission of the University of Chicago Press, on the story "The Skeleton's Song" in *Folktales of Japan,* edited by Keigo Seki, translated by Robert J. Adams, copyright 1963.

"Scared to Death" is based, with the permission of the University of South Carolina Press, on the story "The Leaning Tombstone" in *Charleston Ghosts* by Margaret Rhett Martin, copyright 1963.

To Al Schroeder,
who loves a scary story
almost as much as the author.

R.S.S.

Contents

Introduction

Welcome! Since you've taken a look in this book, I guess it's safe to assume you like to read spooky stories. I must admit that I enjoy a good shudder myself. The thirty stories in this book will introduce you to ghosts, goblins, and assorted other monsters. But beware! These creatures that are lurking in the shadows along a deserted street, or glimpsed in a lightning flash outside your window on a stormy night, or have just put a claw on the knob of the door into this room *(gotcha!)* are pretty creepy customers. Before you read any further, you might want to turn up the lights a bit or hang a clove of garlic on the wall.

Just in case. . . .

Over the years, I've read or heard hundreds of spooky stories, and I have found that some of the best are folktales that have been shared by people in moonlight or candlelight or electric light—sometimes for hundreds of years or more. Many such tales were handed down from storyteller to storyteller countless times, before someone finally wrote them down. Often they were changed slightly with each retelling, as a storyteller added his or her own details and a bit of local color. But the heart of such a story remains the same no matter how many different ways it's told: it has the power to capture our imaginations, give us a thrill of excitement (and chill us at the same time), and make us look at ourselves and our place in the world in a different way. And it might just reassure us that good can triumph, evil doesn't go unpunished, and courage can help us face down even the most frightening monsters.

The stories here come from many different times, from a variety of cultures, and from countries all around the world; but they have one thing in common: they're scary. In these pages, you'll encounter a dancing Japanese skeleton that tricks a murderer . . . a Russian vampire who plagues a peaceful village . . . a Canadian werewolf who haunts a winter forest by moonlight . . . a haunted gold mine in the Old West . . . a clay statue that comes to life . . . a ghost in Iceland, who returns from the dead to claim his bride . . . a goblin pony that takes its riders on a fearful Halloween journey . . . a boy who spies on a witch in colonial America and learns the terrible price of meddling with black magic . . . a brother and sister who battle an African demon . . . and a monster so strange that everyone sees it differently and no two people can agree what to call it.

I've retold these stories in my own way. Sometimes I've just changed or added a few details, shortened a very long tale, or made the old-fashioned language a bit easier to understand, as in the case of Washington Irving's fearsome "Adventure of the German Student." Sometimes I've taken a very brief incident and expanded it to a full-length story, to satisfy my own curiosity about what *might* have happened to the people in the story if the original storyteller had told it in a slightly different way. The story of "The Ghostly Little Girl" and her three best friends is a good example of taking an account that was only a few paragraphs long and making it into a longer story.

Sometimes I have combined several very short tales into a single story: "The Hunter in the Haunted Forest" weaves together into a single narrative three brief Teton Sioux stories of warriors who met ghosts when they were alone in the wild. Once in a while, as with the legend of the *Cegua,* a Central American demon which haunts the roads by night and drives travelers mad with its horrible appearance, I have used a description of the creature and its history as the basis for spinning my own, original story around such lore and legend.

What I've tried to do is make these stories my own, and share them in a way that you, the reader, can enjoy them and make them *your* own. I hope you'll have as much fun discovering these shivery tales now, as I did finding them earlier, and retelling them. For those of you who want to know more about the background of individual stories, I have included "Notes on Sources" at the end of this volume.

So, happy reading! And if you think you hear something scratching at the window or a footstep in the empty room overhead, just remember, it's only your imagination.

Probably.

The Robber Bridegroom

(adapted from the Brothers Grimm)

There was once a miller who had a beautiful daughter. He was a hard worker, so his business prospered, and he grew wealthy. A widower, he gave his only daughter fine dresses and shoes with silver buckles. For himself he bought a splendid cloak, a broad-brimmed hat with a huge ostrich feather, and a gold ring with a picture of his mill engraved on it, because this had brought him his riches.

One night, however, robbers broke into the mill, and stole his hat, cloak, and ring—and all the gold he had saved up. Then the old man said to his daughter, "You must marry soon. The world is full of wicked men, and you should have a husband to protect you. But he must be a wealthy man, because you deserve the fine things I can no longer buy you."

"I don't care if the man is rich or poor," said the girl, Elsa, "as long as I love him and he loves me."

"Tut," said her father impatiently, "if the right kind of bridegroom comes along and asks for your hand, I'll let him marry you."

Soon enough, a suitor turned up who was dressed in the

finest clothes, had boots with silver toes and tops, and rode a grand horse with a bridle trimmed in gold.

"I have seen your daughter when she walks to the village," said the stranger, "and I want her to be my wife."

The miller was dazzled by the man's garments and his horse's trappings, so he said, "She will be your wife."

But Elsa didn't love him as a bride-to-be ought to love her future bridegroom. She didn't trust him; and whenever she looked at him or thought about him, a shudder ran through her.

The stranger came often to the miller's house. Finally, he said to Elsa, "You're engaged to me, and yet you have never been to see me."

"I don't even know where your house is," the young woman answered, feeling a sudden chill in her heart.

Her suitor said, "My house is in the depths of the forest."

"Then I could never find my way there," Elsa said.

"Nonsense," said the stranger. "Next Sunday, you must come and see me. I've already invited some other guests, who are eager to meet you. So that you can find the way, I'll leave a trail of ashes to guide you."

Elsa started to protest, but her father said, "Tut!" Then to the richly dressed stranger he said, "She will be there. I will see to it."

When Saturday came, the girl was about to start out, because her bridegroom had told her the journey would take a day and a night on foot. She felt terribly frightened, though she did not know why. To be sure of finding her way back, she filled her pockets with dried peas and beans to mark her path. At the entrance to the forest, she found the trail of ashes, like a thin, gray thread, and followed it deep into the dark woods. But every step or two, she tossed a few peas and beans to her right or left.

She walked nearly that whole day and night, all the way into the heart of the forest. In the morning, which was almost as gloomy as midnight, she saw a house set by itself in a small clearing. It was so dark and dismal that she feared going any closer. But the trail of ashes led right to the front door, so she went up.

Elsa knocked softly several times; when no one answered, she went in. She saw nobody; there was a silence over all the rooms.

Suddenly, a voice cried:

> "Turn back, young woman! Run away!
> You've come to a robber's house this day."

She looked up and saw that the voice had come from a bird in a cage that was hanging in a window. Once more, it warned her:

> "Turn back, young woman! Run away!
> You've come to a robber's house this day."

She was about to turn and run, when she heard someone singing in a sweet, clear voice deep in the house. The voice was so gentle and sad that Elsa had to see who was singing. She followed the sound from room to room, all over the house, but they were all empty. At last she reached the cellar door. Descending the steep and narrow steps, she found an old blind woman who was sitting in a corner, shaking her head sadly, while she sang mournfully to herself.

"Who are you?" Elsa asked.

"I keep this unhappy house," explained the blind woman. "But what are you with such a young, kind voice doing here?"

"I'm to marry the master of the house," said Elsa.

"Alas! You poor child! You have no idea where you are. You're in the den of a thief and a murderer. Years ago I was brought here with a promise of marriage. Instead the villain blinded me so I could not run away, and has made me work harder than the most wretched slave. Now that I've grown weary and unable to work as I once did, he has brought you here. He will drive me into the woods to die, and he will blind you and make you take my place."

"Come with me," urged Elsa, "we'll run away together."

But as she was guiding the older woman toward the steps, they heard the sound of rough voices above. When Elsa recognized her bridegroom's voice, her heart sank.

But the old woman said, "Hide behind those chests in the corner, and be quiet as a mouse. Don't move, or everything is lost. Tonight, when the robbers are asleep, I'll fetch you. Then we can escape together."

Hardly had Elsa hidden behind a metal-bound chest, when the chief robber came to the head of the stairs and bellowed, "Come up and fix us dinner, or you'll regret it quick enough! My bride hasn't come, and I'm in a rare bad temper. In the morning, I will ride to demand my bride and have no more of these games! Her father is a greedy and foolish man; he will hand her over. And it's going to be harder for her than she can imagine, since she has disobeyed me. Now, hurry and set out some food and drink."

All through the afternoon and evening, Elsa listened to the roaring and stamping and laughter as the men grew drunk and began to argue among themselves. Hidden behind the chests, she trembled and shivered, dreading her fate if she were discovered.

Now one chest that was near her hand was partially opened; she could see gold gleaming faintly in what little light fell down through the open cellar door. Carefully Elsa

lifted out several coins, a belt buckle, and a brooch, all of finest gold. Then, reaching in more deeply, she discovered a massive gold ring with the picture of her father's mill engraved on it. She knew in a moment that these robbers were the ones who had stolen all their gold months before.

Keeping quiet, she dropped the ring in her skirt pocket. Then she waited, while the sounds above continued, though it was growing later and later. She began to fear the robbers would go on crashing about until morning, and the old woman's plan would fail.

Upstairs, however, the blind woman put a sleeping potion in the thieves' wine. Soon, one by one, they lay down and went to sleep, snoring loudly.

When they were all asleep, the housekeeper called down to Elsa, "Come quickly! We must hurry!"

The girl hastily came out from behind the chests and climbed the stairs. She had to step over the sleepers, who lay in rows upon the floor. She was dreadfully afraid of touching them, for fear one would wake, but she got through without mishap.

The other woman was waiting by the open door. Elsa took her hand, and they hurried away as quickly as they could from the robbers' den.

All the ashes had been blown away by the wind, but the peas and beans, being heavier, remained to show them their way in the moonlight.

They walked the whole night and reached the mill the next afternoon. There Elsa told her father everything she had been through and the plan she had for trapping the wicked thief. Then her father hastened to the village to invite all his friends and relations to a feast, while Elsa and the blind woman set out tables and cooked every bit of food in the house.

When the robber and his men rode up to claim Elsa, the

miller welcomed them with a great show of friendship. "My daughter will go away with you this very day," he said, "but first, share a meal with us in honor of my daughter's wedding."

The robbers, who had awakened to find their housekeeper gone, and had been forced to scrounge a wretched breakfast for themselves, were only too glad to sit down and enjoy themselves.

During the meal, the miller asked each person to tell a story to entertain the other guests. When it came Elsa's turn, she was silent. But her bridegroom said, "Come, my sweet, you must tell us a story, too. I won't have people thinking my bride is a dull wit."

"Very well," the girl said, "I will tell you a dream I have had. In it I was walking alone in a gloomy wood, and I came to a solitary house, where not a soul was to be seen. A cage was hanging in the window of one of the rooms. In it was a bird which cried:

"Turn back, young woman! Run away!
You've come to a robber's house this day."

"It repeated the same words twice."

"I don't think I care for this story much," grumbled the bridegroom.

"This was only a dream, my love!" protested Elsa. Then she continued, "I heard someone singing a sweet song, so I walked all through the rooms, but they were empty. At last I went down to the cellar, where I found a blind woman singing to herself. When I told her I had come to marry the master of the house, she cried, 'Alas, you poor child! You're in the den of a thief and murderer!' Then she told me how he planned to blind me, and make me a slave in her place."

"Be quiet! I've had enough of this foolishness!" shouted the bridegroom, rising in his seat.

"This was only a dream, my love!" said Elsa. Then she quickly went on, "The robbers returned at that moment, so the old woman hid me behind some chests in the cellar. While they were making merry upstairs, I looked in one of the chests and discovered—"

"Silence!" bellowed the bridegroom, drawing his dagger to threaten the girl. But she bravely finished, "I discovered a gold ring, with a picture of this mill on it! The ring that belonged to my father and was stolen by robbers months ago! *And here is that ring!*"

So saying, Elsa produced the ring and showed it to the company.

When the bridegroom heard these words, he turned pale as ashes and tried to escape, his men with him. But the guests seized them all and turned them over to the king's soldiers, who took them away and had them hanged for their crimes.

Jack Frost

(from a Russian folktale)

Once upon a time there was a widow who had a daughter of her own and a stepdaughter. Whenever her own daughter said or did anything, the woman would pat her on the head and say, "Clever girl!" But no matter how hard the stepdaughter tried, she was always being called "foolish" or "lazy" by the woman, who often scolded her and sometimes beat her.

The truth of the matter was that the stepdaughter, Maria, was kind and beautiful, while the woman's own daughter, Yagishna, was plain and selfish. But her mother saw only what she wanted to see, so she praised Yagishna continually and made Maria's life a misery. Even an angry storm blows itself out at last, but the old woman's hatred for her stepdaughter never lessened. She said one cruel thing after another, and she was forever grabbing Maria by the collar of her dress to shake her for being "such a burden on us."

One day, in the dead of winter, the stepmother made up her mind to have done with her stepdaughter. She told her aged servant, "Old man, take Maria into the open field where the bitter frost is the thickest and leave her there. I don't want to set eyes upon her or hear her voice ever again. And if you value your life, don't take her to the warm house of your relatives."

The old man begged her not to force him to do such a wicked thing, but the stepmother would not relent. Because he knew that his family would starve if he lost his job, he put the girl on a sled. He tried to cover Maria with an old horse cloth, but Yagishna saw this and snatched it away with a sharp laugh.

"Do as my mother says, or you'll find yourself and all your children out in the cold along with her," she said nastily.

Heavyhearted, the old man drove Maria out to the open fields near the edge of the forest. He set her down on a heap of snow, hugged her, then hastened home as fast as possible, so that he wouldn't see the child's death.

Poor little Maria remained where she was, shivering and softly saying some prayers. Suddenly a strange-looking man came leaping and jumping from the forest toward the girl. He wore a greatcoat of silver-white fur, a high peaked cap of the same silvery fur, and boots of white leather worked with silver. He had thick white eyebrows and a bushy white beard, while his nose was as red as an apple. His coat and hat were spangled with diamonds, and silver bells on a white ribbon across his chest jingled as he bounded toward Maria.

"Little girl, little girl, I'm Jack Frost, the Ruby-Nosed," he said. "I bring the winter wherever I go."

"Oh," she said sadly. "Welcome, Jack Frost! God must have sent you to take me away from this world. It will be hard to leave, for it all looks so beautiful today: the snow is so white and the air is so clean and the ice sparkles like diamonds."

Now he was about to touch her body and freeze her to

death, but he was moved by her wise words and sad eyes. Instead he reached into one of the immense pockets of his greatcoat, pulled out a fur coat, and tossed it to Maria.

She quickly put it on, then squatted on her heels. Sitting in the snow, she watched while Jack Frost went leaping and jumping back to the edge of the forest. In a twinkling, he was back, carrying something in his arms. "Little girl, little girl, I'm Jack Frost, the Ruby-Nosed," he cried. "I have brought something for you."

"Is it my death?" Maria asked fearfully.

But he had not returned to take her life away. He brought her a chest, heavy and deep, and filled with bedding and petticoats and all sorts of warm clothes.

Then Maria sat on the chest in her fur coat, laughing and clapping while Jack Frost danced for her.

A third time he bounded away to the forest's edge; this time, when he came back, he gave her a cloak embroidered with silver threads and studded with pearls and diamonds.

Wonderingly, Maria drew this cloak over her fur coat. She looked as beautiful and elegant as a grand duchess. For a long time she sat there happily singing songs, while Jack Frost danced lightly over the sparkling ice and snow.

Meanwhile, her stepmother said to her servant, "Go, old man, and bring home my daughter so that we may bury her." Then she set about fixing the evening meal for herself and Yagishna.

A short time later, the gate creaked, the doors flew open, and the old servant dragged in a chest, heavy and deep. Maria followed, radiant and regal as a princess.

When the stepmother saw all the riches Maria had returned with, she immediately set an extra place at the table for the girl. She sat her stepdaughter down, pretended to ask her forgiveness, made a great show of giving her the daintiest morsels (even though Yagishna complained about this), until she had gotten the whole story out of Maria.

As soon as Maria was asleep, the old woman called her servant. "Old man," she ordered, "harness the horses and have them ready to go at the first light of dawn. Take my daughter to the same field, in the very same place, and leave her there. Then return for her in the evening, to gather up the treasures she will receive."

In the morning, the old woman struggled to awaken her daughter.

"Let me sleep," complained Yagishna. "It's too cold to do anything else."

"You must go and get treasures from Jack Frost, you lazy creature," her mother scolded.

"Can't we just take Maria's gifts for ourselves?" asked her daughter crossly.

"We will, we will," said her mother impatiently, "but why settle for one treasure when we could have two? Now, get up!"

Grumbling, Yagishna did as she was told. She put on her warmest coat and hat and boots. When she was on the sled, her mother bundled her up in furs and blankets. Then the old servant drove her to the field and left her there, just as the morning sun turned the ice crystals bright as diamonds.

Yagishna sat on her pile of furs and tried to keep her eyes open.

Suddenly Jack Frost came prancing from the edge of the forest.

"Young woman, young woman, I am Jack Frost the Ruby-Nosed," he said.

"Then be quick and bring me a treasure," said Yagishna, who thought he looked foolish with his leaping about and

jingling bells and nose like an apple stuck to the front of his face.

"Young woman, young woman, I am Jack Frost the Ruby-Nosed," he repeated. "I bring the winter wherever I go."

"When you've brought me my treasure," said Yagishna disagreeably, "you can go, and take winter with you. It's ugly and cold. Now, where is my gift?"

"Young woman, young woman, I am Jack Frost the Ruby-Nosed," he cried, dancing closer to the girl. "And here is your gift of diamonds and silver."

And he stretched out his hands to Yagishna.

In the evening, while Maria stoked the fire, her step-mother anxiously watched the door for the return of her daughter.

Suddenly she heard the creak of the gate outside. Without waiting, she flew to the door and saw the old servant standing beside the sled, cap in hand. Impatiently the old woman pulled at the mound of furs on the back of the sled.

"Yagishna, foolish child, come out from underneath. You'll be warm inside in a minute, but first show me your treasure."

To her horror, when the woman pulled back the last fur, she saw her daughter lying there, a cold corpse. Silver snowflakes frosted her eyelashes, and ice like diamond chips beaded her lips where her last breath had frozen.

The shock was too much, and the greedy stepmother fell down dead in the snow.

Maria became mistress of the farm, where the old servant continued to serve her faithfully all the rest of his days.

The Waterfall of Ghosts

(from the Japanese writings of Lafcadio Hearn)

There was once a small village in Japan very near a cascade called the Waterfall of Ghosts. No one could say for sure why it was called this. Some people thought they saw the twisting shapes of ghosts in the mists that rose from the rocks onto which the water poured; some claimed to hear ghostly voices—or the voices of gods or demons—in the roar. It was considered a holy place, so the villagers built a small shrine at the foot of the falls and left a little wooden money box there for visitors to make offerings.

One frosty evening in the last century, the women and girls who worked in the local factory, where they spun hemp into lengths of rope, gathered around the big iron stove after their work was done.

As they warmed their hands by the coal fires, they amused themselves by telling ghost stories. By the time a dozen stories had been told, even the bravest began listening with new ears to the whisper of wind at the doors and window frames. They began to grow uneasy at the idea of walking home through the dark.

Then one of the younger girls, who was enjoying the

little thrills of fear she was getting, said, "Just think of going all alone tonight to the Waterfall of Ghosts!"

Her suggestion provoked shudders, followed by nervous laughter.

"Why," said the girl, unwilling to let the matter rest, "I'll give all the hemp I spun today to any person who goes!"

"So will I!" exclaimed another, caught up in the spirit of the game.

"And I!" another promised.

Soon all but one of the women had offered her day's output of rope as a prize to anyone brave enough to go to the waterfall that night.

The only spinner who did not join with the others was a young woman named O-Katsu, the wife of the village carpenter. "Listen," she said, "if you will all really agree to hand over the hemp you spun today, I will go to the Waterfall of Ghosts."

Her words were met with cries of astonishment; most thought she was joking. But when she repeated her challenge several times, they realized she was serious. Each of the spinners promised to give up her share of the day's work to O-Katsu, if she went to the waterfall.

"But how will we know if she really goes there?" several women asked.

"Why, let her bring back the money box from the shrine," said the old woman the others had nicknamed "Grandmother." She added, "That will be proof enough. She can return the money in the morning, after she has shown it to us."

"I'll bring it, you'll see," boasted O-Katsu, who did not believe in ghosts. In her greed she had also made up her mind to take the money from the offering box before she returned it.

Bundling a warm robe around her, she hurried out into

the street. The night was frosty but clear. The young woman's wooden clogs made crunching sounds on the ice-crusted road as she hurried down the empty street. All the doors and windows of the houses she passed were shut tight against the piercing cold. But O-Katsu only pulled her robe more tightly about her, and thought of the coins she would take from the shrine in a short while, and the hemp she would take from her fellow workers in the morning.

Soon she left the village behind and hurried along the road that ran between frozen rice fields that glittered in the starlight. For nearly half an hour, she traveled through the great silence. Then she heard the distant roar of the Waterfall of Ghosts.

A little while later she began following a narrow path that wound under high cliffs. Her way grew darker and more dangerous as she neared the bottom, but she had visited the falls before, so she knew the way. The roar of the cascade grew louder and louder.

The path ran around a huge boulder and opened onto a stretch of pebbled shore. The sound of the falls was now deafening; she could see the water like a shining ribbon of silk against the black cliffs. In the starlight she could just make out the curved roof of the shrine and the shadowy square of the money box underneath.

She rushed forward eagerly and stretched out her hand to take it.

But the sound of the waterfall suddenly became a babble of voices crying, "Oh! Wicked woman!"

For a moment O-Katsu stood frozen, gripped with terror.

But she was a bold young woman. "It's only the sound of the water," she said to herself. When she looked at the falls, she seemed to see strange, twisted shapes boiling

about the base. But she told herself, "That's only the mist."

She snatched up the money box and ran.

Behind her the chorus of ghostly voices cried, "Oh! Oh! Oh! Wicked, wicked woman!"

O-Katsu did not stop running until she reached the top of the path. There she paused a moment, gasping for breath. Then she ran back toward the village. Around her, snow began to fall lightly on the ice-covered fields, then faster and faster. A wind rose and tried to push her back the way she had come; in its howling she thought she could hear angry voices crying, "O-Katsu! O-Katsu!"

But she kept on, her robe wrapped snugly around her, and only her eyes uncovered. The snow was drifting so high that even her tall clogs could not keep her feet dry. But she was back in the village now, and she could see the lights of the hemp factory ahead.

Before she went any farther, she took shelter in an alley-way between two buildings and opened the money box. She took all but a handful of copper coins and put these in her kimono. Then she walked toward the lighted windows of the factory.

The other women had all stayed to see if O-Katsu would make good her boast. They cried out in amazement when she entered, panting, with the money box from the shrine.

They brought her to the fire, asking breathless questions about what had happened. O-Katsu told them in a few sentences about hearing ghostly voices—though she did not tell them that the voices had called her "wicked." She said nothing about the coins she had stolen. When the woman nicknamed "Grandmother" opened the box and saw only a few coppers in the bottom, O-Katsu was loudest in crying out how miserly people were to leave such a miserable offering at a shrine.

"How brave you are, O-Katsu," said the young girl whose challenge had started the whole business. "You have certainly earned the hemp we promised."

The others all agreed, and they good-naturedly turned their day's output over to O-Katsu. Then they hurried away to their own homes.

When she was alone, O-Katsu took the stolen coins out of her kimono to count them by the ruddy glow of the fire.

But the offering box, on the floor beside her feet, suddenly began rocking from side to side.

"Oh! What is this?" cried the startled young woman.

As if to answer her, the lid of the box suddenly flew open, and a white mist, like steam, issued from it. O-Katsu looked on in horror, as the mist began to take on strange forms and suddenly became a howling cloud of ghosts. Their bodies were drawn out to amazing lengths; their legs dwindled away to nothingness; their necks were long and twisted like snakes; they stretched their long arms out and clutched at O-Katsu with their thin, pale fingers. Around and around the frightened woman they spun, like a horrible whirlpool, screeching, "Wicked woman! Wicked woman!"

O-Katsu thought she might faint. She sank to her knees and begged the ghosts to leave her alone. Then an idea occurred to her. She took the coins she still held in her hands and returned them to the offering box. When all the money had been put back, the ghosts poured themselves like a waterfall down into the box. The lid closed with a snap.

Quickly dressing in her warm robes, O-Katsu took the box and hurried back to the shrine. There she replaced it, with a promise to give the spirits of that place all the money she would get from selling the hemp she had gained by her disrespectful deed.

This she did the very next morning, and she was never troubled by ghosts again.

The Ghost's Cap

(from a Russian folktale)

In a certain village there was a girl who was as full of mischief as she was lazy. Though her mother and father would nag at her to help with the cooking or mending or sweeping, she would slip away to meet with her friends, who were as useless as she was. They would sit on the banks of the river, gossiping and chattering away, while their mothers washed the clothes and spread them on the bank to dry, near the churchyard.

One day Anya and her friends began talking about who was the boldest. The boasting went on and on, until Anya finally declared, "I'm not afraid of *anything!*"

"Well, then," said one young man, Ivan, "if you're not afraid, go at midnight to the graveyard. My father and uncle say there's a ghost who sits on a tombstone there from the stroke of midnight until the first light of morning. Go, make the ghost tell you its name, and I'll believe that no one is as brave as you. And I'll give you the silver buttons off my jacket that you've admired for so long."

"Oh, *those!*" said the greedy girl, with a toss of her braids. "I'd have to have more than *them* to go to the churchyard at midnight and meet a ghost." In fact she did not believe there was any ghost, because she knew that the young man's father and uncle were notorious for the amount of vodka they drank. They were often seeing spirits in the night, after they'd downed too many glasses of liquor.

"If you'll do it, I'll give you two lengths of lace," said one girl.

"And I'll give you twenty *kopecks*," offered another girl.

Soon Anya had extracted promises for all sorts of things from her friends. She vowed to go to the graveyard that very night, at the stroke of midnight, and force the ghost to tell her its name.

When she went home that evening, her mother grumbled, "The dust is piling up in the corners of every room, because you won't do your sweeping."

"Soon," said Anya, taking out her favorite embroidered jacket and beginning to cut off the wooden buttons, thinking how grand Ivan's silver ones would look in their stead.

Her father cleared his throat impatiently. "You'd be better off learning to cook a decent meal and do an honest day's work, than worrying about how you look. You'll die a pauper in rags, if you don't have a care."

"Never," said the girl, thinking about the lace and *kopecks* and other things her cleverness would win her this night.

Her parents just threw up their hands and shook their heads at each other.

Shortly before midnight, when her mother and father were asleep, Anya pulled on her shawl and slipped out of the cottage. She planned to walk to the edge of the church-yard, because she was sure some of her friends would be watching from their windows to be sure she was doing what she promised. When she got there, she intended to turn right around and come home. In the morning, she would tell her friends the ghost was the ghost of Old Peter, who had died the spring before. That would satisfy them, and they would have to give her the things they had promised.

So she strolled to the crumbling, low stone wall around the cemetery. She pushed her way through the rusting gate. The full moon shone brightly, filling the place with pale light. Just inside, she saw what looked like a corpse dressed in white from head to foot, sitting on a tombstone.

Anya wasn't the least bit afraid: she thought it was Ivan playing a trick on her. So she ran up to the figure and, pulling the cap off it, shouted, "You won't frighten me!"

The ghostly figure held its peace, never uttering a word. "Are you a ghost waiting for the stroke of midnight to speak?" she teased, "or are you the boy who will have no silver buttons on his jacket in the morning?"

Laughing, she ran back through the moon-splashed streets. When she got home, she looked closer at her prize, and found it was a moldy white cap, half filled with loose earth.

"Ugh!" she cried, tossing it into a dusty corner of her room. Then she blew out the candle and climbed into bed. Three times she came awake, thinking she heard someone tapping at the window. In the rising wind, she thought she heard a voice whispering, "Give me back my cap! Give me back my cap!" But each time she relit the candle and threw open the shutters, she discovered only darkness. Finally she slept soundly until the morning.

The next day she met her friends on the riverbank. She told them she had gone to the churchyard the night before, and two girls admitted they had been spying on her and had indeed seen her walking down the lane toward the cemetery.

"Did you meet the ghost?" asked Ivan.

"To be sure," Anya said, "it's the spirit of Old Peter, who died last spring. He told me so himself. Then I snatched his cap as proof, and here it is."

She held out the dirt-stained cap, enjoying the way her friends shuddered and pulled away from the trophy. Only Ivan stretched out a finger to touch it. Anya tossed it at him, but he jerked away, so it fell onto the grass between them. "Don't you want your cap back," she teased, "since you lost it last night?"

"I've never seen the thing before," said Ivan. Then he reached into his pocket and dropped the silver jacket buttons into Anya's cupped hands.

"You're a liar," she laughed, "but you pay your debts like an honest man." Then she gathered up the rest of her prizes from her friends and hurried back home to hide them away. She paused only long enough to crumple the white cap into a ball and toss it into the river.

The night, long after everyone was asleep, in the hour just before dawn there came an angry tapping at the shutter of Anya's bedroom window. "Give me back my cap!" a voice moaned. But the girl, sleeping heavily and dreaming of silver buttons and lace, never woke up.

But her mother did, and woke Anya's father. They opened the window and saw a ghastly figure in the moonlight.

"What do you want?" asked the mother, trembling.

"My cap, which your daughter stole."

Just at that moment the cocks began to crow, and the ghost disappeared.

Anya's parents woke her up.

"Foolish girl! What have you done?" demanded her father. Then he told her what he and her mother had seen from their window.

"It's only Ivan," said Anya, pulling the bedclothes up around her head. "He's always playing tricks."

Her parents pleaded with her to give back the cap, but she said she had tossed it into the river on her way home, and that was that.

Alarmed, the girl's father and mother sent for the village priest, told him about their horrible visitor, and begged him to help. "You can perform a service to rid us of this ghost, can't you?" they asked.

The priest considered for a while, then told them to bring their daughter to church the next day.

So on the following day, Anya was dragged to church, protesting loudly that she had buttons and lace to sew on her favorite coat. The priest had asked a number of villagers to come to add their prayers to help lay the troubled spirit to rest.

Just as the service was nearly finished, a terrible whirlwind arose. The entire church was shaken, and everyone was hurled to the floor. But Anya was thrown down with even greater force. A single, bloodcurdling scream escaped from her lips. Then everything was silent, and the whirlwind was stilled.

But when the terrified people picked themselves up and looked toward the altar, there on the bottom step, where Anya had been kneeling, was nothing but a single braid of her hair and one silver jacket button.

The Witch Cat

(folklore of the United States—Virginia)

One windy March day back in 1850, a handsome young man, whose wife had died the year before, arrived in a small Virginia town. He brought with him his young daughter, a wagon full of household goods and tools, and enough money to buy a small plot of land.

The townsfolk were kind and showed him several parcels of land that were for sale. Before he decided, he went walking through the back country and found a nice piece of land beside a wide, still pond.

When he asked about it, people said it wasn't owned by anybody. It had once belonged to a family that had left those parts after a string of misfortunes. No one said much, though they tried their best to get him to change his mind. But nothing would do except that land for his farm.

The people in the neighborhood helped him get started. They had a house-raising to build him a cabin and a barn raising the following week. With the last of his money, he bought a horse, a cow, and several chickens.

He worked hard, clearing the land and getting the fields ready for planting. His daughter milked the cow and fed the chickens. They seemed happy enough, though the townsfolk told one another that such a fine man should get married pretty quick, to give himself the sort of companionship a man needs and give his little girl a mother.

Sometimes, when his day's work was done, the farmer would fish for a while on the banks of the pond, staring dreamily out across the waters that turned gold, then red, then purple as the sun set.

One evening, at twilight, he saw a small skiff coming across the water, poled by a tall, slender figure. The glare of the fading sun made it impossible for him to see whether it was a man or a woman on the water.

But when the boat was nearer shore, he saw the stranger was wearing a bonnet. A moment later, as the skiff landed smoothly, a young woman's voice called out, "Hello! Help me up, will you?"

She extended a delicate hand, pale and fine as bone china, to him. Like a man in a dream, the farmer reached out and took it, helping her out of the boat and onto the shore. The woman pulled off her bonnet and shook her curly black hair free. "That feels more to my liking!" she said. "All that rowing can really wear a body out."

For a moment he didn't answer her. He was fascinated by her wide, green eyes, pale skin, and lips as dainty and red as a rosebud. At last he remembered his manners, removed his hat, and said, "Tom Morgan at your service, ma'am. Are you lost?"

"Not a bit!" she said with a laugh. "My name is Eleanor Faye. I live over across the pond." She gestured toward the far side, where willows and cypresses were tangled together. "I figured it was time I called on my new neighbors."

Still in a daze, Tom invited her up to see his cabin and barn, and meet his daughter Effie. Eleanor "ooh'd" and "ah'd" as he pointed out the new house and barn, and the chicken coop with its coat of fresh paint. But when she reached out a hand to stroke Effie's hair, the child, clinging to her father's trouser leg, began to cry, and wouldn't let the woman touch her.

"Shy little thing, isn't she?" said Eleanor with a polite laugh that showed her white teeth. Tom, feeling badly, tried to get his daughter to apologize, but she ran away suddenly.

"I'm sorry about that," said Tom, "she's not usually shy with strangers."

"No matter," said Eleanor easily, "we'll become good friends before long."

It was now nearly dark. "I have to be going," the woman said. "Next time I won't come by so late."

Tom walked her down to the shore. He offered to row her back across the pond, but she said, "No, I've been a widow for five years and doing for myself. I'll manage fine."

It seemed that her pole barely touched the water before the skiff slid quickly and silently toward the shadowed far shore. Tom stood staring for a long time, until he could no longer see Eleanor or her boat in the gathering dark.

After that, Eleanor came almost every day to visit. Once she brought a jar of homemade preserves; another time, it was a lace tablecloth.

Tom was enchanted, but Effie hid if she could get away. If her father forced her to stay inside when Eleanor visited, she sulked in a corner, staying as far away from the smiling woman as possible. Eleanor would blink her green eyes, which seemed flecked with gold, as if she were holding back tears, but she always made a show of excusing the child's actions.

When Effie's father asked her why she acted the way she did, Effie said, "I don't know. I just don't like her, papa."

This bothered Tom a good deal, because he had fallen under the spell of the young woman and was trying to work up nerve enough to ask her to marry him.

He never went across the pond to her farm. She said she preferred to visit him and get away from her chores. And anything she said made sense to him.

In addition to Effie being difficult, Tom was troubled by something getting at his chickens. Night after night, he would be aroused by a blood-curdling cat scream, followed by a fluttering and squawking from the chicken coop. Each time he ran out to see what the matter was, he'd find one or two of his chickens missing, and feathers scattered all around.

Effie had bad dreams of a huge cat with blazing yellow-green eyes, that climbed through the window of her room and curled up on the foot of her bed, waiting for her to go to sleep, so that it could suck the breath of life from her when she did. One morning, Tom found her barely breathing, and there was a round spot in the bedclothes at the foot of her bed, as if something—a cat, maybe—had curled up to sleep there.

When Tom went into town to pick up supplies, the townsfolk took him aside and whispered to him that Eleanor was a witch who lived beside the pond, because it was enchanted, having been sacred to the Indians who had lived there long before the white men had arrived. They also said she had done away with her husband by black magic, though no one was clear how this had been accomplished.

The young farmer refused to believe them. "You're just jealous o' my good fortune," he said.

Folks in town shrugged and went their own way: they knew what they knew.

His daughter got more sickly, and Tom began to fear for her life. Desperate, he went to the neighborhood "conjur man," named Zeke Franklin. The old man was a white witch who helped people, especially those troubled by black magic.

"I can't say for sure who's witchin' you," said Zeke, "but I'll give you somethin' to help."

He got a little bottle, and into it he put a dried snail, a mummified spider, and the toes from the left foot of a tree toad. He added a bit of bat's wing, then corked it, and tied a string around the neck of the bottle.

"That'll do 'er, I reckon," said Zeke. "Next, you take your huntin' knife, whet it as sharp as a briar, and keep it under your piller."

Tom hung the bottle over Effie's bed that night, and from that moment on, she had no more nightmares. But he kept his hunting knife, honed to a razor edge, under his pillow.

In the morning, Eleanor came to visit him, and expressed disgust at the jar Zeke Franklin had given Tom.

"That's foolishness!" she said, sounding downright angry. "I don't have any patience with nonsense like that."

While Tom tried to explain that the "conjur man's" jar had kept Effie from nightmares, Eleanor ran back to her skiff and poled across the pond without ever once looking back at him.

Frantic, Tom shouted after her; but she ignored him. In misery, he returned to his cabin, where Effie hugged him.

That night something got into the chickens again and tore them apart out of sheer meanness.

"I may have lost a lot," Tom said angrily the next morning, "but I'm not gonna lose any more, that's for sure!"

So he sent Effie into town to stay with neighbors. That night, he moved the few remaining chickens into the barn, and hid behind some grain bags near the window.

He hadn't been in hiding long, when he heard the wind rise, followed by a rumble of thunder. A minute later, rain began pounding on the roof shingles, while the wind howled through the cracks in the walls. Tom was a man not easily frightened, but the power of the storm began to make him uneasy. Then he heard a yowl that sent a thrill of terror up his back.

A moment later, he heard a pounding on the doors, as if huge fists were beating upon it. Tom raised himself into a crouch. At the same moment, a monstrous cat with flashing yellow eyes leaped at him through the window of the barn.

The man sliced the air with his knife to defend himself. The briar-sharp blade caught the cat's right paw, severing it completely.

The cat gave a shriek of pain; yellow eyes blazing, it fled back out through the window.

Tom stumbled out of the barn, like a man in a nightmare. A line of red drops led toward the shore; though the rain was washing the trail away, he was able to follow it easily enough.

At the water's edge, he saw the mark of a boat's prow in the mud. Far out, where the rain-pocked lake was lit by flashes of lightning, Tom saw a skiff skimming the black water toward the opposite shore.

He shouted after it, but the wind and thunder drowned out his cries. In a moment he had launched his own boat and was rowing across the storm-lashed pond.

The storm ended shortly before dawn. The neighbors who had care of Effie came to the farm later, when they had begun to wonder why Tom hadn't come to claim his daughter.

Silence lay over the farm. The tracks of a man's boots led down to the shore of the pond, now silver in the late-morning sunlight.

Some brave villagers rowed across the lake at noon. On the far side, they found Tom sprawled lifeless on the muddy shore. Clenched in his fist was the severed paw of a cat.

In the rude cabin farther up the shore, they found Eleanor Faye collapsed face down on the floor. When they turned her over, they found she was dead, and her right hand was gone.

The Green Mist

(a legend from Lincolnshire, England)

In the old days, folk believed that spring came to the world when a Green Mist covered the land and set seeds to bursting and made fields and trees and flowers grow again.

Once there was a family more eager than the rest for the Green Mist to rise and put an end to winter. Their only daughter had grown sickly during the time of cold and snows. She had been the prettiest young woman in the village, but now she was so pale and thin and weak that she could not stand up on her own feet without the help of her parents or one of her brothers.

Everyone else was sure she would die soon enough, but she thought that if she could only see the spring again, she would live. "Oh, mother," she would say over and over again, "if the Green Mist would only come, I'm sure it would make me strong and well, like the trees and the flowers and the corn in the fields."

Her mother promised her that the spring would come soon enough, and she'd grow strong and pretty as ever. But day after day the girl became weaker and more lifeless,

like an early-blooming flower when winter comes back after a false spring.

Each morning, they carried her bed to the doorway, so
she could watch for the first sign of spring. But the snows
lingered and kept the seeds asleep, and the trees leafless,
and the fields and flowerbeds locked in its frosty grip.

Finally, in a voice hardly above a whisper, the girl said to
her mother, "If the Green Mist doesn't come tomorrow,
then I must die. The earth is calling me, and it will cover
me soon enough. Oh! If I could only live as long as one of
those cowslips that grow by the door each spring, I swear
I'd be content!"

"Hush, now, child! Hush!" her mother cautioned. "You
don't know who might hear you say such a thing!"

The old woman knew that there were always bogies
around—wicked goblins who made mischief and grief for
their human neighbors. No one was ever safe; people
thought these evil creatures they couldn't see were always
spying on them and waiting to play their wretched tricks.

Even as the woman looked nervously around, she
thought she heard thin, piping laughter on the icy breeze.
And the sound of that merriment came from no one of
flesh and bone and blood.

But her worries were quickly forgotten. The next day the
Green Mist rose, like an ocean the color of grass in the
summer sunshine and as sweet-smelling as the flowers in
spring. It covered the countryside, and roused the earth
from its winter sleep.

The girl, watching from the doorway, said, "Now, I'll
live." She sat in the sun, and laughed with joy, and waved
to her father and brothers as they worked in the nearby
fields.

She grew stronger and fairer every day that the sun
shone; sometimes she would stretch her arms up to it as if

she lived by its warmth alone. But when a cloud hid the sun, she suddenly became as pale and wispy as she had been during the long dark winter days and nights.

But there were more sunny days than not, and the cowslips bloomed by the kitchen door. Soon she was running about and laughing like her old self. Every morning she would kneel by the cowslips and water and tend them. Sometimes she would dance for them in the sunshine; sometimes her mother would catch her just staring and staring at the fragant yellow blossoms.

Once, when the old woman leaned down to gather a bouquet of the flowers, the girl cried out, "Oh, mother, don't pick a single one!"

"Why not?" her mother wondered.

"They're pretty enough growing where they are. And I feel that if you plucked a single one, you'd pluck out a bit of my soul with each blossom."

The woman was deeply troubled by these words and the fear she heard in her daughter's voice. She remembered the girl's rash promise that she would be happy living just as long as the cowslips. And she recalled the thin, piping laughter that had followed the girl's words.

Indeed, her child seemed to grow stranger as the cowslips flowered. Yet she also grew more beautiful—and strong enough to do chores around the house or run errands into the village.

One day, in town, she met a handsome young man, who thought her the most beautiful girl he had ever seen. They talked a bit, and he asked if he could come and visit her. She smiled and nodded and told him where she lived.

He came the next day, and they walked together for a long time, hand in hand. In the afternoon, they sat under a tree near the kitchen door; because the day was sunny and warm, the girl fell asleep. While she dreamed, the young

man gathered up the cowslips from beside the kitchen door, and wove these into a wreath. Gently he set it on her head, waking her up.

At first she laughed; but when she pulled the wreath off her head to look at his handiwork, she was horrified to see what he had done.

"You picked the cowslips to make this!" she cried.

"Aye," he said, "a crown of flowers for the prettiest lass in the neighborhood."

But with a moan, she snatched up the wreath and clutched it to her breast. Then she stood staring wildly around at the green trees and sprouting grass and the golden sun and the yellow cowslips most of all. Puzzled, the young man reached for her, but she gave an awful cry, like an animal in pain, and hurried into the house, slamming the door behind her. Nor would she open it when the young man knocked and pleaded with her to tell him what was wrong with his love wreath.

After a time, he gave up calling to her and went sorrowfully back to town.

In the late afternoon, the girl's mother, who had been visiting a neighbor, found her lying on her bed, with the wreath of cowslips in her hand. The old woman put her hand to her mouth to keep from crying out. Then she sat by her child and tried to make her comfortable. But all the day long the girl seemed to fade; nor could her mother coax a single word out of her.

The following morning her family found her lying dead and white and withered, like the shrunken yellow flowers in the wreath still clutched in her hand.

While the old woman clung to her husband and wept, she heard thin, piping laughter through the open window.

Then she knew for a fact that the bogies had heard her daughter's wish. They had let her live as long as the cowslips, but had caused her to fade when the cowslips themselves had died.

The Cegua

(a folktale from Costa Rica)

One evening, a young man from San José, the capital of Costa Rica, rode into a small town north of the city. He was on his way to visit the ranch of a friend situated in a lonely area, but he wasn't sure which road to take out of the town.

He decided to stop in the local *cantina* to quench his thirst and ask directions.

When the proprietor brought him a mug of beer, he told the traveler he still had a fair distance to cover. "But," the proprietor warned, "no one travels these roads after dark. Stay here: I have a room I will let for a few *pesos*—then you can finish your journey in the morning."

The young man shook his head. "I have to reach my friend's ranch tonight."

The older man shook his head. "Only a fool would risk meeting the *Cegua*."

"The *Cegua!*" the traveler exclaimed. "What kind of creature is *that?*"

The *cantina* owner smiled, as if he was unable to believe such ignorance existed. *"Señor,"* he said, "don't folks in

San José know what the *Cegua* is? She is a demon—and heaven keep you from meeting her on the road!"

"I've never heard of such a thing," said the young man. "Bring me another mug of beer, and please explain what you know about this *Cegua.*"

When the older man returned with the beer the traveler had ordered, he brought a second mug for himself. He sat down across the rude wooden table and said, "No one who sees the *Cegua* is left with a sound mind. Strong men, in the peak of health, have gone mad from the sight. Some have even died of fright." He began to rattle off the names of locals who had lost their minds or lives because of this monster.

But the younger man interrupted him, saying, "If she is such a terrible devil, why haven't I heard of her before?"

"She prefers certain parts of our country; we have the misfortune to be one such place," explained the proprietor patiently. "For that reason, no one here rides alone after dark. If someone must travel after nightfall, he always goes with a companion."

"Why? Doesn't she like crowds?" laughed the young man, who was beginning to feel the effects of his long ride and the beer.

"The *Cegua* only appears to someone who travels alone," said the older man gravely, finishing his own beer and starting to rise. "She appears as a beautiful *señorita,* smiling sadly and fluttering her eyes, pleading for a ride—but woe to the traveler who stops to help her! If the unsuspecting rider sits her in front, she turns her head. If he has placed her behind him, she will make him turn to look at her. In either case, his doom is sealed."

"How so?" the traveler asked.

"When he looks, the beautiful *señorita* is gone. The creature riding with him has a huge horse's head, with monstrous fangs. Her eyes burn fiery red, like hot coals, and her breath stinks like sulfur. With a hiss, she will bury her claws in the shoulders of the rider and hang on like a wild animal. A horse, sensing that he is being ridden by a demon, will bolt in such a frenzy that no one can stop him."

"What then?" asked the younger man, no longer smiling quite so broadly.

"Those who are found the next day, if they are still alive, will have gone mad from the sight of her."

"Nonsense," said the traveler, suddenly standing up and tossing down a few *pesos* to pay for the beer. "I must be on my way, if I'm to reach my friend's ranch tonight."

The older man shrugged, gathered up the coins, and turned away. Clearly, he thought to himself, there is no arguing with a fool.

The little town square was deserted. The traveler untied his horse from the hitching post and set out along the road the *cantina*'s proprietor had pointed out to him earlier.

It was a warm night. Not a breath of wind stirred the leaves in the trees on either side of the road. Nothing disturbed the silence, except the *clop-clop* of his horse's hoofs on stones in the roadway.

Suddenly, around a bend, when the town was out of sight behind him and no other building was visible, he saw a slender figure standing in the thick shadows where the trees overhung the road.

Slowing his horse, the young man discovered a beautiful girl, with a pale face framed by the black-lace *mantilla* that covered her head, and which she held under her chin with her left hand. In the moonlight he could see she had curly black hair, huge dark eyes, and deep red lips.

"*Señor,*" she began. Her voice was sweet, but so weak and

weary that he feared she must be near fainting. "I am so tired, but I must go to see my mother, who is ill. Would you take me to Bagaces?"

"Of course," he said, bringing his horse to a stop and climbing down. Bowing slightly and removing his hat, he said, "My friend's ranch is just south of that town. You can spend the night there. In the morning I will escort you the rest of the way."

"You are very kind, *señor,*" she said, in such a faint whisper that he had to lean close to make out her words. Then he helped her onto the horse—which had grown restive during their halt—behind his saddle. He mounted himself, and they took off at a good trot.

A breeze had arisen to freshen the still air and flutter the leaves on the nearby trees. The moon and stars tinted the landscape pale silver. Several times the traveler tried to make conversation with the woman, but she didn't answer. She only leaned her head against his back and clung to his shoulders with her hands, as if she were afraid of fainting and tumbling from the horse.

Abruptly his horse, without any prodding, broke into a gallop. The woman dug her fingers into his shoulder, clearly afraid of falling. The young man was too polite to tell her that her nails were digging into his skin.

The horse gave a cry and charged down the dark road as though something terrible were pursuing them. The traveler pulled back on the reins and shouted, but it did no good. His horse only galloped faster.

Suddenly he felt razor-sharp teeth lock onto his neck so that only the collar of his coat saved his skin. An instant later, he heard a cry that came from no human throat as the awful teeth suddenly pulled away a mouthful of his coat collar.

He wrapped the ends of the reins around the fingers of

one hand, and with his free hand he struggled to pry loose the fingers that were clamped on his shoulder. As shadow, then moonlight, then shadow again, washed over the horse and its two riders, the young man saw that the fingers clutching him were too pale—they were the white of bone, rather than fair skin.

He heard another screech and smelled the creature's foul breath. He felt his strength giving out, while the bony fingers pulling at him seemed to grow stronger. The jaws snapped at the back of his neck, this time drawing blood.

Then, ahead, he could see his friend's ranch. He thought he could hear dogs barking, to signal his arrival. Lights were burning in the *hacienda*. There were figures running up the road toward him, carrying torches.

There was a final, ear-splitting scream from the demon behind him. He felt his whole body jerked backward. The hand that was tangled in the reins pulled backward suddenly, causing his horse to rear up, then fall sideways. Both riders fell with the animal.

The traveler was knocked senseless for a moment. When he came to, his friend, holding a torch, was staring at him, asking if he was all right. He nodded, still shaking from his near-brush with death. When he touched his hand to the stinging at the back of his neck, his fingers came away bloody. He looked around hastily, but all he saw was a crowd of friendly-looking *campesinos*, countrymen, watching him. One was calming his horse, which was on its feet again.

"Where is it—the creature?" he asked his friend.

"What creature?"

"The *Cegua.*"

"My friend," laughed the other man, "you stayed too long at some *cantina*, I think. The *Cegua* is a story to frighten children, nothing more. Still, next time you ride at night, be sure you travel with a companion. These lonely roads can be dangerous in the dark."

The young man said nothing, but he shivered just a little when the night breeze brought the lingering odor of sulfur to his nostrils.

The Ghostly Little Girl

(United States—California)

Near the turn of the century, in the seacoast town of Monterey, California, lived a widowed fisherman, Richard Colter, and his young daughter, Maria. Their home was a weather-beaten shack of boards with a tin roof, on the shore some distance from town.

Maria Colter was a pretty, but strong-willed little girl. Her father worked hard, fishing for sardines, salmon, cod, tuna, and yellowtail in Monterey Bay and the Pacific Ocean, just beyond, so that Maria could go to the Catholic school in town. She was very popular with the other girls who were pupils there, though a few parents did not approve of someone whose father was so poor.

Maria's closest friends were Annie Kelly, Susan Cooke, and Catherine Hopper.

In the early spring, Maria was absent from school for several days. Her three friends asked their teachers about it, but were told only that Maria and her father had sailed out of Monterey Bay three days before. Their boat had last been seen by another fisherman, around noon, beyond Point Lobos.

"But I *saw* her this morning, on my way to school,"

Annie Kelly told Susan Cooke and Catherine Hopper. "She was standing across the street, watching me. I waved to her, but she didn't wave back. I don't think she saw me, because she ran away right after that. I didn't see her again."

But once again Maria's desk at school was empty. As her three friends walked home, they talked about her absence.

"Maybe her father is sick, and she has to take care of him," Annie suggested.

"Maybe she got sick herself," Susan said. "Maybe she was starting to come to school today, and had to go home."

"I think we should go and see what's happened to her," said Catherine decisively.

The girls knew their friend lived with her father in a shanty outside of Monterey. They decided to pay a visit as soon as school was over. But it was a long walk, and they took their time, poking along the beach.

It was very late in the day, when, far down along the shore, they could see a single cabin, the back of which was built on stilts that extended down into the water.

"I'll bet that's Maria's house," said Annie.

"I hope so," said Susan, "because it's getting pretty late. I'll be in trouble if I don't get home by supper."

"Maybe we shouldn't go," said Annie. "I don't see any lights."

"Don't be silly!" said Catherine impatiently. "We've come this far."

"But it *is* getting awfully late," added Susan.

"I just want to see how Maria is. Then we can go right home."

But by the time they reached the run-down shack, a thick, wet evening fog had crept in, heavy with the tang of salt. Walking softly and whispering to each other, the three friends climbed the stairs to the rickety front porch. It was piled high with rotting fishing nets, rusted crabbing cages, buckets, and odd bits of rope and canvas. Around the corner of the house they could see a little pier, but no boat was tied to it. Everything was quiet except for the roar of waves hitting the shore.

"I don't think there's anyone home—let's go!" urged Annie, as the haunting call of a seagull cut through the foggy air. The mist was swirling so thickly around them that they could no longer see the distant roofs of Monterey. Tentacles of fog were tangling in the live oaks and pines far up the hillside.

"Don't be a ninny!" hissed Catherine. Boldly she knocked one-two-three times on the door. When there was no response, she pounded on the door even louder.

"Let's look through a window," suggested Susan.

This seemed a good idea, since clearly no one was coming to answer the door. Tiptoeing to the nearest window, the girls peeked in past ragged curtains.

At first all they saw was an empty room, with a few sad pieces of furniture scattered around. An unlit kerosene lantern stood in the middle of a wooden table. Opposite the window was a single closed door.

Suddenly a strange glow began to seep under the closed door. Then the door opened slowly, and they could see Maria Colter framed in the glow of the unearthly light. She was standing upright, but her eyes were closed, as if she were in a deep sleep.

Without a sound, the girl, like a sleepwalker, crossed the room. A moment later the three friends on the porch heard the cabin's front door unlocked with a loud *click,* then pulled open with a squeal, because the damp had swollen the wood.

Annie, Susan, and Catherine looked at one another for a moment. Then they went to the open door and peered through. The room inside was empty again, with only a faint silver-gray light coming through the streaked windows. The door in the far wall was closed, though they could still see the line of curious light underneath it.

Their friend had vanished.

"She must have gone back into that other room," said Susan.

"Why is she playing tricks on us?" asked Annie, "I don't think we should stay here anymore."

But Catherine walked bravely into the room and yelled, "Maria! We just want to say hello! You can come out." She was reaching for the knob of the closed door when something stopped her. There was a smell of saltwater so strong that they could almost taste the salt. The odor of fish was strong enough to make Susan hold her nose. The roar of the ocean filled the room as though it was circling the house outside.

"Catherine," Annie said, her voice little more than a squeak, "Look! The door!"

Water was beginning to seep under the door, soaking the worn carpet. The three girls stepped back, afraid to let it touch their shoes.

Abruptly they were startled by a crash like a huge wave hitting the other side of the door. It amazed them that the door didn't splinter from the impact. A moment later a second blow shuddered the door.

The three friends just gaped, too frightened to move. In the silence that followed, broken only by the gurgle of the water still seeping out under the door, they heard a ghostly voice from the other side of the door. It sounded like someone calling from underwater.

"Catherine!" it called. "Annie! Susan! I *knew* you'd come looking for me. I'll be with you in just a minute!"

There was a last *boom* against the door; then a deep silence fell over the room that smelled of fish and salt and seaweed.

The door began to open. There was silver light all around it. The puddle of water on the floor looked like a tide pool in the moonlight. They saw a little girl's hand, pale as whitefish, wet, and wrinkled as something that has lain in the water too long.

Terrified, the three girls ran from the shack as fast as they could, out into the thick, wet fog. They didn't stop running until they were back in their own neighborhood. There, while they caught their breath, they tried to make some sense of their frightening experience. Had Maria been playing a trick on them? If so, why? But that didn't explain the strange light and the sound and smell of the ocean inside the house or the crash of waves against the closed door.

Finally, confused and frightened, the girls decided to tell their parents what they had seen.

It was Catherine's father who told them, "Richard Colter's boat sank three days ago. They found his body washed ashore near Point Lobos. His little girl, Maria, drowned with him, but they haven't found her body yet."

The Midnight Mass of the Dead

(a Norse folktale)

There was once a very devout widow who lived in a small village in Norway and went to church every day. For many years Juliana would go with her friend Berta to these services. When Berta died, she went alone.

One Christmas Eve, she thought she would go to the early service on Christmas morning. Since there were fewer people at this mass, she could sit nearer the altar, feeling close to the Christ child on this holiest of days.

Before she went to bed Christmas Eve, she put out coffee, so she could have something warm to drink because she did not want to go to church on an empty stomach.

Juliana's alarm failed to wake her, but she roused herself out of a deep sleep sometime Christmas morning. Moonlight was streaming through onto the bedroom floor when she got up. She looked at her little alarm clock, but it had stopped with the hands frozen at eleven-thirty. She did not know for sure *what* time it was, so she went over to the window and looked down the street to the church. Light was shining through all the windows; and, opening her window sash for a moment, she was sure she could hear singing carried to her ears on the chill breeze.

She hastily set the coffee boiling while she dressed. She downed a cup of the strong, black brew, then got out her long, pink cloth coat, lined and trimmed with rabbit fur, which she only wore on special occasions. Tying a white scarf around her head and gathering up her prayer book, she set out for the church.

Oddly enough it was very quiet on the street, and she did not see a soul on the way. Usually Christmas morning brought many to even the earliest services—souls who might otherwise never go to worship during the year.

When she entered the church, she found a pew very near the altar. But when she glanced around, it seemed to her that all the other people looked pale and strange, though she was not rude enough to stare at them. The woman on her right had deep circles around her eyes, as though she had just gotten over some terrible illness; the man on her left clutched the back of the pew in front of him with fingers so long and thin, they hardly seemed to have any flesh on them at all. It seemed to Juliana that there wasn't anyone kneeling around her that she knew—yet, she had the feeling she had met many of them before, though she could not say where or when.

She settled back into the hard wooden pew along with the rest of the congregation, when the pastor left the altar and climbed half a dozen short steps up to the pulpit. He was not Pastor Solvold, nor any of the city ministers she was familiar with. The visitor was a tall, pale man who preached quite well. Again she had the nagging feeling that she knew him from sometime long ago, but she could not place him.

He spoke of death and those who lay waiting the resurrection under the Christmas snows and who grew impatient with eternity. Juliana found his themes morbid and not at all the message of joy and hope she expected. The preacher rambled on, and she became restless, shifting uncomfortably in her pew. As she let her mind wander, she realized there was not the noise and coughing and throat clearing that she was used to hearing at any early mass. The silence was so absolute that when she nervously dropped her prayerbook, the sound seemed to boom out from the altar to the choir loft. The preacher paused and stared at her with red-rimmed eyes that had no trace of kindness in them at all.

Juliana picked up her prayerbook, but she was feeling so uneasy that her hand was trembling.

When the preacher had finished his sermon, he led the congregation in a hymn. The music was strange, and the words were unfamiliar to Juliana.

"Leaves have their time to fall,
And flowers wither at the northwind's breath,
And stars to set—but all,
Thou hast *all* seasons for thine own, O Death!"

She was so uncomfortable that she could not get any words out. She was aware of the woman on her right and the man on her left staring at her with the same intensity as had the strange pastor.

Suddenly while the singing continued, a woman who was sitting behind Juliana leaned forward and whispered in her ear, "Throw your coat over your shoulders and go quickly! If you're still here when the mass is over, you're finished! This is a service held by the Dead."

Now the widow was so frightened, she wasn't sure her legs would support her. But she recognized the voice of the woman who had warned her, and turned around.

It was Berta, her friend, who had died many years ago. In a flash, she realized that the pastor and other members of the congregation that she had recognized were persons who had died in the parish over the years. She shivered from terror; but Berta gave her shoulder a reassuring squeeze, so she pulled her coat loosely around her and got up to leave.

But just as she reached the aisle, the woman with the sunken eyes and the man with the bony fingers began to screech. These ghastly figures turned in the pew and snatched at her.

Like a sea that has suddenly been churned by winds, the crowd of horrible, pale churchgoers rose in their pews and began clamoring toward the aisle. They yelled and moaned and scratched at her, their hands like claws, with dirt and mold beneath their cracked, yellow fingernails.

Sobbing "No, no, no," Juliana pushed her way down the aisle. Just as she shoved her way through the doors and out onto the church steps, she felt her coat pulled from her shoulders by the creatures chasing her. Without giving it a second thought, she let them have the coat, and ran down the steps into the windy street beyond.

The moment she reached her own door, she heard a clock somewhere chiming one. She fumbled out her key, unlatched the door, and slammed it behind her. Half dead with terror, she set about lighting every lamp and candle in her room. Then she sat on the couch, determined to keep watch through the small hours of the night. But exhausted as she was, she fell asleep.

Juliana awoke late in the morning. Most of the candles had burned themselves out; only a single lamp was still burning on the mantle. Through the gray light, she heard the church summoning the faithful to Christmas morning services.

Had she dreamed it all? she wondered.

But when she went to put on her favorite coat, she could not find it in the closet. Putting on an old black coat, she went out into the street and was greeted by her neighbors, who were hurrying to mass. Yes, she told herself, it had all been a nightmare, and she had simply misplaced her coat. She would find it soon enough.

She had to force herself to mount the steps and enter the back of the church, for all that it was crowded with friends and neighbors. But she turned and fled when the sexton came up to her, saying, "I think this is yours, isn't it? I've seen you wearing it at church before."

He held out to Juliana her pink cloth coat, with the rabbit lining and trim, that had been torn into a thousand strips.

Tailypo

(United States—West Virginia)

Not so very long ago, an old man lived by himself in the backwoods of West Virginia. He had a log cabin with a single room that held a stove, a bed, a table, a chair, and a big open fireplace built of fieldstone.

One night the man sat eating a plateful of beans and bread and regretting that he hadn't been able to catch a single fish in the lake behind his cabin or bag a single possum or deer for his supper. He was startled to look across the table and see the strangest creature he had ever seen, sitting on its haunches in the far corner of the room, staring at him.

It had jaws like a weasel, ears like a fox, piercing yellow eyes like an owl, a monkey's body, and was covered in bright red fur. But mainly it had a huge, long tail that coiled around and around it, the way a rattler coils on itself before it strikes.

"What th—!" cried the man. "How'd you get in here?" He grabbed his carving knife from beside the loaf of bread and went after the animal. The thing gave a screech like nothing the man had heard before; then it scrambled out through a chink between two of the cabin's logs.

But it wasn't quick enough. With a single slice, the man cut the creature's tail off, while the rest of the animal scampered away to the woods. The man walked back to the table and stretched out the tail, marveling at its length. After a few minutes he decided that meat was meat, and that was what he was hungry for right now.

So he cooked up that tail, found it tasted a little like rabbit, and ate it all at one sitting. After that, he plugged up the hole between the logs, went to bed, and soon was fast asleep.

He hadn't been asleep very long when he heard something scratching at the door, just like a cat. Pretty soon, he heard it call, "Tailypo, tailypo; just give me my tailypo."

Now he had three dogs that slept under the house. He whistled for them, and they came charging out and chased the creature far into the woods. But only two of his dogs came back. When the man saw this, he cursed a blue streak. Then he sent the dogs to sleep under the floorboards and went back to bed himself.

A short time later, he heard the same clawing at the front door, as the creature tried to get in. Then he heard it call through a crack in the door, "Tailypo, tailypo; just give me my tailypo."

Once again the man whistled up his dogs from underneath the cabin, and they chased the creature all the way down the road, snapping so close behind that if it had still had a tail, it would have lost it to the hounds.

The man heard the dogs giving chase until the woods swallowed up the sound. But a little later only one dog returned.

Again the man cursed loudly. This time he had his remaining dog sleep at the foot of his bed.

In the smallest hours of the morning, he heard something scrabbling at the window, like a night bird trying to

get in. Through the cracked glass he heard, "Tailypo, tailypo; I've got to have my tailypo."

Quick as he could, he flung the cabin door open and sent his last dog out into the night. He heard the dog charging around the corner of the cabin and heard the creature screeching and scrambling away.

After that, things were pretty quiet. But the last hound never did return.

The man stayed awake a long time, listening, but he heard nothing more. Finally, just before dawn, he fell asleep. But he woke up a few minutes later. He was sure he'd heard something in his room. He looked into the far corner and saw the patch he'd put over the hole was gone. Then he heard something scrabbling up the foot of his bed. A minute later he saw a fox's ears, a weasel's jaws, and two huge yellow eyes—just like an owl's—looking at him.

He tried calling for his dogs, but they were gone. He was too frightened to climb out of bed. He just kept staring while the red, monkeylike creature crept closer, and closer—

"Tailypo, tailypo," it growled, "just give me my tailypo."

"But-but-but," the man stuttered, "I haven't got your tailypo."

Then the horrible creature which was by then sitting on the man's knees, snarled and said, *"Oh, yes, you have!"*

And it jumped on the man's chest and scratched him all to pieces.

There are those who say that the creature got its tailypo back, and some who say it didn't. But the fact is, that old man and his dogs were never seen again in West Virginia or anywhere else.

Lady Eleanore's Mantle

(from a tale by Nathaniel Hawthorne)

When America was still a British colony, a young woman, Lady Eleanore Rochcliffe, traveled from England to become the ward of Governor Shute of Massachusetts Bay. The gentleman and his wife were Eleanore's only surviving relatives, and very happy to have her stay in Province House, the governor's home in Boston.

Lady Eleanore was beautiful, witty, well-educated, and extremely proud of her place in the world. She wanted nothing to do with anyone who was not as highborn and rich as herself. She was not at all sure that the colonies had much to offer her, after life in London at the royal court.

But she was quite impressed when the governor sent an elegant coach, drawn by four sleek black horses, to meet her ship and carry her to Province House. He also arranged for a gallant escort of gentlemen on horseback to ride before and behind her coach.

People in the street glimpsed Lady Eleanore through the large glass windows of the coach and thought she looked very much like a queen—though she was still in her teens. But what caused the most comment was her embroidered mantle, which had been woven by the most skillful seamstress in London. Its gold, silver, and red threads seemed to catch fire from the late-afternoon sun so that the young woman appeared wrapped in a cloak of flames.

When the coachman reined in his four black steeds in front of Province House, a nearby church bell tolled for a funeral. Everyone was upset that its mournful *clang* accompanied Lady Eleanore's arrival.

Just then, as Governor Shute and his wife approached the carriage to assist their ward in climbing down, a pale young man with tangled hair rushed from the crowd and fell in the dust at Eleanore's feet, offering his back as her footstool.

"Get up, sir!" roared the governor, threatening to beat the young man with his cane.

"Don't strike him," said Eleanore scornfully. "When men want to be trampled on, I am happy to give them the favor they deserve."

Light as a sunbeam on a cloud, she placed her foot upon the waiting back, extended her hand to meet that of the governor, and stepped down.

"Who is this insolent fellow?" the governor's wife demanded.

"Gervase Helwyse," replied the governor's doctor, "a youth without position or fortune, but of good mind—until he met Lady Eleanore in London. He fell in love with her, but she would have nothing to do with anyone in such humble circumstances. Her scorn drove him mad."

"He was mad even to dream of approaching so noble a lady as my ward," said the governor, signaling the discussion was at an end.

A few days after this incident, a ball was given in honor of Lady Eleanore's arrival. Province House was filled with the richest and most noteworthy gentry in Boston. The ladies shone in rich silks and satins, spread out over wide hoops; the gentlemen glittered with gold embroidery laid unsparingly on the purple, or scarlet, or sky-blue velvet of their coats and waistcoats. The place was alive with voices, laughter, and music.

But no person drew the eye and admiration of the crowd like Lady Eleanore. And her mantle gave an added majesty and mystery to her. The story went around that it had been made by a dying girl and had the magic power of giving new grace and beauty to the wearer every time it was put on. It was said that the fanciful birds and animals and flowers that adorned it were the product of a mind grown delirious with approaching death.

To some of those looking at the young woman, it seemed that the strange magic of the mantle gave her an almost feverish flush, while others thought it made her skin look as pale as the most delicate bone china. Eleanore herself seemed as changeable: sometimes she chattered and laughed excitedly with certain select guests; just as often she seemed moody and withdrawn and tired to the point of fainting.

While the guests were taking refreshment, Lady Eleanore settled into a large damask chair with a sigh, chatting with the governor's doctor, who noted her sudden weariness with a professional eye.

Suddenly Gervase Helwyse appeared, kneeling at her feet, having slipped unnoticed through a side door. "I beg you, dear lady, throw off that mantle," he cried. "It may not be too late! Throw the accursed thing in the fire!"

But Lady Eleanore, with a scornful laugh, drew the rich folds of the embroidered mantle around her head, so that it threw her features half into shadow and gave her a mysterious look. "Leave me," she mocked. "But always remember me as you see me now!"

At this, he was dragged from the room by the doctor and several other gentlemen and servants, who shoved him roughly out the iron gate of Province House and slammed it shut with a loud *clang.*

As the night wore on, the weariness in Eleanore's manner increased; her face grew flushed; she smiled because it seemed too much effort to speak. The doctor whispered something in the governor's ear that changed the man's cheerful expression to one of fear and worry. A few moments later it was announced that unforeseen circumstances made it necessary to end the party immediately. Puzzled, the guests went home.

The curious events at the ball were quickly forgotten, when, a few days later, the city was thrown into a panic by an outbreak of smallpox, which in those days could not be prevented or cured. At first the disease struck only the proud, the well-born, and the wealthy, though it soon spread throughout the whole city and countryside.

It was pointed out that the first to fall victim were persons who had attended Lady Eleanore's ball at Province House. In fact, the blood-red flag that marked every house where smallpox had entered, had first been seen waving over the door of Province House.

Though no one outside the house had seen Lady Eleanore since the night of the ill-fated ball, it was rumored that the disease had crossed the sea from London in her gorgeous mantle. It was said that fate and misery had been woven into its gold and silver threads by a woman already dying of the disease. People whispered that this had been a punishment of Eleanore for her pride and cruelty.

People cursed her and called each red warning flag, "A new triumph for the Lady Eleanore."

They shunned Province House, and most of its inhabitants fled. So there was no one to stop Gervase Helwyse when he entered one evening. Quickly he climbed the stairs to the upper hallway, throwing open door after door, calling "Lady Eleanore!"

At last, from the gloom of a darkened chamber, a woman's voice murmured, "A drop of water! My throat is scorched!"

Gervase stepped a little way into the room. Spotting the mantle, into which a dead woman had innocently embroidered a spell of dreadful power, he shuddered. Then he drew near the canopied bed, where something stirred behind the silken curtains. He pulled the drapes apart and saw a skeletal figure that tried to hide a hideous face with clawlike hands. "Do not look at me!" the woman croaked.

"Who are you?" asked the young man, fascinated and repelled by the vision. "What are you doing in my lady's chamber?"

"I am one who wrapped myself in pride as in a mantle and scorned you," she rasped, "Now you are avenged. I am Eleanore Rochcliffe."

"Another triumph for the Lady Eleanore!" cried Gervase, driven completely mad by her words. "All have been her victims! It is fitting that the final victim is herself!"

Then, laughing wildly, he snatched up the fatal mantle and ran from Province House.

That night a torchlit procession, led by Gervase, carried the straw figure of a woman, wrapped in a fantastically embroidered mantle, to the square in front of Province House. There the mob burned the effigy, and a strong wind came and swept away the ashes. And it was said from that hour, the disease abated, as if, from first to last, it had some mysterious connection with Lady Eleanore's mantle.

No one knew the lady's fate for certain. But for a long

time afterward, there was talk that in a certain chamber of the mansion, a woman's ghostly form could be seen, shrinking into the shadows and muffling her face with a richly embroidered mantle.

The Soldier and the Vampire

(a Russian folktale)

In the days when the czars still ruled Russia, a soldier was allowed to go home on leave to attend the wedding of his sister. He traveled on foot; and though it was a long journey, it was a pleasant one. It was almost summer, and the days were mild; the countryside he crossed was thick with forests and sweeping meadows filled with wildflowers. He was eager to see his family after his long absence, so he set himself a "double-time" march pace and whistled a lively tune as he hurried along.

Late in the day he came to a mill less than two hours from the village where he had been born. It belonged to an old friend, so he stopped there to beg something to eat and drink, because he had had nothing to eat since morning.

The miller welcomed him warmly and set out a generous meal for the younger man. Soon the two of them were chattering away about this and that.

Suddenly the soldier looked through the window at the darkening sky and cried, "It's almost nightfall. I'll have to make haste the rest of the way home." He started to get up from the table.

"Spend the night here, my friend!" said the miller quickly. "It's so late, you're sure to run into trouble."

"What do you mean?" the younger man asked.

"A terrible wizard died near the village recently," his friend explained. "Every night he rises from his grave as a vampire, wanders the countryside, and steals the lives of the innocent to prolong his own life-in-death. Even a brave soldier like you should be afraid of such an evil creature."

"I've seen evil enough in war," said the soldier gently. "Meeting a monster such as you describe can't seem too bad after the horrors of the battlefield. And I'm eager to see my family as soon as possible."

The miller tried to argue further with him, but the young man's mind was made up. So off he went.

As it turned out, he reached the village without seeing the vampire. But when he reached his parents' cottage, he heard lamenting and weeping coming from inside. Pushing open the door, he found his parents and the young man who was to become his brother-in-law huddled by the fire, trying to comfort each other.

"Oh, my son!" cried his mother, rushing to embrace the soldier, "you've come for a wedding, but you'll go to a funeral instead." She began sobbing against his chest.

His father placed a hand sadly on the young man's shoulder and told him, "Tonight we discovered your sister had been visited by a wizard who has risen from the grave and who plagues us. She sleeps the sleep that will end in death tomorrow night, when the creature uses her life to escape his grave once more. And there is nothing to be done."

"Why haven't you destroyed the body of this vampire before now?" demanded the soldier, distraught at the news.

"No one knows where the creature lies buried during the

day," the young man who was to marry his sister explained. "And at night he is too powerful to resist."

At this the soldier went into the back room. His sister, dressed as a bride, lay on her bed, pale in the moonlight streaming through a single narrow window. Her chest barely rose and fell; she seemed to grow weaker with each breath she drew. Her hands, palms open at her sides, showed red wounds where something had pierced them and drawn off some of her blood.

The soldier left the room quietly and walked to the door of the cottage.

"Where are you going?" his father asked.

"To try and undo the horror that's been done tonight," answered the soldier. Then he marched out into the darkness, before they could draw him back inside.

He walked the road that ran past the village graveyard but met no one. He was almost a half mile beyond it, where the road ran through a thick part of the forest, when a dark figure, smelling of damp and earth, came shambling out of the shadows. The figure fell in step beside him, but the soldier kept walking along, as if he hadn't a fear in the world, though he guessed it was the wizard returned from the dead who was keeping pace with him.

Now the soldier's travels had taken him far and wide, and shown him many things, so he was able to make a sign with his right hand that signaled to the wizard that he was a wizard also.

"Hail, brother," said the shadowy figure, "what are you doing here?"

"I heard that you have found the secret of life-in-death," said the young man boldly, "and that by stealing some of the blood of the living, you are able to cheat death for another day."

"That's true enough," confessed the wizard. "Only tonight I stole the lifeblood of a village maiden. Tomorrow, at sunset, her life will become mine, and she will die so that I can live."

"How is this done?" asked the soldier.

"Come with me, and I will show you," said the wizard. "But I feel the dawn is drawing near, and I must return to my grave before light. You can keep me company on my way."

Together they turned off the path and entered the shadowy woods. For a long time they made their way through the tangled trees and bushes in silence. At last they entered a clearing, where just enough moonlight sifted through the branches to let the soldier see the face of the wizard, which was streaked with dirt and mold. In the center of the open space, the earth lay tumbled about, and the young man guessed this was the sorcerer's grave.

Seating himself on a fallen log, the soldier said, "Now, make good your promise, and tell me the secret of life-in-death."

From the pocket of his rotting waistcoat, the wizard took a small flask of blood. It glowed like fire in the moonlight. "Just before dawn, I will swallow this. Then the girl's life will leave her body and enter mine the following sunset."

"And if those few drops of blood were returned to her, would she awake?"

Smiling, the wizard shook his head. "If I was destroyed utterly, so that not a bit of my soul escaped, then she would be restored. My magic is already at work on her. And now," said the monster, taking a step toward the soldier, "I'll tear you to pieces. Though you know a thing or two, you're no true wizard to be asking me these questions."

Then the soldier realized that the wicked creature had only been toying with him, luring him into the woods to destroy him and maybe steal his life, too.

"In God's name, I won't give you an easy time of it!" cried the soldier, jumping up and drawing his sword.

The wizard gnashed his teeth and howled like a wolf at mention of the holy name and the sight of cold steel, which is one thing such creatures fear. The soldier began swinging his blade wildly. The wizard, who kept leaping from one side to the next, tried to grab hold of the young man with his clawlike hands.

Finally, after they had fought almost to a standstill, the vampire struck the soldier's sword arm and sent his blade flying away into the shadows. Instantly the creature fell on the young man, who struggled and struggled, but felt his strength giving out. "Ah!" he thought to himself, "I'm done for now."

But at that instant the cocks began to crow, and the first light of dawn touched the tips of the tallest trees. The vampire fell lifeless to the ground.

Quickly the soldier took the flask of blood from the creature's pocket. Then he built a pyre of aspen boughs, placed the wizard's body on it, and set it on fire. He drew his sword and circled the edge of the flames.

As the fire grew hotter, the body changed to a mass of snakes, lizards, toads, worms, and beetles. These tried to creep away from the blaze. But the soldier remembered he had to destroy the creature utterly, so not a bit of his wicked soul could escape. He caught each crawling thing and flung it back into the fire, so that not the tiniest insect escaped.

When the body was utterly consumed, he scattered the ashes to the four winds. Then he returned to the village, where he poured the stolen drops of blood back into the wounds in his sister's hands, so that she came awake again.

After that, the wedding went on as planned. And the village was never troubled by the vampire again.

The Skeleton's Dance

(a folktale from Japan)

In Japan, many years ago, there were two young men, Taro and Jiro, who were good friends. When they were old enough, they left the village in which they had been born to journey together to the distant city to make their fortunes.

Now Taro worked very hard and earned a great deal of money. But Jiro quickly fell in with companions of the wrong sort and spent all his time lounging in tea shops during the day, becoming drunk and roisterous at night, and learning the ways of thieves and murderers.

Still, the young men remained friends, though Taro was very sad to see how corrupt Jiro had become. After three years, Taro decided to return home and asked his friend to join him. It was his hope that, away from the city and its wicked ways, Jiro might become again the good man he had once seemed.

In truth, Jiro had borrowed and spent a great deal of money, and many of his former companions were demanding he pay them back. He was eager to escape the city, because he had no intention of making good his debts. So he said to Taro, "I really do want to go back, but I have no clothes for the trip."

Since he now had a good deal of money, Taro happily shared it with his friend. He gave Jiro money enough for clothes and some extra to buy food and lodging along the way. However, when they reached the mountain pass, beyond which lay their home village, Jiro attacked Taro and killed his friend. He took Taro's money, rolled the body beneath a bush, and went the rest of the way home, as if nothing had happened.

The villagers greeted him warmly, and many asked, "What has become of your good friend, Taro."

"Oh," replied Jiro, "that is a sad story. He fell in with bad companions the moment we reached the city. From that day to this, he has done nothing but waste his money in the company of the most wicked men. I begged him to return with me, in the hopes that he would mend his ways once he was home. But he only laughed at me, and made rude remarks about this village, and had his criminal friends drive me away."

At this, there was much indignant head shaking among the villagers, who said that Taro deserved whatever misery happened to him.

For a few days Jiro made a show of being the same good-hearted fellow he had once been. But he quickly began to gamble and waste his money in drunken revels. Soon he had spent all the money he had stolen from Taro. Because he refused to do honest work, he decided to return to the city, where he would give himself another name and live by stealing from wealthy citizens.

On his way back, he again traveled the mountain pass, where he had killed his friend, Taro. As he was striding through the pass, he heard a voice calling, "Jiro! Jiro!"

Puzzled, he looked all around, but could see nothing

except bushes and the rocky mountain walls. Thinking the wind was playing a trick on him, he continued on his way.

But he had only gone a few paces when the voice cried again, "Jiro! Jiro!"

Determined to find the answer to this mystery, he followed the cries to a thicket far back from the road. Parting the brush and peering through, Jiro discovered a skeleton sprawled on the ground. Even as he looked on in amazement, the skeleton sat up and said, "Has it been such a long time that you've forgotten me, my friend? I am Taro, whom you killed and robbed. I have been waiting here, hoping that I would meet you again some day."

Terrified, Jiro turned to run, but the skeleton seized his *kimono* in its bony hand, and would not let him escape.

"Don't be so quick to run away. Tell me what you have been doing since you struck me down."

Choking with fear, Jiro told how he had gone home and spent all Taro's money and was now going to the city to become a thief.

"You haven't changed," said the skeleton. "But you are sure to come to a bad end if you become a thief. I have a better idea. I will dance like this—" Here the skeleton began to dance, rattling and clattering his bones together, waving his arms in the air and kicking with his legs. Then he continued, "You can put me in a box and carry me around with you, and people will pay you to see me dance. Since I won't eat or wear clothes, and money means nothing to me, you can earn a great deal without expense."

"Why should you do this for me?" asked Jiro, though his mind was already filled with pictures of the fortune he could earn.

"I am bound to you in death as in life," said Taro. "Will you accept my offer?"

"Yes," said Jiro. Then he took the skeleton and pur-

chased a beautiful teakwood chest to store it in, and toured the countryside, playing a flute while the skeleton danced in front of wondering crowds. The money poured in, enough so that Jiro could spend it as fast and foolishly as before, and still have some left over.

Eventually word of Jiro and his dancing skeleton reached the most powerful lord of the province. He summoned Jiro to his castle and told him to have the skeleton dance in the vast hall that was filled with his guests.

Jiro opened the chest, stretched Taro's skeleton out on the bamboo matting, and began to play a lively tune on his flute. But the skeleton simply lay there. Jiro played tune after tune, then began to yell and curse, but the skeleton refused to move.

Finally, in a rage, Jiro took his flute and began to beat upon the bones, commanding them to get up and dance.

At that moment, the skeleton sat up, climbed to its feet, and walked to the throne of the great lord. There, bowing humbly, it said, "My lord, I have been dancing all this time, just so word would reach you, and I would be brought before you. In my life, I was your honest subject, Taro. This fellow killed me and robbed me of my money." Then the skeleton told exactly how this had happened.

The lord, who was a just man, was angered at the way Jiro had betrayed his friend. "Seize that man, and take him away to be tried!" he ordered his guards.

At that moment the skeleton fell to pieces before the throne; and three days later Jiro was sentenced to death for his crimes.

Scared to Death

(United States—South Carolina)

Some ten years after the Civil War, the old Charleston mansion named Roseway was ablaze with lights and bursting with music. An orchestra, hired by Stephen Heyward, played waltz after waltz in the huge ballroom in honor of his daughter Sally's eighteenth birthday.

Sally, however, had quickly grown bored with the whole affair and had steered a cluster of handsome young men and beautiful young women to the open area at the foot of the magnificent staircase. There she stood, rearranging her pale yellow skirts that rose, ruffle upon ruffle, to her waist. Her bare shoulders were adorned with a single fall of jet-black hair, which tumbled over her left shoulder. A perfect red rose was pinned to her bodice, setting off the whiteness of her skin.

Even if she hadn't been mistress of Roseway since her mother's untimely death—or hadn't flirted so outrageously—Sally would have easily drawn the attention of the young men now gathered around her because of her beauty. Her dark eyes, ivory skin, and bubbling laughter charmed men of all ages.

At the moment, however, she was quiet. She was looking

unabashedly at tall, dark Peter Beaufort, while listening intently to what Alice Cardross, his fiancée, was saying.

Breathlessly Alice informed the little cluster of friends, "When our carriage passed the graveyard tonight, both horses reared up. I declare, I was so frightened, I almost lost my wits."

"I'm sure nothing serious was at risk," said Sally, with a wicked little smile.

Gallantly Peter said, "It's certainly spooky there—I've heard the place is haunted."

"Yes," said Sally, sounding even more bored than before, "we've all *heard* stories, but have you ever *seen* a ghost, Peter?"

"Don't *you* believe in ghosts?" asked Alice, in a voice barely above a whisper.

"Not at all," sneered Sally. "Only simpletons hold with such foolishness."

"My manservant saw a ghost standing by old Daniel Payson's tombstone," said Peter. "That's the tallest grave marker—the one that tilts to one side. The ghost was the image of Daniel Payson, who's been dead four years."

"Bosh!" said Sally, with an airy wave of her hand. "Your man dreamed it—or was frightened by a shadow."

"You'd never catch *me* going into the cemetery after dark," said Alice, holding more tightly to Peter's arm.

"Why? Whatever on earth is there to be afraid of, *really?*" wondered Sally, ignoring Alice to stare into Peter's face.

Peter, who seemed equally uncomfortable with Alice's clinging and Sally's boasting, said, "Come, now, Sally, you wouldn't go in there after dark, and you know it!"

"Nonsense!" Sally retorted angrily. "I'm not as foolish as some people I know." She looked pointedly at Alice.

Alice, aware that Sally was making fun of her, cried, "If

you're so brave, I dare you to go into the graveyard alone. Tonight. *Right now!*"

"Oh, very well," said Sally offhandedly. "Peter, will you escort me?" She stretched out her hand to take his.

But the young man put his arm around Alice's shoulder and said, "I've never been a man to tempt fate, Miss Heyward."

Nor would any of the other young gentlemen surrounding her risk the unknown terrors of the churchyard—even for a chance to escort the lovely Sally.

"Then I'll go alone," snapped Sally pettishly. "The dead couldn't be any more dreary company than the rest of you!" She sent one of her servants to the cloakroom to fetch her wrap.

"Wait," said Alice. She ran after the servant and returned with Peter's walking cane, which had a gold handle shaped like a goblin's head. While Sally was putting on her wrap, Alice thrust the cane at her, saying, "Take this, and plant it in the ground by old man Payson's crooked tombstone. That way, we'll know in the morning that you really went there."

"Since my word isn't good enough for you, Miss Cardross," Sally said nastily, "you'll find the cane in the morning—when the sunlight gives you enough courage to look for it!" Then, gathering her long cloak around her, Sally Heyward swept out through the front door and into the night.

She marched along the moonlit sidewalk to the cemetery, slashing at the air in front of her with the gold-tipped cane, furious at the memory of how Peter Beaufort had defended his fiancée, Alice Cardross, against Sally's best efforts to belittle the other woman. And she grew even angrier at the thought that he remained unmoved by Sally's charms—in spite of the fact that she had flirted with him throughout the whole evening.

Sally pushed open the high iron gates in the churchyard wall and stepped through. Inside was complete darkness, except for an occasional tall grave marker gleaming palely in the moonlight. Dimly the young woman could see the outline of the church steeple on the far side of the cemetery. Though she couldn't make out the face of the clock in the tower, she clearly heard it chiming midnight.

Up until this moment, Sally had been angry and not in the least afraid. But the thick, chill darkness pressed closely in on her, creating shadows that seemed to writhe and clutch at her when she didn't look directly at them. Deciding, with a last burst of resentment, that this was the wretched end to an already spoiled evening, she wrapped her cloak more tightly about her, and searched hastily for the crooked tombstone.

A part of her was ready to cut and run, but Sally was strong-willed enough to force herself to make good her boast. She would plant the cane before she left or die in the attempt. Keeping this thought in mind, she searched up and down the narrow rows of tombstones, until she discovered the crooked marker, shining faintly in the moonlight.

She raised the cane to thrust it into the damp soil below the marble slab, then froze—

A sigh, then a loud moan, came from the blackness just beyond the tombstone. A sudden gust of wind, chill and smelling of damp and mold, rushed past her. She was certain that she could hear something coming toward her —something that moved stiffly and wetly and never drew a mortal breath.

Stifling a scream, Sally thrust Peter's cane into the ground; then, gathering up her cloak, she turned to run.

Something caught her; something held her and wouldn't

let her run. She heard a moan and smelled the breath of the open grave. But the more frantically she struggled, the more firmly the horror held her in its grip. Too frightened to scream, she clawed frantically toward the narrow aisle of tombstones that led back to the gate. But something was tugging at her throat now. In a final spasm of terror, she flung herself forward, only to feel herself dragged back toward the crooked tombstone. At that moment something burst in her head, and she sank to the ground, mercifully unconscious.

When Sally failed to return, Peter and Alice led a party of anxious friends and relatives into the churchyard.

There they found Sally, a short distance from the crooked tombstone, dead, her eyes wide open in fear. The end of her cloak was pinned solidly to the ground at the foot of the marble slab—held in place by the deeply planted cane with the gold goblin's head. The unfortunate young woman had scared herself to death.

To this day, people talk of *two* ghosts that haunt the old churchyard. One is the tall shadowy figure of a man; the other is a woman in a pale yellow dress with a long cloak, who wears a single red rose in her bodice.

Swallowed Alive

(a British folktale)

Dorothy Mately lived in the British town of Ashover in the county of Derby during the seventeenth century. She was a widow who made a living working for a lead mine located nearby. She would take the ore which had been dug out of the mine, break it with a hammer, and wash this to separate out the traces of lead from the other minerals.

She was a big, homely, rough-spoken woman who upset many of her neighbors with her continual cursing and swearing. She was also rumored to be a liar and thief, but she would deny this loudly if anybody accused her. Her favorite expression was "Let God open the earth and have it swallow me, if what I tell you isn't the truth."

On the morning, of March 23, 1660, while she was busy washing ore in a stream near the mine, a young miner, just off his shift, decided to take a quick plunge in the water to clean off the day's grime from working below. He slipped off his trousers and laid them on a rock while he swam in the brisk mountain stream.

When he climbed out a short time later, he discovered his clothing had been tossed about, and his pockets had been searched. Several coins, which had been in the young man's pocket, were missing. Since they were all he had to live on until the next payday, he frantically searched for the thief. But the only one he spotted was Dorothy, hard at work with her tub and sieve, seemingly unaware of the hue and cry the lad was raising.

Because there was not a sign of anyone else around, he accused her of stealing his money and demanded she give it back.

Holding her ore hammer tightly in one hand, Dorothy stood up and loudly denied she knew anything about the missing coins. As usual, she ended this by saying, "Let God open the earth and have it swallow me, if what I'm telling you isn't the truth."

As it happened, a God-fearing man from Ashover was passing nearby and overheard the argument. He knew Dorothy's reputation, and he knew that her accuser was an honest, hard-working young man, who would never call someone a thief without good reason. He took a step forward in the hope of helping to resolve the argument when Dorothy suddenly cursed the miner and threatened him with her hammer.

Startled, the young man turned and ran.

The passerby walked over to Dorothy and said he had witnessed the whole event. He demanded that the woman restore the money she had stolen.

Because the newcomer was a man of some importance in the village, Dorothy did not threaten him. She merely insisted on her innocence and made up some story about having seen two men lurking near the stream shortly before the theft was discovered. The man did not believe a word of this and told her so, threatening to involve the authorities in the matter.

At this, Dorothy raised her hammer in her right hand over her head and cried, "Let God open the earth and have it swallow me, if what I've told you isn't the truth!"

Disgusted, the fellow turned to continue on his way. But he had gone only a few paces, when he heard Dorothy scream. Looking back, he was dumbfounded to see her spinning round and round like a top, all the while sinking into the ground with her tub and sieve, her hammer still raised over her head.

Even while he stared, the woman disappeared into what seemed to be a whirlpool in the solid earth. Suddenly it stopped, and the man cautiously crept to the edge of the opening. Below him, he saw Dorothy some nine feet down; the woman was buried almost to her waist in the loose earth, which had completely covered her working tools.

The villager frantically tried to think of a way to help her. Lowering his coat toward her, he said, "Take hold of this, and pray God will pardon your sin and let you live."

"I have no sin to forgive," she said, stretching her fingers toward his dangling coat sleeve. But immediately she began spinning and sinking again. In a moment she was far below her rescuer's reach. She screeched for help, now buried almost to her shoulders in the soil.

"I hope God will have mercy on you," the man called down, "for I'm afraid you will never be seen alive again."

But Dorothy only struggled harder to raise herself out of the soft earth. Suddenly a large stone apparently tumbled from nowhere, and struck her soundly on the head, silencing her screams and curses. As if this was a signal, loose earth from the mouth of the opening began pouring down on her and quickly buried the wretched woman, while the man scrambled back from the crumbling edge.

When workmen from the mine eventually dug Dorothy Mately's lifeless body from the pit, they found she had sunk some twelve feet down. There was no sign of her hammer, tub, or sieve.

When her body was laid out on the grass, the miners found the young man's stolen coins in her apron pocket.

The Deacon's Ghost

(a folktale from Iceland)

Many years ago, in Iceland, a deacon served in the parish of a small town, nestled in the side of a beautiful little valley. He was very much in love with a girl named Gudrun, who lived in a farm on the opposite side of the valley, across the river from his own tidy little house near his church. They were engaged to be married in the spring.

He had a handsome horse with a gray mane. He called the horse Shadow and rode him every day.

A short time before Christmas, the young man rode to Gudrun's home and invited her to join in the Christmas Eve celebration at the church. He promised to come for her on Shadow, so they could ride back together. She was delighted and said she would watch for him in the evening, so they could leave without delay. Then she brought him tea and cakes, and they passed a long afternoon planning for their future life together.

Earlier in the day he had ridden safely across the frozen river because the ice was so thick. But even while the deacon and his betrothed were talking, an unseasonable thaw had set in. The river became a flood; much of the ice broke up and was whirled downstream in huge drifts.

When the young man left the farm late in the day, he was so full of happy dreams that he did not immediately notice how much the river had changed. As soon as it became clear to him what the situation was, he searched rapidly for a means of crossing the treacherous stream. Spotting a bridge of ice that still spanned the river, he urged Shadow onto this. But when they reached the middle, the bridge crumbled beneath them and tumbled the horse and rider into the stream.

The next morning a search party was sent out when it was found that the deacon had not returned home. Later in the day Shadow was discovered running free across a frosty meadow. Shortly after that, the searchers found the corpse of the deacon, which had drifted to the bank after the man had drowned. All the flesh had been torn off the back of his head, so the skull shone through.

Sadly they brought the body back to the town, and the deacon was buried a week before Christmas.

As it happened, the river continued to flood so dangerously that no one from one side of the valley could cross to the other. No one had been able to bring word to Gudrun of the deacon's death. Having no idea of the tragedy that had befallen, she happily looked forward to Christmas Eve when her lover would come for her and take her across the river to the celebration at his church.

On Christmas Eve, while she was still dressing in her finest clothes, Gudrun heard a knock at the door. A moment later one of the maids opened the door but saw no one there. Since the moon was quite hidden by clouds, the girl went to fetch a light. But holding a lamp high over her head, she could discover no one. Puzzled, she returned to her work.

A short time later the knock was repeated. Gudrun, who

was just pulling on her winter cloak, called, "It is someone waiting for me."

She pulled open the door and saw Shadow standing a short distance away. The figure of the deacon, his hat pulled low over his eyes, stood beside the horse. She hurried to him, and without a word he helped her climb onto Shadow. Then he mounted in front of her, and they rode off in the direction of the river. As they rode, the moon slid out from behind the clouds, so it was very easy to see again.

When they reached the stream, Gudrun saw that it was frozen over again, except for a narrow ribbon of black water in the middle, where the current kept the frost from hardening.

Quickly the horse trotted onto the ice, then leaped over the rapid stream in the middle. At the moment they lighted on the far side, the deacon's head bobbed forward so that his hat slipped over his eyes for a moment. Gudrun saw a large patch of bare skull gleaming white in the middle of his hair.

"What has happened to your head, my love?" the girl asked.

"Ride a little farther with me, and you'll understand" was all her lover would say as he set his hat back in place.

Troubled, Gudrun looked eagerly toward the lights of town, gleaming across the frosty fields and drifting snow.

But instead of going to the church, which was ablaze with lights, the deacon turned Shadow toward the churchyard beside it. He brought them to a halt outside the ice-crusted hedges. Without a word, he dismounted and helped Gudrun down.

Shivering, the girl asked, "Why have we stopped here, my love?"

He put out his hand, which felt as cold as the ice all

around, to lead her through the hedge gate, saying, "Walk a little farther with me, and you'll understand."

The young woman let him lead her amid the snow-dusted tombstones, wondering what strange notion had taken possession of him. But when they had reached the center of the cemetery, she saw that they were heading for an open grave, which had frozen earth piled up all around it.

"My love, why are you showing me this?" she asked in a voice made small by her fear.

"Just rest beside me there, and you'll understand," the deacon said.

Sick with horror, Gudrun broke free and began to run to the church porch, screaming for help. Suddenly she felt her cloak snatched from behind. For a desperate moment she was held prisoner; then she loosened the clasp and ran on toward the church, where shouts and bobbing lights showed people were coming to help her.

Just as she stumbled into the arms of her rescuers, she looked behind her. She saw the deacon jump headlong into the open grave, with her cloak hugged to him. The piles of dirt on either side tumbled in after him, filling the grave once again.

But the troubled ghost of the deacon came night after night to try and drag Gudrun away with him, so that she had to be guarded from sunrise to sunset. The priest from a neighboring parish tried to lay the spirit to rest; but nothing worked until a man from the north, who knew something about ancient spells, came and drove out the demon who possessed the man's body. After that, the deacon remained at rest, never to haunt Gudrun again.

Nuckelavee

(a folktale from the Orkney Islands)

The people of the Orkney Islands, off the north-eastern coast of Scotland, tell many stories of a monster called Nuckelavee, who lived in the sea but never missed a chance to plague humankind whenever he could. When he came onshore, he appeared as a horse and rider—though, in fact, a closer look showed man and horse were all part of the same creature.

His human-looking head was ten times the size of a normal man's, while the horselike head had an enormous mouth that jutted out like a pig's. Most horrible of all, he seemed to have no skin, so those who came near and lived to tell of it, swore that you could see black blood flowing through his veins, and every movement of his white muscles.

If crops withered away, or livestock fell off the high rocks that made up the shoreline, or a disease plagued the islanders, the folk blamed Nuckelavee. They said his breath was poisonous, bringing blight and disease wherever he trod.

The only thing the monster feared was fresh water, and he would never cross a running stream. Nor would he ever visit the land when it was raining.

There was once an old man named Thomas, who met the monster late one night. Though there was no moon, the air was clear and the stars gave considerable light. Thomas was going home from an evening in the village, and his path lay close by the seashore.

Just as he began the most dangerous part of his journey, where the road ran along a ridge, with the sea on one side and a deep, freshwater lake on the other, he saw a huge shape ahead, moving toward him.

He sensed instantly that it was no natural thing he was facing. He could not move to either side, because of the water that hemmed in the path; and he had heard that turning one's back on an evil thing was the worst thing a man could do.

"The Lord be with me and take care of me," Thomas whispered to himself. Then, since he was always regarded as brave or foolhardy (depending on the person one talked with), he decided, as the best of two evils, to face whatever was coming toward him. So he walked slowly but steadily forward.

He quickly discovered to his horror that the gruesome creature approaching him was the dreaded Nuckelavee. Thomas could see quite clearly that the lower part of this terrible monster was indeed like a horse, with flippers extending from his legs. The mouth seemed large as a whale's mouth, gleaming with sharp teeth in the starlight and giving off breath that poured out like steam from a giant teakettle. The horsehead had a single eye, glowing red as a coal.

Out of the back grew what seemed to be the upper half of a man, with a head as big as a barrel and arms that reached nearly to the ground. The whole creature looked sculpted from red, raw flesh, in which Thomas saw blood black as

tar, running in yellow veins, and great white sinews twisting, stretching, and contracting as the monster moved.

In mortal terror—his hair standing on end and his body
feeling as if it was filmed with ice—Thomas forced himself
to keep moving. He knew it would be useless to try to
escape and determined to die facing his enemy, rather than
with his back to the monster.

Then, for all his fear, the man remembered what he had
heard of Nuckelavee's dislike of fresh water. So he edged
closer to the side of the road near the lake.

The awful moment came when the lower head of the
monster was just inches from him. To the terrified man, the
mouth of the creature yawned like a bottomless pit. The
red eye seemed to burn into his mind. Slowly the long arms
were stretched out to seize Thomas.

At the last possible instant, the man ducked under one
arm and ran forward, splashing through the shallows of the
lake. Some of the water sprinkled the foreleg of the monster. The horsehead snorted like thunder, and the monster
shied over to the far side of the road.

Without looking around, Thomas began running with all
his might; behind him he heard Nuckelavee turn and gallop
after him; the mannish head bellowed with a sound like a
typhoon ripping across the sea.

Ahead of Thomas was a little stream, by which water
from the lake overflowed into the sea. The man knew if he
could only cross the running water, he was safe; so he
strained every muscle to reach safety.

Behind him he felt the wind of Nuckelavee's clutches as
he narrowly escaped the monster's grip. Just as he reached
the bank of the little stream, the long arms snatched at him
again. Thomas made a desperate leap, felt his cap and part
of his coat torn away by Nuckelavee, then landed safely on
the far side, just out of reach of the monster.

Nuckelavee gave a deafening, unearthly yell of disappointment and rage, as his victim raced to safety beyond the water.

Thomas continued to run until he knew for certain that he was safe. When he finally stopped to glance back toward the grotesque Nuckelavee, he could still hear the creature's terrifying roar, but the sight of the monster would be only a memory from now on.

The Adventure of the German Student

(from a tale by Washington Irving)

Gottfried Wolfgang was a young man of a good family. He had gone to school for a time in his native Germany, but he had become so obsessed with studies about spirits and devils and who knows what that it began to affect his mind and health. He was especially tormented by the idea that a demon was haunting him, trying to catch him and ensure his ruin.

He became thin and gloomy. His friends, determined to help him, decided that the best cure was a change of scene. So they sent him to finish studies amid the splendors and gayeties of Paris.

Unhappily Wolfgang arrived just as the French Revolution was breaking out. The terrible scenes of violence that followed shocked his sensitive nature, disgusted him with society and the world, and made him even more solitary in his ways. He kept to himself in a lonely apartment in the old part of Paris where most students who attended the university lived.

In his loneliness, he would often daydream of the face of a beautiful woman. Her imagined features made so strong an impression on him that he dreamed of her again and again. She began to haunt his thoughts by day and his sleep at night. He fell passionately in love with this shadow of a dream.

One stormy night young Wolfgang was returning to his lodgings. The hour was late, and a storm had just begun. Loud thunderclaps rolled through the dark narrow streets, filled with driving rain. Lightning danced over the peaked roofs above him and shed flickering gleams over the open space in front of him. This was the square where public executions were performed—a place he dreaded to cross even in the sunlight.

The rain came down harder, driven by a freezing wind. Wolfgang rushed out into the square, but stumbled and fell to his knees. As he picked himself up, he was horrified to find himself close by the guillotine—the dreadful instrument of death that stood ever ready to claim fresh victims.

Shuddering, the young man was turning from the horrible engine when he saw a shadowy form cowering at the foot of the steps that led up to the scaffold. Several vivid flashes of lightning revealed the figure more distinctly: it was a woman dressed in black. She was seated on one of the lower steps of the platform, leaning forward, her face hidden in her hands. Her long, tangled hair was streaming with the rain that fell in torrents.

Wolfgang paused. There was something touching and terrible in this solitary figure of woe. He guessed she was some heartbroken mourner whose relative or lover had been cut away from her by the dreadful blade. His heart went out to her suffering.

He approached her and said gently, "Mademoiselle, you will catch your death out here."

She raised her head and looked wildly at him. He was astonished to see, in the bright glare of the lightning, the very face which had haunted him in his dreams. Her fea-

tures were pale and grief-stricken, but she was ravishingly beautiful.

Trembling with unexpected emotion, Wolfgang urged her, "You should not be out here at this hour, exposed to the fury of such a storm. I beg you, permit me to take you to some friends."

In answer, she merely pointed to the guillotine, and shook her head. "I have no friend on earth," she said sadly.

"But you must have a home," said Wolfgang.

"Yes—in the grave!"

The heart of the student melted at these words.

"If a stranger can make an offer, without danger of being misunderstood," said he, "I would offer my humble rooms as shelter, and make myself your devoted friend. I am friendless myself in Paris, and a stranger in the land—but whatever help I can give you, it is yours for the asking."

There was such an honest earnestness in the young man's manner that the homeless stranger nodded her head, as if too wearied by her suffering to do more.

Sharing his cloak with her, he led her from the square and the sight of the horrible instrument of execution.

On entering his apartment, the student, for the first time, felt how shabby his rooms were. They were cluttered with books and papers and all the other things a student uses. Hastily he cleared off a chair by the fireplace. Then he lit candles and a small fire to let his visitor warm herself, for her hands were cold as ice.

In the firelight, he had a better opportunity of studying her; and he found himself even more intoxicated by her beauty. Her pale face had a dazzling fairness that was set off by the clusters of raven hair framing it. Her eyes were large and brilliant, though something like wildness swam in their depths. Her whole appearance was striking, but she was dressed in a simple black dress with only one item of jewelery: a broad black band around her neck, clasped with a diamond pin.

"I will spend the night with another student, whose apartment is above," Wolfgang offered. But he was so fascinated by the woman's charms, there seemed to be such a spell upon his thoughts and senses that he could not tear himself from her presence. Instead they sat and talked, while the rain continued to beat against the windowpanes, and thunder rattled the shutters.

She spoke but little and never mentioned the guillotine. Her grief abated, but she would not say what had caused it. For the most part she contented herself, listening to him and staring into the fire.

Wolfgang, in the infatuation of the moment, confessed his love for her. He told her the story of his mysterious dream and how she had possessed his heart before he had even seen her.

She seemed strangely affected by his recital and admitted, "From the first, I was drawn to you by a power I cannot account for either."

The young man saw that his kindness, which had first won her confidence, had now apparently won her heart. It was a time for wild actions, and Wolfgang suddenly knelt beside her chair, saying, "You have no home or family. Let me be everything to you—or, rather, let us be everything to one another. Marry me—here is my hand," and he grabbed her delicate hand in his own, distressed to feel how cold it still was. "I pledge myself to you forever!" he said, in the heat of his own passion, "upon my very soul."

"Forever? Upon your soul?" said the stranger solemnly.

"Forever!" repeated Wolfgang. "My heart and soul are yours."

The stranger clasped his fingers tightly in her own.

"Then I am yours," she murmured and kissed him. "And you are mine . . . forever." Then she whispered, "Now, help me to the bed, for I am growing so tired, so very tired."

Alarmed at the weakness in her voice, Wolfgang escorted her to the little bed in the next room. She fell asleep the instant her head touched the pillow. Quietly he withdrew and spent the few hours left of the night dreaming of the life he and the stranger would build for themselves.

The next morning, while she was still sleeping, the student went out to look for a more spacious apartment suitable for his bride. The storm had passed, and the streets gleamed with sunlight, reflecting brightly off lingering puddles. He quickly found new lodgings, arranged to take possession of them immediately, and returned to his rooms.

But when he threw open the bedroom door and called to the woman, he found her lying with her head hanging over the bed, with one arm thrown over it. He spoke to her and received no reply. He advanced to awaken her from her uncomfortable position. Lifting her hand, he discovered it was cold, without a trace of pulse. Her fair face was now pallid and ghastly. He knew in an instant that she was a corpse.

Horrified and frantic, he awoke the house. In the confusion that followed, someone had sense enough to summon the police. As the officer entered the room, he started back the moment he saw the body.

"Great heaven!" he cried. "How did this woman come here?"

"Do you know anything about her?" asked Wolfgang through his tears.

"Of course!" exclaimed the officer. "She was guillotined yesterday."

He stepped forward, undid the black collar around the neck of the corpse, and the head rolled on the floor!

The student began to shriek, "The demon! The demon has gained possession of me! I am lost forever."

Vainly they tried to calm him. But he was possessed by the frightful belief that an evil spirit had brought the dead body back to life and tricked him into pledging away his soul forever.

With a cry he ran out into the street and was never seen in Paris again. Years later the rumor circulated that he had returned to his native Germany, where he died in a madhouse, still believing himself possessed by a demon.

Billy Mosby's Night Ride

(United States—New England)

In the early 1800s, in a small town in a remote part of New York state, a young boy named Billy Mosby, whose parents had died, was raised by his grandparents, Enoch and Anne Mosby.

Billy helped out on his grandparents' farm, getting up early to milk the cows and feed the pigs and gather the eggs. Though he sometimes grumbled when his grandfather rousted him out of bed before sunrise, he liked his new life and found little to complain about.

He was afraid, however, of his grandparents' neighbor, Francis Woolcott, who lived a half mile down the road from them. Every afternoon, when the sun was westering and long shadows had begun to creep down the hillsides, Billy would watch from a window as Francis Woolcott, like a tall, dark shadow, strode down the dusty road toward the grove of ash and chestnut trees at the end of the road.

He lived in a cabin, which he had let fall nearly to ruin. But he never wanted for anything. The farmers whispered that he was a witch—and feared him so much that they gave him pork, flour, meal, cider, or anything that he might need. If they didn't, neighbors said, he would make a horse come to a dead halt in the middle of plowing, or make a man run around, flapping his folded arms like wings and clucking like a chicken. But even worse, rumor said, was the fact that the old man could conjure up thirteen night riders—demons straight from hell—when the moon was growing old. They would go anywhere he told them to, and do all sorts of mischief. Whenever he heard about the demon riders, Billy felt a thrill of fear—and an eagerness to see these creatures of the night (from a safe distance, of course).

Woolcott never bothered Billy's grandparents. They were polite to the man when they met him in the lane, and thought the talk of witchery was so much foolishness. "Good Christian folk should be about their business and not wasting time scaring each other with such nonsense," declared Anne Mosby.

But Billy kept an open mind; there was so much talk in the neighborhood, he couldn't believe *everybody* was wrong. He kept his thoughts to himself, however: he knew there was no arguing with his grandparents once their minds were made up.

But Billy's curiosity about Francis Woolcott grew the more he tried not to think about the strange old man.

"I've got to see for myself," he decided one evening. So after his grandparents were asleep in their room, he slipped out his bedroom window and ran down the road to Woolcott's cabin. A three-quarter moon overhead gave plenty of light to see by.

But when he was near the dark cabin, Billy saw the old man open the front door. The boy ducked behind a bush; but, peeking from behind some leaves, he saw that Woolcott was carrying bundles of oat straw in his arms. With a quick glance up and down the road, the shadowy figure headed toward the grove of ash and chestnut trees at the end of the lane.

When it seemed safe, Billy followed. Something told him that tonight he would find out the truth about Woolcott's witchery.

The man went directly to a clearing in the center of the grove. There he carefully laid out thirteen bundles of oat straw in a circle. Standing inside this ring, Woolcott extended his arms and began to turn, muttering words that Billy, watching around the trunk of a chestnut tree, could not hear.

As the witch spun faster, the bundles of oat straw began to put off sprouts so they looked as if they were growing into gnarly plants. But the "roots" quickly became horses' legs, the bundles themselves became the bodies of sleek black horses, and the strange "blossoms" became their heads and tails.

Then a cloud passed across the moon, and the clearing was suddenly dark. When the moonlight returned, Billy saw that there was now a rider on the back of each horse. They were wrapped in black cloaks and had their broad-brimmed hats drawn down so that the boy could see nothing of their faces.

Quickly Francis Woolcott began giving instructions to these mysterious horsemen, sending them off in different directions. Sometimes a night rider would go alone; sometimes two would gallop off together. When all but one had been sent away, Billy, leaning closer to try and hear what Woolcott was saying, stepped on a dry, fallen branch that gave a loud *SNAP!*

Instantly the man at the center of the clearing came bounding across and grabbed the boy before he could run. Woolcott's hand was like a claw on Billy's shoulder as he hauled the boy into the clearing, where the last night rider silently waited.

"Please don't hurt me!" begged Billy. "I promise I won't tell."

"Tell whomever you please," said the man. "It doesn't matter a jot to me." Then he fixed Billy with a thoughtful stare and stroked his chin. "It might just be I could use a brave lad like you as an apprentice. You've got curiosity enough to kill a cat nine times over. And you seem bright enough." Now Woolcott was rubbing his hands together eagerly. "Yes, you have all the makings of a fine apprentice. So we'll begin your lessons tonight: since you were curious about my friend, ride with him awhile—satisfy your curiosity."

Before Billy could even ask what an "apprentice" was, the old man picked him up with surprising strength and swung him onto the saddle, behind the shadowy rider. "Now go!" the old man yelled.

Without a word, the rider urged his midnight steed to a trot and guided the animal out of the clearing to the road. Billy found he was stuck to the sleek, black horse as though he were a part of it. He glanced once over his shoulder and saw Francis Woolcott standing in the clearing, watching him. The rider in front said nothing; but Billy felt him urging his horse to a gallop, the moment they were free of the trees.

In uncanny silence they rushed down the lane. The silky black cloak of the man in front of him whipped back around Billy, obscuring his view much of the time. The horses' hoofs made no sound on the rock-strewn roadway; the only sound was the wind rushing past the boy's ears. They raced like hurricanes across fields and through woods—leaping bushes, fences, even *trees* without effort.

Billy lost all track of time and distance. He began to think they were going to ride forever, when they reached the gates of a farm Billy had never seen before. The house was quiet and dark.

Reining in his horse in front of the barn, the night rider cried:

"Tangle the horses' tails this night;
Let the hogs all sing and dance upright."

The doors of the barn flew open, and two horses charged into the yard. They whinnied in terror, and Billy could see their tails were so twisted together that they began running in a circle, which only frightened them more. Behind them, in the shadows of the barn, he saw the nightmarish forms of three pigs, squealing and prancing around on their hind legs, as though they were trying to sing and dance.

Lamps were lit in the farmhouse; Billy could hear shouts. The night rider wheeled his horse and galloped away from the farm. They traveled fast as a whirlwind through unfamiliar countryside. Long after the moon had set, Billy began to recognize landmarks. In the starlight he saw that they were nearing the cluster of chestnut and ash trees where his adventure had begun.

But at the very edge of the grove, Billy's rider suddenly vanished; the black horse turned into a bundle of oat straw under him, and he tumbled to the ground with a *thump*.

He lay for a long time, just catching his breath. Then he got to his feet, grabbed the bundle of oat straw, and ran to tell his grandparents what he had seen. Before he reached home, he looked at the oat straw and thought, "They'll never believe me." So he crept quietly back into bed and said nothing, though in his mind he relived the amazing night ride again and again.

The next evening, sitting at the kitchen table helping his grandmother shell peas, Billy asked, "What's an 'apprentice'?"

"A beginner, a learner," Anne Mosby answered, "a boy who works for someone so he can learn the man's trade." She looked at her grandson curiously. "You thinking of hiring yourself out to someone?"

"No," said Billy, "I just heard the word somewhere, and I wondered what it meant."

But as he worked at the peas, his mind began to race. He imagined what it might be like to wave his hands and have pigs dance in the moonlight or bundles of oat straw turn into night riders on magical horses. If he could ever get up the nerve, he thought, he might, just *might*, ask Francis Woolcott to make him an apprentice. It was a frightening thought, but it was also an exciting one.

But there were no more stories of the thirteen night riders after that. Though Billy eagerly watched the road past the farm, old Francis Woolcott, who was ninety years old, no longer visited the neighbors and took away the farmers' goods with him. The boy heard several people mutter, "He's died or gone to the devil, and not a moment too soon."

No one would go near the silent, tumble-down cabin. When Billy suggested he and his grandparents should go take a look, Anne and Enoch told him to mind his own business.

When his need to know what had happened and his fear that he might never learn the secrets of night riding got the better of him, Billy slipped away one afternoon to the little house that looked completely deserted. He knocked several times; when a faint cry came from inside, the boy pushed open the door.

The cramped room inside smelled stale and sour. Old Francis Woolcott lay under a pile of filthy bedclothes on a cot in one corner. At first Billy thought the old man was dead, his eyes were closed so tight. But they popped open, and Woolcott asked sharply, "What are you doing here, boy?"

"I . . . well . . . ," Billy mumbled.

"Speak up!" Francis Woolcott demanded.

"I want to become your apprentice," the boy managed to get out.

"Then you're a fool, boy," said the old man bitterly. "Why would you want to learn such things?"

"I want to call up night riders of my own," Billy said eagerly. "I want to be able to turn people I don't like into chickens."

"There's a price on such secrets, boy," whispered the old man, suddenly turning his head to watch the door. "There's a terrible price which nobody should have to pay. But I'm going to, soon enough."

"What do you mean?" asked Billy, wondering if maybe the old man had gone out of his head.

"He's coming for me soon," croaked Francis Woolcott. "I'm dying, but I won't have any peace."

"Maybe I'd better go get my grandfather," said Billy, frightened by the other's fear. He turned to go, but the old man grabbed his wrist with a clutch like a circle of iron.

Billy heard a sudden clap of thunder, unexpected on what had been a pleasant summer day. Staring out the window, he saw rain pelting down from a sudden storm. In the shadows, the dying man's face had such a horrible look that Billy gave a small cry of alarm. With each peal of thunder, Woolcott trembled more and more.

"He's coming," the old man said again, struggling to sit up in bed. Then he gave a cry and fell back on his pillow.

Billy heard the loudest crash of thunder yet. Then, over the sound of the wind and rain, he heard galloping hoofs in the road. They stopped just outside the cabin.

Francis Woolcott, terror-stricken, tightened his hold on the boy, and tried to say something that Billy couldn't make out. The door was flung open, and a night rider stood like a monstrous shadow in the doorway. The old man gave a final, strangulated cry, then let his hand drop limply away from Billy's wrist.

There was a violet flash of lightning; for an instant Billy caught a glimpse of the rider's face. He saw horns, skin the color of raw beef, and eyes that burned like coals. The room smelled of sulfur, and the sound of rain on the roof was deafening. Then the figure strode to the bed, picked up the old man as if he weighed no more than a bundle of oat straw, and carried him through the door.

The panel slammed behind them. There was a peal of thunder, then the sound of galloping hoofs disappearing into the rain.

But when Billy had calmed down enough to leave the cabin that now held only him, he found the road outside was dry. At home he found his grandparents hadn't noticed any rain or heard any thunder. When he tried to tell them what he had seen, they scolded him for making up outlandish stories.

Later Anne asked her grandson, "You still thinking about becoming someone's apprentice?"

"No, ma'am," said Billy, "not now, not *ever!*"

The Hunter in the Haunted Forest

(a Native American legend)

Once a young hunter of the Teton tribe went seeking game in a forest that was supposed to be haunted. His relatives and friends tried to discourage him from going there. But he said, "I have a wife and two children to feed. Winter is coming, and luck has been against me. We have very little to eat. If I don't bring back game, my family will starve."

"We will share what we have with you," promised his relatives.

"No," he said, "if the winter lingers, and my family eats too much of your food, we will all starve. I have heard there is much game in those woods because no one goes there."

"That is because ghosts roam its paths at night," said his friends. "Anyone who goes there does not come back."

But the young man's mind was made up. He took a small quantity of *wasna*, which is grease mixed with pounded buffalo meat and wild cherry. His father gave him some tobacco to take with him, also.

Then he set out. After two days he reached the edge of the haunted forest. Just as he entered its shadows, the Thunder Beings raised a great storm, so he was forced to seek shelter from the pounding rain. Hurrying along the path, he came to a clearing. In the center was a small tepee made of deer hide.

Just as the hunter was about to lift the flap and go inside, he heard two persons talking.

One voice said, "Hush! There is someone outside. Let us invite him in. We will offer him food and invite him to stay the night here. Then, when he is asleep, we will kill him and follow his ghost along the spirit's road"—which is what the Teton people called the Milky Way.

"Yes, yes," the other voice agreed eagerly.

Then the hunter fled, because he knew they were ghosts inside the tepee. And he knew from their talk that they had not found their way out of this world, but walked a dark trail—probably because they had been wicked when they were alive.

So he ran until he thought his lungs and heart would burst. For a time he was sure he heard the ghosts following him; but when he could run no more, he looked back and realized the sound was only the rain dripping from tree branches onto the leaves spread over the forest floor.

As sunset approached, the rain stopped and the sky cleared. The hunter found what shelter he could under a fallen tree. He tried to sleep, but voices gathered around him and whistled, *"Hyu! hyu! hyu!"* though he could see no one. When the moon rose, the voices scattered like leaves in the wind and left only silence behind. He pulled his blanket over his head and tried again to sleep.

When the hunter awoke the next morning, he decided to go deeper into the woods. But though he found plentiful signs of game all around, he was unable to see a single deer or elk. Disappointed, when night came he found a small clearing and built a fire to warm himself. He ate a bit of *wasna,* then leaned back against a tree trunk to smoke some of the tobacco his father had given him.

He had only taken a puff or two when an old man, wrapped in a red robe, appeared at the edge of the clearing, making the sign of peace. The hunter invited him to sit, and the old man settled down on the other side of the clearing.

The young man, happy to have human company, offered the other some *wasna*. The old man refused, but he asked eagerly for some of his tobacco. The hunter held his pipe out to the other; but when the old man took it and held it by the stem, the younger man saw in the firelight that his fingers were nothing but bones.

Then the stranger let his robe slip back from his shoulders, and all his fleshless ribs were visible. The ghost (for the hunter knew this is what the old man was) did not open his lips when he pulled on the pipe; the smoke came pouring out through his ribs.

When he had finished smoking, the ghost said, "Ho! Now we must wrestle. If I throw you, you will go home empty-handed, to face cold death this winter. If you can throw me, you will catch more game than you can carry, and your family will stay well fed and healthy until the spring."

Since there was nothing else he could do, the young man agreed. But first he threw an armful of brush on the fire; then he put even more brush near the flames.

The ghost rushed at the hunter. He seized him with his bony hands, which hurt the young man painfully, though he did not cry out. Then he tried to push off the ghost, but the skeleton's legs were very powerful, and were locked around the hunter's own.

With great effort, the hunter was able to twist nearer the fire. When the ghost came near it, he grew weak. But when

he was able to pull the young man back toward the darkness, he became strong again.

As the fire burned low, the ghost's strength grew. The man began to get weary, but the thought of his family slowly starving to death gave him added vigor. He was able to force the ghost near the fire again. Then, with a last effort, the hunter yanked one foot free and pushed the pile of brush into the fire. It blazed up instantly, lighting the whole clearing. The ghost let out an ear-piercing scream, and then his skeletal frame began to crumble, until it was nothing more than a pile of ashes.

But the ghost had spoken the truth. The next day the young man caught all the game he needed—more than enough to provide his family for the long, cold winter ahead.

Brother and Sister

(retold from an African folktale)

There was once a stubborn girl who refused to marry any of the young men who came to ask for her hand. The men offered her father cattle and goats in exchange for his daughter, but the young girl would have none of them. Finally her parents grew angry and said they would marry her to the next suitor who came for her.

Soon after this there was a great dance in the village, and all the young men from other villages came. A very tall and handsome man arrived, wearing a headband of gold. All of the unmarried girls tried to catch his eye—but the young woman who had refused to marry was the first to speak to him. When it came time for dancing, he saw to it that he danced close to her. And she fell in love with him.

Later the young man asked for the daughter's hand in marriage, and her mother and father joyfully agreed.

But during the feasting that followed, while everyone laughed and shouted and ate sugar canes, oranges, bananas, and guavas, the girl's little brother saw that the stranger had a second mouth at the back of his head, which was the sure mark of a demon.

He told his mother what he had seen, but she only said,

"What foolishness to think that this fine young man is evil. You are wicked to make up such a story. Be quiet, and share your sister's happiness."

When he went to his father, his father only said the same thing, adding that he would beat the boy if he made trouble. Nor would any of his friends do anything but laugh at him.

So the wedding was celebrated. After several days, the girl and her new husband set off for his home, which was a great distance away.

But her brother, who was worried because of what he had seen, followed them.

As the couple walked along, the husband asked, "Can you still see the smoke from your parents' village?"

"Yes," his new wife answered.

Then he shrugged and they walked on in silence. A little farther along, he asked, "Can you see the hills behind your parents' home?"

"I can see the tops just above the trees," she said. Then they walked farther still.

At last he said, "Can you see the smoke or the hills that mark your old home?"

"No," she replied, "they have disappeared."

"Then we are in my land." And he brought her to a one-room mud hut. It looked like one of the *madili*, temporary houses her people lived in when they were away from their real homes; but the grass thatch was black with the soot of years. There was no *shamba*, vegetable garden, near it. The hut was surrounded by a *boma*, a fence built of thorn branches, like an enclosure where cattle were kept, with only a single small opening in it for a gate. Far away the girl could hear the sound of a rushing river.

There were only a few poor mats and broken pots inside.

The young wife was very disappointed. But because she loved her husband, she only said, "Have you any green maize or beans or sweet potatoes, so that I can fix a meal for you?" For it was growing very late in the day.

"I will eat soon enough," said her husband.

"But," the girl persisted, "surely you have some *shihango?*"—the roasted meat her people kept on hand for emergencies.

"I will eat very soon," her husband replied. Then he sat in the door of the hut and would say nothing else. She set to work cleaning the place, which seemed as dirty as an animal den. When the shadows lengthened, the man rose suddenly and walked down the path into the woods. His new wife called out to him not to leave her alone or risk the dangers of the forest, but he ignored her. Soon the shadows under the trees swallowed him up.

Now the little brother was hidden at the edge of the woods, watching. He secretly followed the man. In a clearing he saw him beginning to change into a hyena. Then the creature threw back its head and shrieked, and the boy, still hidden, heard answering shrieks from all around. In a moment the boy guessed that his sister had been lured to this place to be eaten by the demon and his forest kin.

So the boy raced back to the hut and told his sister what he had seen. At first she refused to believe him. But her husband's strange actions and the howls of approaching hyenas forced her to believe.

Because they did not dare try to outrun the beasts, they rearranged the thorny branches that made up the *boma*, fence, around the hut, to block the only opening. When the animals reached the hut, they found it completely circled by a wall of thorns. At first the creatures only snarled and padded around the outside of the fence.

Then the demon, who was far larger than any true hyena, sprang over the wall of thorns.

The boy and his sister had hidden in the hut and tied the wooden door shut with strips of hide. But the hyena was hurling itself against the door, and they knew it wouldn't last long. So they climbed out the single small window at the back of the hut and onto the roof, just as the beast burst through the entrance. There they found a low-hanging tree branch just within reach.

"Now we must climb for our lives," the boy said.

His sister boosted him up, because he was lighter. Then, when he was safely lying at length on the branch, he stretched down his hand and helped her up. A moment later the hyena realized what they had done and scrambled onto the roof after them. But the sister and brother climbed high up into the branches of the tree, where the beast could not follow.

Then the creature leapt back over the *boma* with a cry. The other hyenas gathered in a circle around the trunk of the tree. Led by the demon, with their powerful jaws they made short work of chewing through the tree.

But the boy and his sister fled to another tree, just as the trunk of the first was bitten through, so it toppled with a *crash.*

As quickly as they reached a new tree, the hyenas began biting its trunk to pieces, so they were forced to flee again. This went on until just before dawn, they came to a tree that grew beside the fast-flowing river. To the right and left there were no trees close enough or big enough to help them. And the beasts had bitten halfway through the last tree.

"Now we must swim," cried the boy.

Before his sister could say anything, the tree fell into the swift river with a *splash.*

They began swimming for the far shore. Snarling, the demon hyena plunged into the water after them. The remaining animals, howling and snapping, ran up and down along the bank, but wouldn't go into the water.

"We can't both get away!" gasped the girl. "I will let him catch me, and you can escape."

"We're almost to the shore!" her brother answered. "Keep swimming."

Just as they reached the sandy bank, the dawn began to break, and the demon turned back into human form. Now it was the tall young man who was swimming after them— but his eyes were those of an angry beast, and he growled like a forest creature.

The brother and sister began throwing rocks at him, so that he could not land. He bellowed at them and threatened them, but they just kept pelting him, so he couldn't get near.

When he began to tire, he turned and swam back toward the other shore.

But the current was too strong and fast for him in his weakened state, and he was carried away and drowned.

Then the boy and girl returned home, where they were welcomed happily by their parents. The little boy was called a hero, and the tale of their terrifying adventure became well known throughout the land.

The Lovers of Dismal Swamp

(United States—Virginia)

There is a swamp in Virginia with an open stretch of water at its very heart. Some people call this Drummond's Pond, but it's also known as the Lake of the Dismal Swamp.

For almost two hundred years, folks say, it has been haunted by two sad ghosts. And this is their story:

The daughter of a family that had settled near the marsh contracted swamp fever. For days she lingered, while the young man who planned to marry her sat by her bedside, holding her hand tightly. By never letting go, he seemed to think that he could hang onto her life, which was slowly slipping away.

But she died and was buried on the edge of the swamp.

The young man was so grief-stricken that he refused to go to the funeral. For days he refused to eat or sleep; nor would he listen to any words of comfort. After much pleading, his family and friends convinced him to begin taking care of himself, and he did recover a measure of health. But his mind was never the same.

He began to fancy that his bride-to-be was not dead, but

had merely wandered into the silent, shadowy depths of Dismal Swamp. "She's waiting for me there," he told his friends. "She's hiding because she knew Death was looking for her."

Later his family heard him mutter, "I'll go and find her. And if Old Death comes looking for her, I'll hide her in the hollow of a cypress tree until he goes away."

The young man's family feared that he might harm himself, so they kept him confined to the house and watched him day and night, to keep him from going off to look for his lost love. But one day he slipped away and ran into the swamp.

For a time he heard his father and brothers and friends calling his name as they searched for him. But he only plunged farther into the marsh. Finally the sounds of pursuit were swallowed up in the distance, and the silence of Dismal Swamp all around him was broken only by the cry of a waterbird or the splash of a frog and the persistent buzz of insects.

For days he wandered, eating berries, sleeping on hillocks of dank grass or curled in the roots of trees. His face and hands and clothes were torn by brambles; his boots were caked with mud; several times he narrowly avoided a run-in with a poisonous water snake that slithered over the wet earth.

At last he reached Drummond's Pond late one evening. A will-o'-the-wisp hovered over the surface of the water, far out from shore.

"There she is," he told himself. As he stared through the falling darkness at the bobbing light, he cried excitedly, "I see her! She's standing there holding a lantern!"

Quickly he began gathering together fallen cypress boughs to fashion into a raft. When the flimsy craft was

ready, he launched it onto the water, using a long tree limb stripped of its leaves to pole toward the center of the pond.

He was sure he could see his girl, floating so her feet rested lightly on the black surface of the lake, smiling at him. In her right hand she held a lantern high like a pale beacon to guide him; with her left hand she beckoned him to join her.

"I'm coming, darling!" he called and shoved the long pole even deeper into the murky depths. But his eagerness and a sudden wind that swept across the water, raising waves, undid him. The hastily built raft came apart, and he sank, splashing and crying out his love's name into the dark water, never to rise again.

But hunters who have found themselves near Drummond's Pond when the sun is setting claim to have seen a ghostly raft drifting quietly over the black waters. At the front sits the wraith of a young girl, holding a lantern that gives off pale light. Behind her is a ghastly young man, who poles them along as they vainly search for a way out of Dismal Swamp.

Boneless

(based on folklore of the Shetland Islands)

For a long time people in the Shetland Islands told stories about a creature they could only call "Boneless," or simply, "It," because no two people who had encountered it ever saw quite the same thing. When asked to describe it, one person said it looked like a large jellyfish, another said it was like a lump of wet, white wool, a third said it looked like a pale animal without legs, while a fourth described it as a ghastly white human body without any head. Yet for all that people often claimed it had no legs, it could move faster than a dog; some swore it could fly faster than a hawk, even without wings.

It was most often seen around Christmas time, when the nights are the longest, and goblins and other strange creatures have the greatest power to plague people.

There was a certain farm that "It" troubled every year at Yuletide. The creature would frighten the animals in the barn and make its presence known to everyone in the house, frightening the children and servants so that they huddled in terror all Christmas Eve. Sometimes the farmer or his wife would catch a glimpse of something milk-white

and wet as a fishbelly pressed up against the window of the
kitchen or the parlor. But it would be gone in the blink of
an eye, so that neither could say for sure what he or she had
seen.

As a result of this mischief, everyone was so tired and
cross the next morning that Christmas Day was ruined.
The inhabitants of the farmhouse spent the short day nap-
ping and dreading the early onset of night, when the thing
would come to haunt them again.

One Christmas Eve, however, the farmer vowed to his
wife, "I'll not put up with this again. When 'Boneless'
comes, I'll chase it away for good and all."

His wife pleaded with him not to risk angering "It." The
thing hadn't hurt anyone, it just gave them the frights. But
if her husband made it angry, she reasoned, who knew
what such an "unnatural creature" might do?

But her husband's mind was made up. When evening
came, he asked his wife to gather the children and servants
in the dining room, with the curtain drawn, while he sat in
the parlor, reading a Bible by the light of a candle. An axe
rested against the leg of his chair.

Toward midnight, he was suddenly alarmed by a sound
like a huge mass of wet meat slapped against the front
door. Snatching up his Bible in one hand and his axe in the
other, he yanked open the door and rushed out.

There was a pool of wetness gleaming on the doorstep in
the moonlight, but nothing else. Far down the road he saw
something pale like a puddle of moonlight and large as a
calf, moving down the road toward the cliffs that over-
looked the sea. With a shout of triumph, he chased after
the thing.

Just as "It" was about to slip over a cliff and escape into
the sea, the farmer shouted, "The Good Lord guide my
hand!" and hurled his axe, which stuck fast in the slimy

creature. After that, the thing made no movement or sound.

Not daring to go any closer on his own, the man ran back home, where he gathered his servants and persuaded them to accompany him to the spot. There "Boneless" was, like some large pudding, with the axe still sticking in it.

"What's to be done with it now?" asked one young man.

"Bury it," said the farmer, shaking now that the deed was done.

So the men fetched shovels and hastily began to fling earth over the carcass. None of them could tell what it looked like; as they worked to bury it, they got into arguments, because the creature looked different to each pair of eyes. Some were not sure if it was truly dead; and no one, not even the farmer himself, would go near enough to recover the axe. So the tool was buried along with "It."

When no trace of the creature could be seen, they dug a wide trench around the mound of earth, so that neither man nor beast would disturb it. But in fact the people of the neighborhood never went near the spot after that.

In the spring, however, a visitor to the island, who had stopped for the night at the farmhouse, heard the story, and eagerly asked the farmer and his wife for details. Believing it only a local superstition, but curious nonetheless, the stranger went to the mound the next day. He found a part of the ditch wall had collapsed, so that it was easy enough to scramble across to the heap of earth.

Digging with his hands to find out what lay hidden in it, he suddenly saw a thick, curdled light gathering in the hollow he had scooped out. This turned suddenly to a milky mist that gathered around him, dense as a fog from the sea, but pale as if steeped in moonlight (though it was still midday).

Frightened, he backed away from the mound and hurried across the crumbling earth to the other side of the ditch.

He had just reached safety there when *something* rose out of the hole, rolled across the trench, and vanished into the mist in the direction of the ocean.

By the time the visitor had reached the farmhouse, the strange, milk-white mist had become an ordinary gray fog, and he had calmed down somewhat. He was sure that what he had seen was something quite natural which had just appeared unnatural because he had been more frightened by the stories of strange creatures than he wanted to admit.

"Surely what I saw was nothing more than an otter or a seal," he said, "something that happened to be near the mound when I chanced to be there."

But the farmer merely shook his head. "We all know there's many kinds of life that live in the air, on the earth, or in the water. And we, poor mortals, have not the power to understand the like of some of them."

The stranger did not get into an argument with his host, though he thought the man a superstitious bumpkin and was angry at himself for believing, even for a moment, such a story.

Two nights later the traveler, who had become somewhat lost, was hiking along a stretch of road high above a cove. He had just located the pinpoints of light that marked the village he was seeking and was heading toward it. He could hear waves breaking on the rocks far below him. Suddenly in the moonlight, he saw something long and white stretched across the road. It wasn't fog, though it had a wet, kind of misty look to it. He couldn't see the lights of the distant town any longer.

The whiteness began to slither toward him, as if it were

alive. Without hesitating, he turned and began to run back the way he'd come. But the thing overtook him in an instant. It wrapped itself around him so that he felt like he was being smothered in a heavy, wet blanket. It was as cold as if it had been soaked in the night sea, and smelled of rotten fish.

Then he felt his waist, legs, and ankles caught in nooses like an octopus's tentacles. His bonds glowed like ropes of moonlight, but were tough as the hardiest seaweed. They began dragging him toward the cliff edge, the ocean below, and certain death.

He tried to call for help; but he was so scared, the sound caught in his throat, as surely as if an assassin's cord had tightened around his neck. He scrambled for a claw hold on the stony path, but his fingernails scraped and slid over the hard rocks without giving him any purchase.

Just as he felt his feet, his knees, then his thighs being yanked over the edge of the cliff—in the instant before he tumbled off into the hungry darkness—he managed to hook his left arm around a sharp outcropping of rock. He flung his right arm around it also, and hung on for dear life. From this dizzying perch, he dared to look below him.

Half of him dangled into space, lassoed by silvery ropes stretching down into the darkness, twisting together into a single cable that linked him to a luminous splotch in the waves hundreds of feet below.

The deadly ropes pulled tighter. He tightened his grip on the rock in response. He had the sickening feeling that he might be torn in two if he—or the horrible thing that had him in thrall—didn't let go.

"Oh, sweet Lord," he prayed—

—and felt the thing loosen its grasp, just a little.

He recalled how the farmer had used a Bible and a

prayer to help defeat the thing once. *A prayer, a prayer,* he told himself, *I need a prayer.*

But in his fright, he could remember nothing except a prayer he had said as a child:

> "Now I lay me down to sleep,
>   I pray the Lord my soul to keep;
> If I should die before I wake,
>   I pray the Lord—"

At the second mention of "the Lord," the loops of moonlight loosened, then dropped away.

Looking below, he saw ribbons of light coiling down, hitting the churning waves with a sizzle like a candle flame extinguished in a saucer of water.

For an instant, circles of cold fire spread outward, one after the other like ripples in a pond. Then all the light was gone. There was only the empty black surf pounding below him.

Painfully he climbed back onto the road, where he lay for a long time, just catching his breath.

When he reached the town, the traveler was too shaken to do anything more than ask when the earliest boat was leaving for the mainland. He left the next day for London, never to return to Shetland.

The Death Waltz

(United States—New Mexico)

In 1851, when New Mexico was still a territory and had not yet become a state, Fort Union was built ninety miles northeast of Santa Fe, to protect people from Apache Indian raids. The fort helped keep the trails open, so that huge, red-wheeled freight wagons, pulled by teams of mules or yokes of oxen, could bring hardware, calico, and other goods to Santa Fe, while taking furs, hides, and Mexican mules and burros back to St. Louis, Missouri.

Fort Union was the only spot for miles around where an effort was made to keep up the appearances of gracious social life, such as was found east of the Missouri River. There were a number of very beautiful young ladies attached to the post, and the most attractive of them all was Elizabeth Bidwell, the sister-in-law of Captain Moore. She had recently come to Fort Union to stay with her sister, the captain's wife, because their parents were dead, and the maiden aunt who had raised Elizabeth had become ill.

Young Elizabeth enjoyed the excitement that came from living on an outpost where the threat of an Indian attack lurked always in the background. She was doubly delighted by the attentions the young officers paid to her, since there were few women who were both pretty and unmarried in that wild country.

One lieutenant named Frank Sutter, recently transferred from the east, was especially attracted to Elizabeth's charms. He devoted himself to winning her hand, in spite of the other handsome officers who buzzed around her like bees discovering the sweetest blossom in a garden.

Frank Sutter's experience with the world was not large enough so that he could tell whether a woman was responding seriously to his attentions or was merely flirting with him. He would walk with Elizabeth in the afternoon, when the sunny, clear air would turn in the blink of an eye to heavy rain that sent them scurrying for cover—then disappeared as quickly as it had begun to fall. They would sit together in the evening, watching the sky turn red, pink, orange, and yellow to the west, while the mountains to the east of the fort turned dark, purple, mysterious.

At such times, Frank would talk to Elizabeth about many things—but he didn't dare tell the young woman, whose hand rested lightly on his arm, just what he felt for her.

Elizabeth laughed, and fanned herself, and complained about the heat, and chattered on about how bored she was growing with life at Fort Union and how eager she was to return to Missouri and the social life there. Such talk cut Lieutenant Sutter to the quick, but he never let his pain show.

Then one day, messengers came racing to the fort with news of a series of Apache raids. Captain Moore ordered a detachment of troops to chase and punish the guilty Indians. Lieutenant Sutter was put in command of the expedition.

The night before they were to set out, however, he called on Elizabeth Bidwell. Drawing her to a private corner of the porch, he dropped to his knee and said, "Elizabeth, if you didn't guess it before, I'm telling you now: I'm in love with you."

She smiled at him, then turned her head away and patted her heart. Finally she said, "Why, Lieutenant Sutter, I'm *overwhelmed* by the honor you're giving me."

"And do you have some affection for me?"

"You don't even have to ask," she replied, blushing.

"Then, Miss Bidwell, will you do me the honor of marrying me when I return?"

He was the handsomest young officer in Fort Union, and his prospects were excellent. Elizabeth answered without thought or hesitation, "Of course I will."

"But, if the fortunes of war deprive me of life—"

"Hush!" she said, "Don't even think such a thing! If you should fail to return, I *swear* I will never marry another."

"Then," he said, rising to his feet and kissing her hand, "you can be assured nobody else will have you. I will come back and make my claim."

The lieutenant and his troops departed the next morning. On the evening of their second day on patrol, they overtook the band of Apaches that had gone on the warpath. In the heat of battle, Frank Sutter became separated from the rest of his men. When the dust had settled and the Indians had scattered into the dusk, the troops searched vainly for the young lieutenant, but he had vanished. When they could turn up no trace of him, they returned to Fort Union and reported him missing in action.

Other people at the fort noted (not very kindly) that Elizabeth Bidwell, Frank Sutter's bride-elect, grieved very little for the missing bridegroom-to-be. And it came as no great surprise to anyone when she announced her intention of marrying a man recently arrived from the East, who would take her back to St. Louis with him.

Her sister and brother-in-law arranged a wedding for her on the post. When the big day arrived, there was a short ceremony in the chapel; then everyone retired in the evening to the mess hall, which was decorated for a ball.

Outside a sudden thunderstorm rolled through nearby canyons, and sent rain splatting against the roof and walls of the mess hall. But inside all was festivity: there was good food, lots to drink, and loud laughter everywhere. A band was playing with more enthusiasm than tunefulness, but everyone was having a fine time. At the heart of everything was Elizabeth Bidwell, smiling and fanning herself and swirling her skirts of roseblush pink.

Suddenly, when the dance was at full swing, the outside doors of the hall slammed open with a *bang*, letting in a draught of air that made the candles gutter and burn low.

A bloodcurdling cry, neither human nor like any other bird or creature anyone could name, echoed through the common room, carried on the invading wind. All eyes turned to the open doorway. Framed by the doorposts was the body of a dead man, dressed in the stained uniform of a cavalry officer. Across his forehead was a gash left by a tomahawk. His eyes were wide open and burned with a fiery light.

As everyone retreated to the edges of the dance floor, the horrible apparition walked across the floor to the new bride, and pulled her from the arms of her husband. Like the rest of the company, she stood gaping, too shocked to move. The corpse led Elizabeth to the center of the floor; she moved as stiffly as a doll, her mouth working but no sound coming out. Suddenly the thing that had been Lieutenant Sutter clasped the young woman closely to him. Then he gave a signal to the musicians.

Afterward the shaken men protested that they did not know what they were doing. But at the corpse's command, they began to play a waltz, so strange and haunting in its melody that some people burst into tears upon hearing it, while others pressed their hands to their ears to keep out the sound.

On the floor the couple whirled around and around and around. Elizabeth could not take her gaze from the dead lieutenant's burning eyes, but she grew paler and paler. The musicians, possessed by some compulsion from beyond the grave, played faster and faster, until the music became so frantic that the spinning couple out on the floor became a blur of pink skirts and blue uniform.

Then the music slowed from a pace that no human could dance to, back to a waltz, and down to a dirge. The young woman hung limply in the corpse's arms; her slack jaw and empty eyes showed that she was as dead as her partner.

Gently the dead man lowered her body to the floor. For a moment he stood staring down at her; then his eyes circled the horrified company. He threw back his head and gave the same fearful cry they had heard earlier. Then he turned and marched stiffly out into the driving wind and rain, while the doors of the mess hall slammed shut behind him.

When people could move again, Elizabeth's bridegroom rushed to her side, but his efforts to revive her were futile.

The corpse had vanished into the storm that battered Fort Union for a day and a night.

Several days later a troop of soldiers which had been sent to the scene of the earlier battle located Frank Sutter's body where it lay at the bottom of a small gulley, with a single tomahawk gash across the forehead.

He was returned to the post and buried beside Elizabeth Bidwell, in the little cemetery outside the fort.

The Ghost of Misery Hill

(United States—California)

There was once a miner, Tom Bowers, who worked a claim on Misery Hill, near Pike City, in California. Tom was a loner: he never liked having people around him, he only went into town when he needed supplies, and he never took a partner. "Nobody's going to work my claim but *me!*" he told anyone who offered to buy into his claim.

During the winter he laid in supplies and kept to himself, while the snowdrifts piled up high around his cabin. People in Pike City always knew spring had arrived when Tom came down from Misery Hill to purchase a fresh batch of foodstuffs.

But one spring, long after the last traces of snow had melted, the inhabitants of Pike City noticed that Old Tom hadn't turned up with his poke of gold dust to buy beans and salt pork, bread and coffee. After a good deal of discussion, a group of miners and townspeople rode off to investigate.

They found Tom's cabin empty; the pot-bellied stove was stone cold, and some bits of fried bread had gone moldy in the big iron skillet on top of it. Clearly no one had been in the one-room shack for a long time.

Certain now that something had happened to the old miner, the men followed the path that ran from his cabin to the brink of the steep slope where he had done his prospecting. But they found the end of the trail had vanished—had been blotted out by a huge landslide.

Fearing the worst, they dug into the pile of earth and rock; and, after half a day of hard work, they found the old man's body. Then, having solved the mystery and having nothing better to do with Tom's remains, they buried him properly in a shallow grave not far from the mouth of his old mine shaft.

A few miners thought to work Tom's mine on Misery Hill, but the story soon grew that the ghost of Tom Bowers was often seen prowling around, carrying his old pick, near his mine. Soon everybody avoided the spot.

There was one miner, Jim Brandon, who got himself so far into debt when his own claim ran out that he became desperate. He moved into Tom's long-empty shack and began to work the abandoned mine. Soon enough he made it pay well enough to clear up his debts and accumulate a nest egg for himself.

But after several months, he began to notice signs that someone else was working his claim by night. Every morning he could see that somebody had tampered with the sluice—a long wooden trough he filled every day with freshly dug gravel. When water from a nearby stream was run down it, bars along the bottom of the sluice would catch any gold the gravel might hold.

Jim searched high and low for a clue to his midnight visitor but found nothing. Thinking some of the other miners might be playing a trick on him, he challenged them. But they all swore they knew nothing about it.

After this, things were quiet for a few days. Then one morning, Jim again found that someone had been loading the sluice with gravel and running water through it. When evening came, he loaded his rifle and, hiding himself in a nook from which he had a clear view of the claim site, he kept watch for the intruder.

For a long time he heard nothing but the wind whistling through the pines, and the Yuba River rushing over rocks nearby. He could see the distant ridges of the Sierras gleaming in the starlight, but though he strained his eyes, he saw nothing moving near the mine entrance.

Then, by the light of the newly risen moon, he saw a notice shining on a nearby tree trunk, as though someone had just tacked it into place. Curious, he walked over and found the odd sign was as easy to read as if it was glowing by itself, not just reflecting the light of the full moon. It said,

Notice!
I, Tom Bowers
Claim this ground
for placer mining.

Sure now that he was the victim of practical jokers, Jim grabbed for the paper to tear it down—only to feel an electric jolt run from his fingertips to his shoulder. His arm fell numbly at his side.

The notice vanished.

At the same time there came to his ears the sound of gravel being dumped into the sluice. A moment later he heard water gurgling into it, then the rattling and bumping of rocks being tumbled down the length of it.

Shaking his arm back into use, he angrily grabbed his gun and headed toward the sluice. Out of the corner of his eye, he saw the message was glowing again on the tree trunk, but he ignored it. He heard the sound of a pick biting into gravel, now, and nothing mattered except finding out what was going on.

Leveling his rifle, he rounded an outcrop of rock and saw Tom Bowers, swinging his pick near the entrance to the mine. The miner turned to glare at Jim, and the frightened man saw at a glance that he was a ghost. Tom's tall, skinny frame glowed just like the notice on the tree. His head and face were half-covered, with lank, white hair; his eyes blazed from black sockets.

Scared nearly out of his wits, Jim raised his rifle to his shoulder and fired.

The gun's report was followed by a bellow from Tom's ghost. Looking through the rifle smoke, Jim saw the spectre charging at him, his pick raised in both his hands.

"Oh, *Lordy!*" cried Jim and, still clutching his rifle, he took off running, with the angry ghost only a few paces behind.

The living led the dead a wild chase up hill and down, into and out of woods, over streams and ditches, and through scrub, toward Pike City.

In town the miners were all gathered in the saloon, celebrating a new gold strike. Suddenly everyone froze when they heard an ear-splitting scream. Then there was a sound like a body falling, followed by the clang of metal hitting on metal—then silence.

Everyone tumbled outside to see what had happened.

In the middle of the road, they found Jim Brandon's rifle pinned to the ground by the point of a pick sunk clean through the barrel. On the pick's handle were carved the initials "T.B."

No one ever saw Jim Brandon after that night. But for years afterward, miners working near Misery Hill reported the sluice at Tom Bowers's claim ran every night, just like clockwork.

The Loup-Garou
(The Werewolf)

(from French-Canadian folklore)

In the old time in Canada, people believed the werewolf, which they called the *loup-garou,* haunted graveyards and prowled the woods and waited in the brush beside lonely trails to catch unwary travelers and gobble them up.

There was an old couple living on a farm far out in the country. One wintry night Marthe took very ill, and her husband, Pierre, had to go to fetch the doctor in town. This meant a long, long journey through the woods. But Pierre was too worried about his wife to hesitate. He hitched up his horse to his sleigh and set out through the lightly falling snow.

As he went along, he could hear nothing except the *scrunch, scrunch* of snow under the sleigh's runners and the horse's hoofs. The old man wasn't thinking of anything except getting help for Marthe as fast as he could.

They were now a long way into the woods. Moonlight shone on the snow, which lay thick on the ground and on branches of the pine trees all around. Sometimes from deep in the shadows would come the sharp report of an ice-heavy branch snapping and dropping to the ground. Once, Pierre heard an owl hooting. Except for these sounds, silence lay heavily over the forest.

The road ahead was level and easy enough for the horse. But suddenly the animal began to slow down. Pierre shook the reins and shouted, "Giddup!" but the horse was hardly moving at all now. It was as if he was pulling a two-ton load, rather than the little sleigh with its single passenger. The old man flicked his whip, but the horse merely shook its head and made a frightened little whinney. The poor animal was breathing rapidly, his warm breath making clouds like the steam from a steamboat's chimney; sweat was running down his flank.

Now Pierre could feel some of the horse's fear sinking into him. Then there was a low growl just behind him that stood his hair on end. Turning, he discovered what looked like a great big black dog or wolf, its teeth and the claws of its forepaws sunk into the back of the sleigh, its hindpaws dragging on the ground, bringing the sled nearly to a halt.

For one terrible moment Pierre stared directly into the creature's burning yellow eyes. Then, almost without thinking, he cracked his whip across the monster's snout. The wolf gave a howl of pain and loosened its hold on the sleigh for a moment. In that instant the horse lunged forward and ran as if all the devils from hell were in pursuit.

Looking over his shoulder, Pierre could see the shadowy creature bounding down the road close behind. The man knew that unless his guardian angel was riding with him that night, it was all over for him.

He didn't need to urge the horse to go faster: the animal was so scared that he galloped like a hurricane. But for all that, the monster was getting closer.

And closer.

And—

The creature gave a tremendous leap and landed on the back of the sleigh. The *thump* of the impact and the sudden weight on the end of the sleigh sent it sliding first to one side of the road then the other. For a moment Pierre thought he was going to crash; but miraculously the sleigh kept upright on its runners and found the center of the road again. The horse, now crazy with fear, somehow managed to keep from falling in the icy road, often blocked with drifts of snow.

The wolf was growling as it crept toward the old man, who had turned to face the beast. Pierre tried using his whip again, but the monster caught it in his huge jaws, severing it as if it was no more than a twig and tossing it over the edge of the wildly careening sleigh.

Old Pierre felt for his hunting knife, and pulled it free, just as the wolf sprang at him and slammed the man to the bottom of the sleigh. His forepaws were on Pierre's shoulders, pinning him to the floorboards; the man felt his bones were likely to break under the weight of the monster. For one terrible instant he felt the creature's whiskers brush his face like needles, felt its hot breath on his throat, saw its yellow eyes only inches from his own—

Then, with a prayer, he jabbed at the thing with his hunting knife. Though his movement was hampered by the weight of the monster on top of him, he managed to nick it just enough to draw blood, so a spot of red appeared on its pelt.

Instantly the creature reared back, howling like nothing Pierre had ever heard before; then, to the old man's astonishment, the wolf turned into a man. Right away, Pierre knew that this was, indeed, a *loup-garou*, because the stories say if you draw blood from the *loup-garou*, he'll turn back to a man right off and run away.

Pressing his big, pale hand to his side, the man suddenly

leapt off the sleigh. Pierre saw him rolling down a hillside through the snow, where the forest shadows quickly hid him.

Then the sleigh was out of the woods and heading toward the sleeping town ahead. Shaking, Pierre returned his knife to its holster and took hold of the reins, gradually easing the horse back to a trot, saying, "Easy, easy."

When they reached the gate of the doctor's house, Pierre quickly roused the man, who thought at first the old man was the one who was sick, because he was so pale and trembling. But when Pierre told what had happened, the doctor gave him a shot of whiskey. Then they roused the village priest, who gave them holy water and a cross as protection for their journey back through the woods.

Pierre never saw the *loup-garou* again. But Marthe, when she recovered, made him promise never to travel through the woods alone at night again, and the old man was only too happy to give her his word that he never would.

The Golem

(based on Jewish folklore)

There was a rich merchant who lived in a city in Eastern Europe in the sixteenth century. He had heard of the golem, a manlike creature fashioned out of clay that Rabbi Elijah of Chelm and Rabbi Yehuda Loew of Prague had created to serve them. Desiring such a servant for himself, the merchant went to his friend the rabbi, who was a wise man. The good rabbi had studied the magical books of the Kabbala and had discovered many secrets that had been hidden from men's eyes since the beginning of time.

And the most wonderful—and terrible—thing he discovered was how to create a golem. After much persuading, the merchant got the rabbi to agree to bring such a creature to life. The rich man fashioned the likeness of a man out of yellow clay his servants fetched up from the riverbank. He lovingly shaped the hands and feet and head, and carefully sculpted a human face. Then the rabbi said magic formulas from the *Book of Creation* over the figure, walked around it seven times, and wrote the Hebrew word *Emet,* which means "Truth," on the creature's forehead.

Instantly the clay body turned red as fire, and the creature came to life. Hair sprouted on its head, and nails

appeared on its fingers and toes. It climbed clumsily to its feet and stood watching the two men. The rabbi stood for a long time looking at his handiwork and stroking his beard. At last, without saying a word, he left the rich man's house.

The merchant was delighted to have the perfect servant, who would never tire, needed nothing to eat or drink, would require no pay—and could not even complain, because the power that had brought him to life did not give him the power of speech. He ordered the golem to draw water from the well and sweep the courtyard. Silently the clay man went about his tasks.

And for a time he proved an admirable servant. But each day the golem grew a little bit taller and broader, and slower to take the merchant's orders.

Still he was a tireless worker. And when he had grown bigger, the rich man sent him to carry goods to nearby towns and fetch back items the merchant needed for his own business, which prospered. Soon he became the richest man in the city.

When he walked out in the afternoon, the golem trudged silently behind him, to frighten off robbers who might come for his gold or shoo away beggars who also wanted some of his money. No one, looking at the tall, hulking guard of red clay would dream of making the merchant angry.

And still the golem grew a little bit more each day; and each day, the merchant saw in the creature's eyes something that made him uncomfortable, though he could not give it a name.

He asked his friend the rabbi about this, but the old scholar merely shrugged and said, "I can bring the clay to life; I can tell you how to destroy it; more I cannot say."

"I will never destroy my servant," said the merchant, "I am a man of real position now. People tremble when they see me coming; they make way when they hear my servant's footstep on the street."

Soon the golem was nearly twice the height and bulk of a man. In the evening, when the merchant sat at his table, being waited on by the clay figure, he would sometimes grow oddly uneasy as the creature shuffled back and forth to the kitchen. The glow from the fireplace would sometimes light his servant's face in such a way that the thing seemed to watch him with a look of anger. At such moments he was glad that his friend the rabbi had not been able to give the golem the power of speech.

The man's other servants ran away, frightened of the golem. But now the creature was so big it did the work of several, and the merchant could command it to labor all through the night, while he slept—so he counted himself better off. His friends would no longer come to visit, but he was so absorbed with the demands of his growing business that he hardly noticed.

Still the golem grew. Now it had to stoop to enter by even the great front doors of the merchant's house. And the merchant sometimes had to tell his clay servant several times over to do even the simplest task. One morning he had to scream until he was nearly hoarse before the golem took up the broom to sweep and a bucket to clean the ashes from the hearth.

When he returned in the afternoon, he found the broom snapped in half in the middle of the floor and the pail crushed and tossed into the ashes of the fireplace. Angrily the merchant shouted for his servant, but the golem did not come. The man searched all the rooms of the house, but found no trace of the creature.

He went outside, and found the clay being, which was now twice as tall as the tallest man, standing in a far corner of the garden. He ordered the golem to return to the house and finish the tasks he had started, but the thing only stood looking down at him. Something in the way it stared at him made the man take first one and then another step back.

The merchant made one last attempt to regain control of matters. "Since you're out here already," he said, mustering as much authority as he could, "you can draw water from the well for the evening meal."

He was relieved to see the golem start for the well. But instead of drawing water, the creature began to smash the well to bits. Then it turned and began uprooting the fruit trees in the garden.

The merchant tried in vain to get it to stop. But the red clay figure, now almost as high as the wall surrounding the garden, continued its work of destruction, moving closer to the house. Frantic, the man ran about, ordering the creature to stop. But the golem no longer heard him—or if it heard, it no longer would obey.

Terrified, the rich man ran through the rooms of his house, calling for help, but his servants were long gone and no one else dared come near the place. Behind him, he heard splintering wood and a sound like stone grinding on stone. Afraid for his very life, he ran out into the street and hurried to the home of his friend the rabbi.

"Tell me what to do to stop the golem!" he shouted, as soon as he entered his friend's study.

Startled, the rabbi asked what had happened, and the man quickly explained.

"You must erase the first letter from the word *Emet,* which is written on the golem's forehead," the rabbi said. "Then the word becomes *met,* 'death,' and the creature will cease to exist."

The man hurried back home, to find the huge clay figure rampaging through the house, pulling down curtains, smashing holes in the walls, breaking the elegant furnishings into kindling. Seeing his home in ruins, the merchant cried in a loud voice, *"Stop!"*

This time, the golem obeyed. It halted in the center of the room, looking at its master. After a few moments, when he was convinced he again had control of the creature, the merchant dared to come closer. He looked at the word *Emet* written on the golem's forehead, but it was now quite out of reach, because the monster had grown so tall.

The creature waited, staring down at the man.

"I have some things you must do," the merchant began, letting his voice grow softer with each word, "but I have so worn my voice out that I can only whisper what you are to do." Now his voice was little more than a whisper itself: "Bend down and hear my commands."

Stiffly the golem leaned down toward its master. As soon as he could reach its forehead, the merchant rubbed out the *E*, turning *Emet* to *met*, "Truth" to "death."

At that moment, the golem broke apart. But the lifeless mass of yellow clay it once again became fell and crushed the merchant to death.

Lavender

(United States)

Not so long ago, two college freshmen were driving along the road one evening on their way to a dance at a neighboring women's college. Bill, who owned the sleek red convertible, was driving slowly because the road was unfamiliar. Eric, who had a roadmap unfolded over his lap, said, "We're sure not on the highway any longer. We made a wrong turn back there somewhere."

"You're one lousy navigator," laughed Bill, "but what the heck! We're taking the scenic route."

"Yeah," Eric responded, not too enthusiastically, "but I'd just as soon get off this road before it gets too dark." He looked nervously out the car window at the shadows gathering under the trees on either side of the road.

"Hold on!" cried Bill, slamming his foot on the brake. "I think our luck just changed for the better!" He pointed through the windshield to where a slim, young woman stood by the side of the road, flagging them down. In the half-light of evening, they could see she was wearing an old-fashioned lavender dress. Since so many of the women they knew wore old-style clothes they had bought at thrift shops or antique stores, the young men saw nothing un-usual in the way the girl dressed.

Bill brought the car to a halt on the dusty shoulder of the road. "Need a lift?" he called to the attractive young woman.

"I'm going to a dance at Gabriel College," she answered. "I'd appreciate a ride."

"We're going there ourselves," said Bill. "Why don't you hop in and come with us?"

"I believe I will," she said and smiled, climbing into the back seat of the car, while Eric held the door open for her. He was struck by how pale her face was, and how cold her hand felt when it brushed his. There was a faint fragrance of lavender that clung to her, which reminded Eric of his grandmother. But all he said was, "We're lost: I'm the world's worst navigator."

"That's fixed easily enough," their passenger said. Then she gave them careful directions that soon guided them back to the main highway. The three young people talked and joked all the way to Gabriel College. Eric forgot his uneasiness and cracked awful jokes that had Bill groaning. But the young woman in the back seat laughed as though he were the world's greatest comedian.

As they were pulling into the parking lot at the college, Bill suddenly said, "Say, we don't even know your name."

"Oh," she laughed, "just call me 'Lavender,' since that's my favorite color." Then she pushed open the door of the car and climbed out. The music of drums and guitars thrummed across the parking lot. "Hurry," she pleaded, holding a hand out to Bill and Eric, "I don't want to miss a moment of this night!"

Bill took her right hand and Eric, her left. The three of them ran like small children toward the bright lights and loud music.

Inside, while Eric watched Lavender dance with Bill, he thought, *I could fall in love with someone like her.* Then he felt himself blushing, because he'd never felt that way about anyone before. *And,* he reminded himself, *you don't even know her name.* But the mystery that clung to her like the fragrance of lavender only made her seem that much more alluring. Then it struck him, *I'm already in love with her.* Watching Bill on the dance floor with the beautiful, lavender-gowned girl, he guessed that Bill was falling in love with her, too.

How he would sort this out with his best friend was anybody's guess. But "Lavender" was worth it—of that he had no doubt.

When the dance ended, Bill suggested they go someplace for coffee; but the girl only said, "I have to go home." To Eric, she sounded very, very tired.

Bill protested this, but she simply said, *"Please. I have to go home."* Something in her voice left no room for further argument.

As they crossed the parking lot, she began to shiver. Eric gallantly gave her his sportcoat, and she gratefully wrapped it around her shoulders. But she seemed to shiver just as much. He was tempted to put his arm around her, but something about her made him hold back—for all he cursed himself for being a shy fool.

It was very late when they left the highway and started up the side road where they had first met "Lavender."

With an odd, faraway sound in her voice, she directed them to a run-down shack way at the end of a rutted dirt road. There was a single light burning in one window.

When Eric and Bill offered to walk her to her door, she said quickly, "No, I have to go alone!" Again her tone of voice stopped their objections cold.

She waved once—a graceful lavender shadow in the mingled moonlight and starlight—then hurried toward the lighted window like a moth drawn to a flame. With a sigh Bill popped the car into reverse and headed back down the driveway.

It wasn't until they were almost back to their own campus that Eric said, "Hey! She never gave me back my jacket."

"I wondered when you'd notice," chuckled Bill.

"Why didn't you say something?" Eric demanded.

"Don't worry," laughed Bill, "this gives us an excuse to go back tomorrow, find out her real name, and get to know our mysterious 'Lavender' better."

"Oh, yeah," said Eric, eager for a chance to see the young woman again.

Shortly after noon the next day, Bill and Eric drove up to the cabin at the end of the rutted road. They had to knock several times before a very old woman in a faded housedress answered. She glanced from one to the other with watery eyes.

"We've, um, come to see a young lady who calls herself 'Lavender,' " Bill explained.

The old woman shook her head. "I don't know anybody named 'Lavender,' " she said.

But when Eric described the young woman they had met on the road the evening before, she suddenly pressed trembling fingers to her mouth and whispered, "That was *Lily.*"

"So, where is she?" Bill wanted to know.

"She's been dead for many years," said the old woman, wiping a tear away from her eye. "Lily was my daughter, but she died in a car accident on her way to a dance. She's buried in the cemetery two miles down the road." The woman gave a sigh and dabbed at her eye with a crumpled Kleenex. "You're not the first to see her: she often tries to come home. I leave a light burning all night, every night, just hoping some night she'll make it all the way back to me. But that's never happened."

"But—" Eric started to say.

Bill grabbed him by the arm and steered him back to the car. When he had pushed his friend into the front seat and started the engine, Bill said, "Don't you *see?* It's a joke. She doesn't want to see us anymore, so she put the old woman up to telling that story. We've just been given a brush-off, so let's forget the whole thing."

"But my coat . . ."

"You needed a new one, anyway," said Bill. "I'm not going back to that dump ever again. I know when I've been had!"

They drove for a while in silence. Suddenly Eric shouted, "Stop! Pull over!"

Startled, Bill did as his friend said, bringing the car to a halt outside the walls of a small country cemetery. Before Bill could stop him, Eric had leapt out of the car and run through the rusted iron gates that hung ajar. With a soft curse, Bill shut off the engine and climbed out.

He caught up with Eric as his friend was walking up and down rows of gravestones, reading each.

Abruptly Eric stopped, pointing at a small, white gravestone.

"What . . . ?" Bill began, then he fell silent.

Engraved on the tombstone was the name *Lily Abbott*. The dates inscribed showed that the woman had died more than thirty years before. Lying neatly folded on the grass below the stone was Eric's sportcoat.

"It's a trick," Bill said weakly.

But neither one of them believed it.

The Goblin Spider

(a Japanese legend)

There was once a famous samurai named Raiko, who was sent by the Emperor of Japan to rid the country of a terrible goblin spider plaguing the countryside near the city of Kyoto. This famous warrior went searching for the monster with his companion, Tsuna. When they reached the plain of Rendai, which was supposed to be haunted, the two men suddenly saw a skull floating in the air in front of them.

"Have you come to destroy the spider?" the skull asked.

"We have," answered Raiko.

"The monster killed me many years ago," said the skull. "I have waited a long time to see the beast punished. I will show you where to find it."

Before they could question their ghostly friend any further, the skull flew away in front of them, as though it was driven by the wind. The two knights followed as fast as they could. But when they had almost caught up with their strange guide, it suddenly disappeared.

Looking around them, the two men discovered nearby the ruins of a palace. Entering the littered courtyard through a crumbling archway, they saw a strange old woman, sitting on a broken pillar across from them. She was dressed in white, with lank white hair; her face was a mass of wrinkles, delicate as spiders' webs. When she raised her heavy eyelids, her eyes glittered like an insect's, black and cold, at Raiko and Tsuna.

"Warriors, you are not welcome here," she said to them. "I am two hundred and ninety years old. For all my life I have served the demon who haunts this place. Be warned: if you linger here, the monster will slay you as he has slain countless other men—some as brave as you or as foolish."

"We won't be frightened away," said Tsuna.

"Begone, hag," commanded Raiko, "and tell the creature you serve that we are here by the will of the Emperor, who commands us rid his kingdom of the goblin spider."

At this, the old woman broke into a cackling laugh. "I will send some friends to entertain you, while I tell my mistress you have come to see her."

With that, the hag melted into a pale mist and vanished through a crack in the courtyard flagging. At the same moment, dark storm clouds began to gather above the shattered palace; flashes of lightning lit the ruins all around them. A short time later, rain began to patter onto the flagstones of the court.

"Hsssst!" warned Raiko, grabbing his companion's shoulder. "Listen!"

Now Tsuna could hear it also: ghostly footsteps all around them. Suddenly a great company of demons poured out into the rain: some were huge with horns, three toes, three fingers, and three eyes; some looked like animals but walked like men, with faces that were a horrifying mix of beast and human; one had its eyes in its hands, and kept its palms up so it could see; another was a serpent with a woman's head, its long hair flying and its tongue flickering out to taste the rain; small creatures, like frogs or monkeys with a shock of red hair, pranced around the legs of their taller companions.

Both samurai drew their swords. In an instant the gruesome horde was upon them, but their flashing swords kept the monsters at bay. On and on they fought, while more monsters came from the shadows to join those already battling the two heroes. Toward morning, the rain slackened, and the thunder died away somewhat, but still the demons kept up the attack.

Then, over the sounds of battle and the dying storm, Raiko heard a distant cock crowing.

A shudder ran through the monstrous company surrounding them. When the cock crowed a second time, the hideous creatures began retreating to the shadows of the ruins. Hissing and snarling and screeching, the goblin army fled the approaching dawn.

When they were alone in the vast courtyard, Raiko and Tsuna hugged each other and each complimented the other on his bravery.

Then they heard a single pair of footsteps climbing an unseen staircase. In a doorway on the far side of the courtyard, a beautiful, pale woman dressed in white appeared. She looked as slender and graceful as a willow, curving in the breeze. Silently she beckoned the two men to come nearer.

But when they were close to her, she was suddenly wrapped in a fierce white light, brighter than the sun, which blinded the two men. Tsuna gave a cry, dropped to the ground, and pressed his hands to his eyes. Then he rolled to one side. Raiko turned his head aside and raised his left arm to shield his eyes; with his right arm he drew his sword.

The dazzling light grew fainter by degrees. Looking into it from an angle, Raiko saw that the beautiful woman had become a ghastly creature: a thing with a tiny body and a head two feet long that floated at the end of a reedlike neck. Her arms were white as snow, long and thin as ropes that were snaking out toward the half-blinded warrior.

Just as the awful creature touched him, Raiko shouted and struck at her with his sword. She turned into threads of silk that disappeared down between the stones of the courtyard, just as the old hag had vanished earlier. Raiko found that he was covered with cobwebs as thick as wire. As he pulled the sticky strands off, Tsuna, who had also recovered from the blinding, joined his friend. Together they discovered that Raiko's sword was smeared with *white* blood.

The sun had returned now; the last of the rainwater was seeping away through the cracks between the flagstones.

After watching this for a while, Raiko clashed his sword on the stone several times, then said, "There is a vast hollow space below us. That is where the hag and the other creature fled. Surely that is where the goblin spider has its den."

"There must be a way down through the building," suggested Tsuna.

"To be sure," said Raiko. "But the monster must fear the sunlight, or else it would have come after us itself—not sent others to warn us away. We would be smart to bring the sun with us."

"How?" asked Tsuna.

"Like this," said Raiko, and he sank the point of his sword between two flagstones and pried one loose. The ancient mortar crumbled easily; stone after stone came free and was tossed into a far corner of the courtyard.

Suddenly from the shadowy depths below, a voice cried, "Stop! The sunlight burns me! Go away, I grant you your lives."

But the two men only worked harder, revealing a vast room under the courtyard. Peering into the spot where the shadows were deepest, Raiko saw a monster with many legs, covered with long, silky white hair. It had an enormous head, split with terrible jaws, and huge, black eyes that glittered darkly as it watched the two men.

"I am sick and in pain!" groaned the creature. "I will make you pay dearly for the suffering you have caused me." It scuttled around the pool of sunlight that Raiko and Tsuna had created by prying away the chamber roof stone by stone.

Then Raiko dropped to the floor below and battled the monster, keeping always in the square of light. The creature charged and retreated and charged again, but it was afraid of the sunlight that glinted off Raiko's armor and helmet and lay like a band of fire along his sword's blade.

Still the battle raged for more than an hour, before Raiko dispatched the monster with a blow of his sword that sent the creature's head rolling across the den. It came to rest beside a pile of human bones and skulls that showed how many unfortunate subjects of the Emperor had fallen victim to the monster.

Carrying the monster's head on a pole between them, Raiko and Tsuna returned to the Emperor's court, where they were highly praised and richly rewarded for their courage.

The Halloween Pony

(from a French folktale)

Grandmother put another log on the fire. Outside the little house which was not far from the sea, the wind was howling so fiercely that it set the windows rattling. "Listen to that!" said the old woman. "There's a storm brewing for sure."

She stirred the coals in the fireplace with a heavy poker until the new log caught and began to blaze. Satisfied, she turned to her three grandsons, who were sitting on the floor gazing thoughtfully into the flames. "Besides," she added, "this is Halloween. Witches are abroad tonight, and the goblins, who are their servants, are wandering about in all sorts of disguises, looking for children to snatch away."

But Tom, the eldest boy, said, "I won't stay here, frightened of a little wind and old stories. I promised Colette I'd call on her tonight. She swore she wouldn't get a wink of sleep, if I didn't visit her before the moon had gone down."

"I have to go and catch lobsters and crabs," said the middle boy, Louis. "Not all the witches and goblins in the world will keep me from that."

All three brothers announced they were going out for one reason or another and ignored the warnings of their

Grandmother. Only the youngest child hesitated a minute, when she said to him, "You stay with me, my little Richard, and I'll tell you stories of fairylands and magic animals."

But he wanted to pick blackberries by the moonlight, and so he ran out after his brothers.

He caught up with them on the rise, beneath the old oak tree.

"Grandmother talks about wind and storm, but I've never seen the weather finer or the sky more clear," said Louis, "I'll bring home plenty of crabs and lobsters tonight."

"See how big the moon is," said Tom. "Perhaps I can coax Colette to go for a walk with me."

Then Richard, who was starting for the blackberry patch, suddenly cried, "Look!" and he pointed to a little black pony standing quietly at the foot of the hill.

"Oh, ho!" said Louis, "that's old Frederic's pony; it must have escaped from its stable and is going down for a drink at the horse pond."

"Now, now, my pretty little pony," said Tom, going up and patting the creature with his hand, "you mustn't run away; I'll lead you to the pond myself."

With these words, he jumped on the pony's back.

"Take me, too," called Louis, and his brother helped him up.

"Don't leave me behind!" cried Richard, and his brothers helped him mount. Soon all three were astride the little black pony, which waited patiently till they had settled themselves. Tom clung to the pony's neck; Louis held Tom's waist; and Richard held Louis's shirt.

"Now, giddup!" urged Tom, and the little pony headed directly for the horse pond.

On their way, each brother met a friend and invited him to mount the pony. Soon there were six boys, holding to one another and laughing. The pony didn't seem to mind the extra weight but pranced merrily along under the brilliant moon.

The faster it trotted, the more the boys enjoyed the fun. They dug their heels into the pony's sides and called out, "Gallop, little horse! You've got six of the bravest riders in the world on your back!"

Soon they were racing along through the grassy fields near the seashore. The wind rose, sending clouds scudding across the face of the moon and whipping the pony's long black mane back across the eyes of the boys in front. Very close now, they could hear the waves pounding against the rocky shore.

The pony did not mind the noise at all. Instead of going to the horse pond, he circled around and cantered rapidly toward the seashore.

Louis, the middle brother, began to regret his wish to catch crabs and lobsters, and Richard, the youngest, found that he was no longer interested in blackberries. Both held onto their seats on the pony that was galloping at breakneck speed down toward the beach.

The eldest boy, Tom, seized the madly charging pony by the mane and tried to make it turn around. But he tugged and pulled in vain, for the pony galloped, fast as the howling wind, straight on toward the sea, pausing only when the first waves splashed over its hoofs.

The six riders thought to slip off the pony's back, while it lingered at the water's edge; but they found they were stuck fast to the creature's back.

Then, rearing up once, the little black pony neighed loudly, ran back and forth through the sea foam gleefully, then suddenly charged into the billowing waves, while its riders cried out in terror.

"The pony is bewitched!" wailed Tom. "We should have listened to Grandmother's warning."

The pony advanced farther and farther into the sea; the waves rose higher and higher until they covered the children's heads and the pony vanished beneath the swells.

Some say the children were drowned; some say the goblin pony carried them to a strange city of coral and pearl at the bottom of the sea. But they were never seen on dry land again.

Notes on Sources

THE ROBBER BRIDEGROOM. This is a favorite tale from the Brothers Grimm, which has frequently been translated. I've shortened it a bit, edited a few incidents, but have kept the general thrust of the story intact.

JACK FROST. I have freely adapted this traditional Russian tale, including incidents from several variant readings. This "red-nosed" Jack Frost is not the good-natured sprite who paints traceries of frost on winter windows: he is the blood-chilling, potentially deadly embodiment of a fierce Russian winter, when icy winds, blinding snow, and remorseless cold threaten death by freezing to the unfortunate.

THE WATERFALL OF GHOSTS. The story was originally published in English under the title "Yurei-Daki" in Lafcadio Hearn's *Kottō: Being Japanese Curios with Sundry Cobwebs,* first issued by the Macmillan Company, New York City, in 1902. Hearn (1850–1905) drew on old Japanese books for the ghostly tales in this volume. The writings of Lafcadio Hearn have been reissued in uniform paperback editions by Charles E. Tuttle Company, Rutland, Vermont, and Tokyo, Japan.

THE GHOST'S CAP. A retelling of an Icelandic folktale, "White Cap," originally gathered by Jón Árnason (1819–88), a librarian and teacher who assembled the monumental *Icelandic Legends* (1864), translated by George Powell and Eiríkur Magnússon, two volumes, second series, London: Longmans, Green and Co., 1866. Reprinted in *Scandinavian Folk and Fairy Tales* (1984) edited by Claire Booss, New York: Avenel Books, distributed by Crown, New York. I have enhanced this story with material from parallel tales from the Scandinavian and Russian.

THE WITCH CAT. This is a favorite American tale of witchcraft, yet another play upon the theme of shape shifting (see notes on the stories "The Loup-Garou" and "Brother and Sister"). Numerous variants of this story have found their way into folk literature; and I have drawn on several of the more interesting retellings for this version, including Nancy Roberts's excellent account in her *Ghosts of the Carolinas.*

THE GREEN MIST. Derived from Mrs. M. C. Balfour's account in her *Legends of the Lincolnshire Cars,* published in 1891, reprinted at length in Katherine

Briggs's *An Encyclopedia of Fairies,* Pantheon Books, a division of Random House, New York City, copyright 1976. (Originally published as *A Dictionary of Fairies* by Allen Lane, Penguin Books, London.)

THE CEGUA. I have created this original story around the horrific image of *La Cegua,* an apparition described in the tale of that name by Maximo Soto Hall (1871–1941), reprinted in *Leyendas de Costa Rica,* gathered by Victor H. Lizano, published by Soley & Valverde, San Jose, Costa Rica, in 1941. The name of this demon with an animal's head suggests the Spanish verb "cegar," "to blind" that also has the metaphorical meaning "to darken the light of reason" or "to make mad." It also suggests "yegua," or "mare." Such ghostly encounters (a man riding past a cemetery suddenly finds a skeleton seated behind him; a taxi driver picks up a spectre) form the basis of Hispanic folktales grouped under the heading "el pasajero del más allá"—"the passenger from the beyond."

THE GHOSTLY LITTLE GIRL. A much expanded version of an account found in Randall A. Reinstedt's *Ghostly Tales of Old Monterey.* The city of Monterey was California's historic first capital, and Mr. Reinstedt has explored its rich vein of ghostly lore in the work cited above and in his *Ghosts, Bandits, & Legends of Old Monterey.*

THE MIDNIGHT MASS OF THE DEAD. A considerably reworked and expanded version of a story collected by Peter Christen Asbjørnsen (1812–85), a lifelong student of Norse folklore, and first published in Norway in 1870 in Asbjørnsen's *Norske Huldreeventyr og Folksagn* (1845), accounts of dealings with spirit creatures from Norse folk traditions. Experts cite some twenty-five variants of this legend in Norway alone—and versions are familiar throughout north-central Europe.

TAILYPO. This is my own version of a classic American story, sometimes known as "Tailypoe," which has been retold countless numbers of times, with West Virginia or Tennessee as the preferred setting.

LADY ELEANORE'S MANTLE. This is a substantially edited version of the Nathaniel Hawthorne story of the same title, which was first published in *The Democratic Review,* December 1838. It was later included, in a much abbreviated form, in Charles M. Skinner's *Myths and Legends of Our Own Land,* two volumes, Philadelphia and London: J. B. Lippincott, first published in 1896. Reissued by Singing Tree Press, Book Tower, Detroit, in 1969.

THE SOLDIER AND THE VAMPIRE. A considerably reworked version of a traditional Russian folktale available in several translations. I have selected key incidents from various sources and have rearranged events and chronology to tighten the pacing and heighten the dramatic effect. For translations of the original tale, the reader might consult the version in *The World's Great Folktales,* arranged and edited by James R. Foster, New York: Harper & Brothers, 1953, or the version in *Passport to the Supernatural,* Bernhardt J. Hurwood, New York: Taplinger, 1972.

THE SKELETON'S DANCE. Originally published in Keigo Seki's *Nihon no Mukashi-banashi (Japanese Folktales)*, three volumes, Tokyo: Iwanami Shoten, 1956–57. The editor of the University of Chicago's selection of translations from the complete work comments that twelve versions of the tale have been recorded in Japan.

SCARED TO DEATH. I have adapted Margaret Rhett Martin's version of this story, which she has titled "The Leaning Tombstone," from her collection, *Charleston Ghosts*, University of South Carolina Press, copyright 1963.

SWALLOWED ALIVE. This bit of Derbyshire folklore is adapted from the account John Bunyan (1628–1688) includes in his *The Life and Death of Mr. Badman Presented to the World in a Familiar Dialogue Between Mr. Wiseman and Mr. Attentive* (1680). In this work by the author of *Pilgrim's Progress*, Mr. Wiseman presents the story of Dorothy Mately as an actual historic occurrence for the instruction of Mr. Attentive and a warning against "such wickedness [as] cursing and swearing."

THE DEACON'S GHOST. Retold from a tale, "The Deacon of Myrká," in *Icelandic Legends* by Jón Arnason (see note on "The Ghost's Cap"). According to Icelandic folklore, white wizards lived in the north, where they continued to practice pagan magic, away from Christian settlements—presumably such a wizard finally laid the ghost to rest.

NUCKELAVEE. Adapted from *Orkney Folklore and Traditions*, a collection of articles by Walter Traill Dennison (died in 1894), who originally published them in the *Scottish Antiquary* in the 1890s. These pieces were subsequently gathered and edited by Ernest W. Marwick and are available in a reprint edition from Herald Press, Kirkwall, Orkney, 1961.

The name "Nuckelavee" translates as "Devil from the Sea," (coming from the same root as "Old Nick," the Devil). Dennison obtained his story firsthand from "Thomas," who claimed to have survived this close encounter of the nightmare kind.

THE ADVENTURE OF THE GERMAN STUDENT. Edited and adapted from Washington Irving's *Tales of a Traveller*, first published in 1824. This selection is one of the supernatural stories appearing in the first section of the book, "Strange Stories by a Nervous Gentleman," and is considered by some critics to be Irving's most terrifying tale. The story, he wrote, was "founded on an anecdote related to me as existing somewhere in French," but he admitted he was never able to discover its source.

BILLY MOSBY'S NIGHT RIDE. I have elaborated considerably upon the account entitled "Francis Woolcott" in Charles M. Skinner's *Myths and Tales of Our Own Land* (op. cit.).

THE HUNTER IN THE HAUNTED FOREST. A combining and reworking of three brief Teton Sioux tales originally included in *Myths and Legends of the Great Plains*, selected and edited by Katharine Berry Judson, A. C. McClurg & Co., Chicago, 1913.

BROTHER AND SISTER. In retelling this favorite African traditional tale, I have borrowed from variants of a story popular in Kenya, Zambia, and Malawi, fleshing out my version with details from collateral readings. I have changed the familiar ending, where the brother causes a drum or wooden bowl or a miniature boat to float into the air while he and his sister hold on to it and escape the werebeast, in favor of a pursuit and escape that relies on human abilities rather than inexplicably acquired magical powers.

THE LOVERS OF DISMAL SWAMP. My own version of a classic American folktale dating back to colonial times, set in and around the Dismal Swamp, near Portsmouth, Virginia. I have combined several accounts of the tale, including elements from the Irish poet Thomas Moore's poem "The Lake of the Dismal Swamp," composed during a visit to the United States in 1803, and Charles M. Skinner's similarly titled prose version in his *Myths and Legends of Our Own Land* (op. cit.).

BONELESS. An original story suggested by several brief, historic accounts cited in Katherine Briggs's indispensable *An Encyclopedia of Fairies*, (op. cit.).

THE DEATH WALTZ. Retold from *Myths and Tales of Our Own Land* by Charles M. Skinner (op. cit.).

THE GHOST OF MISERY HILL. Expanded from the tale "The Spook of Misery Hill," included in *Myths and Legends of Our Own Land*, by Charles M. Skinner (op. cit.).

THE LOUP-GAROU. A French-Canadian legend adapted from an 1894 account in dialect originally published in *Danvis Folks*, by Rowland E. Robinson, Houghton Mifflin Company, Boston and New York. It has been reprinted in B. A. Botkin's *A Treasury of New England Folklore*, Crown Publishers, copyright 1947, 1965.

The term *loup-garou* comes from the Old French *leu garoul: leu* = wolf + *garoul* = werewolf.

THE GOLEM. This is my own "Golem" story, based on a reading of several of the medieval Jewish tales of the clay figure brought to life, which has formed a popular theme in legend and literature.

The two most popular accounts are the *Golem of Chelm*, which tells how Rabbi Elijah of that town created such a creature, but was so appalled by its destructive tendencies that he removed the magic parchment he had placed in the creature's forehead and it crumbled into dust. The second account, the *Golem of Prague*, tells how Rabbi Yehuda Loew brought the clay being into existence, to protect the Jews of that city from persecution. When its work was done, the rabbi returned it to a lifeless clay statue again; according to legend, it remains hidden in a synagogue in Prague, waiting to be summoned to life when it is needed again.

The Hebrew word *golem* refers to anything incomplete or not fully formed, since the creature was never completely human. Some critics have suggested that legends of the *golem* contributed to the background of ideas Mary Shelley drew upon when writing her 1818 novel *Frankenstein,* but no clear-cut evidence has surfaced to indicate she was familiar with this body of folklore.

LAVENDER. This popular American ghost story pops up in versions all across the United States, from New Jersey to California. A prime example of "urban folklore," the events are frequently presented as having happened to someone the storyteller has known personally.

THE GOBLIN SPIDER. A Japanese traditional story, one of many built around the legendary hero Raiko, whose exploits are widely anthologized. This particular variant of the well-known "Goblin Spider Episode," is loosely based on a summary in *Myths and Legends of Japan* by F. Hadland Davis. Mr. Davis prefaced his account with the comment, "This version appears in the *Catalogue of Japanese and Chinese Paintings in the British Museum* by Dr. William Anderson." I have no date for the latter work.

THE HALLOWEEN PONY. Freely adapted from "The Goblin Pony," a French folktale retold by Andrew Lang in his *The Grey Fairy Book,* originally published by Longmans, Green and Company, London, 1900, and reprinted by Dover Publications, New York, in 1967.

ABOUT THE AUTHOR

Robert D. San Souci is the author of four previous children's books for Doubleday. After receiving his bachelor's degree in English from St. Mary's College in Moraga, California, and then completing two years of graduate study in education, Mr. San Souci pursued a career in publishing. He now writes full time from his home in the San Francisco Bay area of California.

ABOUT THE ARTIST

Katherine Coville has worked as a full-time illustrator for the past ten years. Her work in both full color and black and white has appeared in over twenty children's books. In her spare time the artist enjoys making miniature toys and dollhouses. The mother of three, Ms. Coville resides in Syracuse, New York.

More Short & Shivery

Contents

Contents

Contents

Introduction

Welcome, old friends and new, to this second collection of some of my favorite scary tales, retold from the ghostlore of many different peoples and places. Since the first volume of *Short & Shivery* was published, I've had a chance to visit with young readers all around the country who have helped me decide what stories to include here. I am thankful to these friends in Alabama, California, Colorado, Delaware, Illinois, Kansas, Massachusetts, Michigan, Nebraska, Ohio, Oklahoma, Oregon, Washington, and elsewhere—this book is dedicated to all of you.

I hope you enjoy this book as much as the first *Short & Shivery*. One of the nice things about the present volume is that it lets me share stories there wasn't room for in my earlier book. I've also made an effort to include stories from parts of the world not covered in the first book. In the pages that follow are ghostly tales from Brazil, China, Haiti, Italy, Mexico, Nigeria, Papua New Guinea, Scotland, and Spain—as well as many parts of the United States.

You'll meet Bishop Hatto, who *really* had a problem with mice . . . Jubal Lescot, who learns why children shouldn't go poking around cemeteries at midnight . . . Tom Walker, who should have read the not-so-fine print in his contract with the Devil . . . and poor Georgette, who finds a bundle that should *not* be unwrapped until Christ-mas—or *ever*!

Here are such bone-chilling creatures as the duppy, the yara, the draug, and the windigo who haunt lonely houses, forests, rivers, and seashores all over the world. You'll also run into a helpful skeleton, a rolling head, a golden arm, and some witches' eyes—all of which refuse to rest in peace (or pieces).

For those who want to learn more about these stories and where they came from, I have included a section of "Notes on Sources" at the end of this book.

So settle back, relax—no, on second thought, don't plan on getting too relaxed! Truth in advertising means that I have to warn you that these are *not* warm-and-fuzzy sto-ries. They have proven popular—often for centuries—precisely because they have provided readers and listeners plenty of thrills and chills. They are guaranteed to raise a healthy crop of Halloween-style goose bumps in *any* sea-son.

In short, the stories in this book have teeth. Sharp ones. But then, isn't that what you're looking for? It must be, since you're reading these words right now. Well, you've been warned: "Reader, beware!" Proceed at your own risk.

"Hold Him, Tabb!"

(United States—Virginia)

Before the railroads were built in Virginia, supplies had to be carried from one town to another on wagons. One afternoon, late in December, a number of supply wagons traveling together were caught in a sudden snowstorm.

The drivers pushed on through the freezing cold and heavy snow until they came to an abandoned farm very near the road.

"Looks like a good place to sit out the storm," said a man named Tabb.

"I heard that the house is haunted," said another driver, heading toward the barn. "I'm going to bed down in one of the stalls with the horses."

Several other drivers said they had heard some pretty bad things about the house, too; one man said he'd heard that, for almost twenty-five years, not a single person who had stayed overnight remained alive to see the dawn. Most of the men decided they preferred to sleep in the barn with the animals.

"Well," said Tabb, who was braver than the rest, "I'm not afraid of any haunts. And I'm not about to sleep with horses and cowards when there's a real house just up the hill."

When he'd finished unhooking his horses, Tabb marched up to the house, which looked forlorn and run-down but not in the least daunting.

Inside he found a big potbellied stove and a healthy supply of wood. He built a cheery fire, cooked and ate his supper, and finally bedded down on a couch he dragged near the stove. He slept peacefully through the night, without being disturbed by anything except an odd bit of wood snapping inside the stove.

Just before sunrise he woke up, stretched, and said, "What a bunch of fools those other fellows are to have stayed down with the horses, when they could have stayed in here, just as warm and comfortable as me!"

No sooner had he finished speaking than he heard a rumbling laugh overhead.

Looking up to the ceiling, he saw a large man dressed in white clothes stretched out under the rafters, as though he were sticking to them.

Before Tabb could make a move, the man in white dropped right down on top of him. They started tussling, rolling back and forth across the floor, knocking the furniture in the room every which way. The two made so much noise that the men in the barn heard it and ran up the hill to see what was the matter.

Not daring to set foot in the house, they all clustered at the windows, prying open the shutters and leaning in. They saw the struggle going on. Tabb and the man in white seemed about equally matched: One minute, Tabb would be on top; the next, the man in white.

One of the drivers cried, "Hold him, Tabb! Hold him!"

"You can bet your soul I will!" yelled Tabb. "I've got him for sure!"

A minute later, the two fighters came crashing through a window, sending the drivers scattering.

"Hold him, Tabb! Hold him!" another driver shouted.

"You can bet your life I will!" cried Tabb. "I've got him right where I want him!"

The next moment, the man in white began whirling Tabb around and flung him onto the roof of the house. Then the stranger jumped up after him, so the drivers had to stand some distance away just to see what was happening.

"Hold him, Tabb! Hold him!" they yelled, one after another.

"You can just bet your boots I will!" said Tabb, panting. "He won't get away from me!"

Now the two wrestlers on the roof were so knotted together that the drivers down below had a hard time telling which arm or leg belonged to which. Then, as the drivers watched open-mouthed, the fighters began floating up off the roof.

One of the drivers cupped his hands around his mouth and bellowed, "Hold him, Tabb! Hold him!"

"I got him; and he's got me, too!" shouted Tabb.

Then the man in white carried Tabb straight up into the air until they were both out of sight.

And nothing was ever seen of Tabb after that.

The Witches' Eyes

(Spanish American—American Southwest)

Many years ago there was an elderly widower named Don Pedro who eased his loneliness by spending one or two evenings each week visiting two sisters—themselves his own age or nearly so—who lived across the road from his house. Though his other neighbors warned him in harsh whispers that the women were *brujas*—witches—the old man ignored these taletellers. He sipped chocolate with cinnamon, played a card game called *canoncito,* or shared *cuentos*—stories—of the old days with his friends Doña Inez and Doña Teresa.

Don Pedro knew that one sister was several years older than the other, but he was never certain which was the elder—and he was too polite to ask. The two dressed alike in skirts of stiff black material and carried identical fans of ebony silk. They might have been twins—save that one had eyes the deep color of coffee flecked with gold, while the other had paler, tea-colored eyes, likewise gold-flecked.

Always, just before midnight, the women would lay down their cards or stop their storytelling and murmur, "Pedro, you must go home now."

Though he would beg to play just one more hand or hear a story to its end, they would shake their heads firmly and say, "You must go *now.*"

When he mentioned this to his neighbors, they said, "*Sí,*

sí, this proves they are witches. They must be rid of you to begin their night's mischief."

"Do you suppose they go flying about under the moon?" asked Pedro, laughing at the thought.

His neighbors would grow red in the face at his laughter, and shrug their shoulders.

But Don Pedro found that the suspicions of his friends were feeding his own curiosity. Often, when he was unable to sleep, he would sit at a window and watch the silent *casa* —house—across the road. But the only thing out of the ordinary he noticed were the comings and goings of two lean cats, one with dark brown fur and one with tawny fur, that prowled the women's moonlit garden. One night they seemed to sense that he was spying on them, for they arched their backs and hissed in his direction. This disturbed Pedro so that he returned to his bed, though sleep did not come to him until dawn's light streaked the sky.

The next morning he decided to take a little gift of *pan dulce,* a sweet bread, across the road to his neighbors. He noticed that both women had dark circles under their eyes.

"*Buenos días.* I chanced to be up last night and saw two cats near your door," he said. "Are they pets?"

"There are no cats here!" said the sister with coffee-colored eyes.

"You must have been dreaming, Pedro," added the other sister. Her tea-colored eyes glittered with a harshness the old man had never seen before.

"No doubt I was mistaken," said Don Pedro, and he handed over his gift with a hasty "*Adiós.*"

.   .   .

There was a further mystery. Sometimes while the three talked and played cards in the evening, one or the other sister would mention something that had happened in a distant town. Days later, Don Pedro would learn that they had spoken the truth. But how could they know so quickly about something that had happened a day's journey away?

When he questioned them, they merely laughed and said that they had heard the news in the market square.

Then, one night, Pedro was awakened by the sound of a cat howling. Staring at the darkened *casa* across the way, he clearly saw two cats scurry from the stoop and around the corner of the house.

Determined to find answers to his questions, Don Pedro marched across the road and knocked loudly on the door of the sisters' dwelling. The place remained silent, the whitewashed adobe gleaming under the midnight moon. He knocked several times, yet neither woman came in answer.

Afraid for his friends' well-being, he tried the door. It was unlocked, and he pushed it open.

"Doña Inez, Doña Teresa," he called, "are you well?"

Inside, the rooms were empty. The only light came from moonlight streaming through the lattices and the faint glow of embers in the corner chimney. In the red light of the coals, Don Pedro saw to his horror that two sets of eyes—like the glass eyes from a china doll—sat on a dish on a stool in front of the hearth. One pair of eyes were deep brown; one pair, tawny; both were flecked with gold.

"Oh!" cried Don Pedro, blessing himself. In his haste to escape, he stumbled and lost his balance. His foot shot out and knocked the stool over. The dish tumbled into the fire. Instantly there was a puff of brown and a puff of tan smoke that flew up the chimney. The frantic man used a poker to search the coals and ashes. But though he rescued the dish, not a trace remained of its awful contents.

Frightened, Don Pedro hurried home. A little later he heard two cats begin a terrible howling. He did not need to look to guess that it was coming from inside the house across the road.

The next day, Don Pedro did not know what to do. It was his regular evening for calling on the sisters. He was afraid to face them—but he was more afraid that if he didn't, they would suspect him of being the one who had made such mischief the night before. At last he decided to bluff his way through a visit.

He dressed especially well, and took two roses from his small garden. Then, with a trembling hand, he knocked on the door—remembering all too well how that door had opened onto a frightful scene only a few hours before.

"*¡Pase usted!*" called Doña Inez, and her sister also invited him, "Come in!"

As he entered, he noticed that the lattices were still shut. The room was dark. No lamps had been lit, and the fireplace was cold. The two women murmured polite words but kept their faces turned away or hidden by their black silk fans. When they moved, they seemed clumsy, as though even the dim light bothered their eyes.

"Alas, Don Pedro," said Doña Inez in a sad voice, her face averted so that she was gazing at the cold hearth, "I am afraid that we will no longer be able to share our evenings with you."

"Yes," said her sister, sighing behind her fan, "we have other duties that must occupy our time from now on."

"I see, of course," said Don Pedro, who only wanted to

be away from the house. His nervousness had gotten the best of him. As he fumbled for the door, he was aware that Doña Inez had turned to gaze at him suspiciously, while Doña Teresa had momentarily lowered her fan.

At that moment, he pulled open the door. The sudden light revealed the sisters staring at him with the round eyes of cats. "Go! Close the door!" they hissed, turning away in pain.

Don Pedro quickly drew the door shut and fled.

That night and every night thereafter he locked his doors and windows at evening, and did not unlock them until the sun was high above the eastern mountains. And he slept with his rosary clutched tightly in his hand.

Sometimes he thought he heard the sounds of cats' paws at his door or window. But he prayed a "Hail Mary" aloud, and the sound went away.

Shortly thereafter, his strange neighbors departed in a carriage hung with black velvet curtains. They never returned, and the house remained empty for as long as Don Pedro lived.

The Duppy

(Haiti)

Jubal Lescot was only six when his Aunt Albertine died. The old woman had been sharp-tongued, and quick to accuse the child of misdeeds—more often imagined than real. So the boy was more relieved than sorry. He was glad not to have her scolding him all the time, calling him "lazy" and "good-fo'-not'in'."

Albertine Lescot was buried in a small churchyard on a hillside near the shanty where she had lived with her brother and his family. Through the banana trees, mimboms, and palm fronds that grew all around the cemetery, the mourners now and then got a glimpse of the distant roofs of Port-au-Prince, the capital of Haiti.

Before the funeral, Jubal overheard several of the neighbors saying that a duppy—a kind of ghost—was sure to rise from the old woman's grave at cock crow on the third night after her burial.

"What's dat duppy?" he asked his mother.

"Somet'in' you don' never want t' meet up wit'," she told him. "Somet'in' dat can take hold o' you if you not careful—or if you don' believe."

"It a ghost, but not a ghost," his father said. "Everyone have evil in him; but when he alive, his brain and his heart control dat evil. After de spirit go away, dat evil part be lef' behin'. If it don' have nothin' t' keep it from doin' whatever it want, it go out into de worl', where it do terrible t'ings."

"So we get a magic man t' put a spell on dat duppy an' keep it stayin' in de grave," his mother explained. "It a bad t'ing to let a duppy stay 'mong Christian folk." Then she shook her finger at Jubal. "Any child dat ain' a foolish child will keep in his bed wit' de shutters close', 'til magic make dat duppy res' quiet fo' all time," she warned him.

Because he was a curious boy, Jubal quietly got out of bed on the third night after Albertine's funeral. While his parents slept in their little bedroom behind a heavy blanket that served as a door, Jubal stepped out into the warm night.

In the moonlight—so bright it almost felt hot—the boy had no trouble picking out the trail that led from the shanty to the neighborhood cemetery. There he found he wasn't quite brave enough to set foot inside the graveyard. So he climbed a huge mango tree that overhung the rusty iron fence surrounding the burial ground. From here he had a clear view of his aunt's grave, halfway up the slope.

He perched where several massive branches joined, to watch. But as time slipped by and the night grew darker around him, Jubal remembered the warnings his parents had given him. He began to think he would be better off back in his bed. He was already risking a scolding and a spanking for leaving the house after dark. Now he began to be afraid of what else he might be risking, alone in the dark, spying on ghosts.

No! he told himself, *I come dis far, I ain' gonna give up now.* So he clung stubbornly to his perch as the night yawned toward morning. He dozed a little, unaware for the most part that he had slept at all.

Then, in the last hours before sunup, Jubal saw a huge bubble of white light squeeze out of the mounded earth of his aunt's grave. It made a wet, popping sound as it floated free of the ground.

The moon had set, but it seemed to Jubal that the earth

had given birth to a second moon. Inside the man-sized globe of light swam a lazy swirl of shadow, like a just-forming chicken in an egg held up to a candle. It was lit by an unhealthy glow that seemed to seep out, rather than shine, from inside. The surface had a damp look to it.

For a moment the slimy bubble hovered just above the grave. Then, as if it sensed the boy in hiding, it began to move toward the mango tree. The lower half of the bubble slid right through the stone and metal grave markers that dotted the hillside.

Jubal knew that it was coming for him. He scrambled down from the tree and began running through the thick jungle toward home. With only starlight to help him pick out the thread of the path, he stumbled often over roots and rocks. He did not dare look back, because he knew he would see the terrifying bubble of white light stained with shadows following him, getting closer.

Light from behind made the path ahead easier to see; he knew that meant the deadly glowing thing had almost caught up with him. When he rounded a bend in the trail and saw that he was near home, Jubal began to scream for help.

Then, trying to force his aching legs to go faster, he tripped. He tumbled forward into a puddle that soaked his clothes and filled his nose with a rotten smell.

He heard a sound like a rushing wind coming down the path behind him, followed by another sound, as though a great fire was sizzling and crisping the leaves on the trees.

Too scared to move, Jubal buried his face in his arms and waited for the duppy to touch him, to burn him to ashes.

Something grabbed him roughly by his shirt collar and jerked him, screeching like a crazy gull, to his feet. He windmilled his arms, keeping his eyes tightly shut.

He felt himself shaken fiercely by the shoulders while

his father shouted, "Open yo' eyes, boy! And shut yo' mout'! What givin' you such fits?"

Carefully, Jubal opened his eyes and looked around the starlit glade. They were alone; the forest was silent and dark. "Tell me what you be doin' here," his father said angrily, his strong hands never loosening their grip on Jubal's shoulders.

"A duppy, Papa," Jubal said when he could catch his breath. "It be tryin' t' touch me and kill me!"

"Why it be chasin' you?"

"At de graveyard—" Jubal began.

But his father interrupted him. "You been spyin' on dat duppy? Don' you know dat vexes him?" He looked nervously around the clearing. "Get 'long home, quick as you can. In de mornin', you gotta fetch de priest t' lay dat duppy t' rest."

As they hurried along, with many glances back over their shoulders, Jubal's father said, "I should whip you so's you never forget what you done tonight. An' so's you won' do it no more. But I can see by yo' face dat you won' go vexin' no duppy ever again."

And Jubal, seeing their cabin ahead, with his mother standing anxiously in the doorway, felt he was the luckiest boy alive—just to *be* alive.

Two Snakes

(China)

In ancient China, there was once a man who decided to hunt on a certain mountain people said was the home of many strange creatures. But the hunter paid no attention to these old stories. He climbed high up the wooded slopes in search of game. Though he often heard the calls of birds and the sounds of animals in the thickets, and though he kept his bow and arrow at the ready, he did not catch sight of a single pheasant or deer.

At night, discouraged, he built a rude shelter of branches, telling himself that the next day would bring him the bounty that had so far eluded him.

As he huddled in his cloak, trying to fall asleep, he was startled to hear the sound of a heavy footfall in the clearing outside. Peering out of his lean-to, he saw a tall, thin figure dressed in white robes. The man, who was more than ten feet tall, spoke in a thin, piping voice.

"I have come to ask your help," the stranger said. "I am going to fight against my enemy tomorrow. Help me, and you will be abundantly rewarded."

The hunter was delighted. "I am more than willing to help," he said. "What must I do?"

"Tomorrow at mealtime, go to the stream that flows to the east of here," the visitor said. "My enemy will be coming from the north, and I shall be meeting him from the south. Remember that I shall be the one in white, and he will be the one in yellow."

"I promise," said the hunter, puzzled at the words.

With a nod, the tall figure turned and disappeared into the shadows of the forest.

The hunter spent the next morning looking for game, but again returned to his shelter empty-handed. The gnawing hunger in his belly reminded him that it was mealtime. It was time to make good his promise to his night visitor.

He had only traveled a short distance when he came to the stream, just as the stranger had described it. From the heavy growth on the north bank he heard a crackling and hissing like wind and rain. Listening, the hunter could make out the sound of bushes being uprooted and trees falling. Then he heard a similar sound from the south side of the stream.

Suddenly two huge snakes, each nearly a hundred feet long, burst forth from the underbrush—a yellow one from the north, and a white one from the south. They met in the middle of the stream and encircled each other with their powerful tails.

At first the hunter thought them evenly matched. Their coiled bodies churned the stream to muddy froth, while their immense tails lashed the water and bank with sounds as sharp as thundercracks. Neither seemed to have the advantage in the deadly struggle. Each opened its immense jaws as if to swallow the other, but now the yellow, now the white snake fended off the attack by twisting its body or using its own jaws.

Gradually, however, the white serpent seemed to weaken. The hunter, concealed a short distance away, decided that his visitor must have been the white snake changed to human form. True to his promise, he drew his bow and shot the yellow one. A second and third arrow also hit home, and the snake fell back, mortally

wounded. The swift-flowing stream soon carried it out of sight.

Then the white snake turned and retreated into the underbrush on the south bank. Not knowing what else to do, the hunter returned to his shelter to wait.

At dusk, his visitor of the night before came to thank him, saying, "You may stay here and hunt on this mountain for one year. From now on, you will find all the game you want. But I warn you: You must leave this place when one year has gone by. Never come again. If you do, bad luck will befall you."

"I promise," said the hunter.

With a nod, the tall figure vanished into the gloom.

It all came to pass as the snake had promised. From that moment on, the mountain woods and meadows provided the hunter with unlimited game, while the streams poured fish into his nets. Whenever he returned to his village, he would sell a portion of his bounty. Soon he became quite rich.

He marked the time carefully. When a year was up he came down from the mountain one last time, vowing never to return.

But as the years passed, the man was careless with his wealth. His money was gone, and his hunting and fishing barely brought him enough to eat.

At night, sitting in his hut, eating a bowl of watery rice with a single piece of fish in it, he would gaze into the distance at the forbidden mountain. He would see in his mind the glades where herds of deer grazed and the streams that teemed with fish.

Then he would remember the warning the strange visitor had given him, and turn away with a sigh.

But when there was nothing to eat except roots and bark, and his belly rumbled as loudly as mountain thunder, the hunter finally said to himself, "Surely enough time has gone by, and my hunger is so great, that the white snake would not punish me if I returned to the mountain for only one day."

The very next morning, he set out with his bow and nets. As soon as he entered the woods, he found the game as plentiful as ever. Soon he had a number of fat pheasants slung over his shoulder.

Suddenly, rounding a bend of the path he was following, he came face to face with the tall figure in white.

"Oh, my foolish friend!" cried the figure. "Didn't I tell you that you must never come here again? Now my enemy's sons have grown up. They are sure to take revenge on you, and I can do nothing to prevent it."

These words struck fear into the hunter. He begged the tall man to tell him how to escape.

"Too late," said the other, disappearing into the green shade of the forest.

At the same time, the hunter heard a sound like wind and rain moving through the trees toward him. Throwing aside the string of pheasants, he fled down the path.

For a time, the sounds kept growing louder. But he redoubled his efforts, until he was running faster than a startled hare. Gradually the sounds of pursuit began to fade. Finally they ceased altogether. With a cry of relief, he stumbled into a clearing, and realized that he was only a few paces from the edge of the woods at the foot of the mountain.

But when the weary man was halfway across the open space, three men dressed in yellow satin robes, all of them eight feet tall, suddenly slipped from the trees opposite him.

To his dismay, he saw their yellow garments slide off, like shed snakeskins. The three opened their impossibly huge mouths and kept on opening them, even as their hands and feet melted into their bodies, and their bodies lengthened and coiled.

The deer and birds, frozen in place, heard the sounds of three sets of powerful jaws clamping shut.

Then there was only silence upon the mountain.

The Draug

(Norway)

There are many stories told in Norway concerning the draug, a ghostly sailor with a mass of seaweed where his head should be. Sometimes he is no more than a menacing shape in a storm or mist. Sometimes he can be clearly seen as he sails his half-boat by night or swims in the ocean waters by moonlight.

The word *draug* means "a living dead person." Fishermen say it is the spirit of someone who was drowned at sea and who is now doomed to haunt the seaways, looking for victims to drag down and share his misery.

In 1864, in a small Norwegian village, the town magistrate, Ola Hagen; his wife, Solvy; and a crew of four oarsmen were charged with delivering a local criminal for trial. The court was in a town far down the coast.

They set sail in a small, open boat early on a September morning. The weather was fine, and they enjoyed a leisurely journey watching the unrolling panorama of steep, rock-walled fjords—many with waterfalls rushing down to the sea. From time to time they saw thick woods, or occasional patches of green farmland nestled beneath the cliffs.

Sturdy, good-hearted Solvy welcomed this brief escape from the duties of tending her house and vegetable garden. She sang sweetly as she kept watch over the waves ahead or spelled a rower at his oar. Her husband, Ola, leaning upon the rudder, skillfully guided the boat past the often treacherous rocks. He joined Solvy in a chorus, and their high spirits soon had the oarsmen singing, too.

Suddenly their prisoner, who had been lost in his thoughts, shouted, "Why are you mocking me this way? The devil take your accursed singing!"

Solvy said gently, "We were singing to pass the time—not to add to your troubles."

But the man said, "Bah! To the devil with every one of you!"

"Be quiet!" ordered Ola as Solvy blessed herself. She glanced around as though a horned devil might burst forth like a porpoise from the waves. Just to mention the evil one, she knew, might summon him. But the sea remained untroubled.

The prisoner turned away and said nothing more. But the pleasant mood was broken. They continued on their way in silence.

Toward evening, as they passed through a dangerous channel, they heard a forlorn cry.

"It's a seabird, nothing more," Ola assured his companions.

But his wife suddenly drew in her breath and pointed over the gunwale. To their horror, they saw a dark shape swimming around and around them. Abruptly it dove under the boat, setting the craft rocking to and fro. Then it shot from the water with a shriek and splashed back before any of the startled crew could see clearly what it was.

The boat was buffeted from side to side again. The youngest oarsman cried out, "Surely it is a draug who means to sink us!"

The craft pitched and rolled yet again.

"Come about!" ordered Ola Hagen. "We must head for shore!"

"Look! A light!" his wife said. "Perhaps there is a farm-house where we can find shelter for the night."

The four oarsmen bent their backs to the task, while the boat continued to rock as though in a storm. But the air was calm and the sky clear. If the frightened crew had not been rowing for dear life, they might have counted the glittering stars overhead.

When they entered a small inlet, their underwater tor-mentor suddenly left off its attacks. The boat sped smoothly across the sheltered water. In a moment they had moored their craft beside a fisherman's boat. Hur-riedly, Ola and Solvy, the four oarsmen, and the prisoner in manacles hurried up the slippery path to knock on the door of a stone hut. From its single window, the butter-yellow light of an oil lamp streamed out to welcome the newcomers, who kept looking back over their shoulders at the still, starlit water of the cove.

Once only, a dark shape leaped out of the depths and back again—so quickly that Solvy, the only one who saw it, was not sure that she had really seen anything. But she shuddered nonetheless.

Then the door was pulled open. The fisherman inside, who recognized the magistrate and his wife, bade them all, "Come in."

When they had told their tale, the fisherman nodded and said, "On a moonlit night such as this, the draug shrieks so loudly that you may find sleep impossible."

After they had warmed themselves by the fire and had eaten some of the man's fish stew, the weary travelers set-tled down for the night on straw pallets beside the hearth. Though the walls of the cottage were solid stone, and the fisherman drew the shutters tight, none of the visitors was able to sleep. They were kept awake by piercing shrieks that continued until daybreak.

. . .

The travelers wearily shared some of their bread and cheese with the fisherman for breakfast, then continued on to their destination. There they turned the prisoner (who was only too glad to be away from the sea) over to the authorities. Because it was already late in the day, they decided to delay their departure until the next morning.

With fresh provisions and determined to return home before sunset, the six set out at dawn. As before, Ola claimed his place at the rudder, while Solvy took up watch in the prow. The steady rhythm of the four rested rowers and a full sail sent the small boat skimming across the waves.

But as the day lengthened, a strong headwind arose and slowed them. Soon, taking note of the westering sun, Solvy said, "I'm afraid we won't reach home before nightfall." Then she cautioned, "We should look for a place to tie up the boat and find shelter for the night."

Just then, however, the wind shifted in their favor. Ola said, "The breeze is helping us now, and the current is strong. I think we can still outrun the dark." So the oarsmen put even more effort into their rowing.

Indeed, landmarks along the shore showed that they were nearing home. With safety drawing closer, the youngest rower boasted, "I, for one, am not afraid of the draug. Let him throw his worst at me, I will throw it right back."

At that moment, the boat heaved as something large slammed into it from underneath. Shrieks erupted from the water all around them. The rowers strained at their oars, while the sail belled in the rising wind. But they were unable to make any headway. Something was holding them back.

"Something has fastened itself to the rudder!" cried Ola. At the same instant, a horrified Solvy, turning back to look at her husband, saw that water was pouring over the stern of the boat.

The sturdy mast groaned and seemed in danger of snapping as it resisted the sail's pull. The rowers churned the water with their suddenly useless oars. The boat remained in place as more water gushed over the gunwales.

"Ola! The boathook!" shouted Solvy.

Her husband grabbed the pole and began jabbing its metal point at the formless thing he could just make out under the surface. The sea seemed to boil all around the boat, and the air was filled with bloodcurdling screams. But the thing retreated from the sharp blade of the boathook. The vessel was released. It lurched forward, nearly pitching Ola out of the stern.

"Head for shore!" cried Solvy. "It's our only hope!"

For a few moments it seemed that they had escaped.

Then a black shape exploded out of the water beside the boat. In an instant it had seized the youngest oarsman and dragged him into the sea with a splash. His companions frantically searched the water for any trace of him, but all they could see was a circle of bubbles like tiny pearls, surrounding a single dark curl of seaweed.

The others reached shore safely, and huddled beside their beached craft through the night. In the morning, the survivors found their way home. Shuddering, Ola said, "The draug has claimed one victim. Let us beg merciful God that no others will fall prey to this horror for a long time to come."

The Vampire Cat

(Japan)

The prince of Hizen, in Japan, once fell in love with a beautiful and intelligent lady of his court named O Toyo. One evening, while the two strolled together in the fragrant palace gardens, the young woman noticed that they were being followed by a large black-and-white cat.

"How pretty!" O Toyo exclaimed.

But when she extended a hand to stroke the cat, it suddenly hissed at her, then ran away.

When they parted company a short time later, with soft murmurs of affection, O Toyo returned to her chamber. At midnight she was suddenly awakened by a strange sound. To her surprise, she discovered the black-and-white cat, grown to the size of a tiger, crouched in a corner, watching her. Before the frightened young woman could cry out, the creature leaped upon her. Breathing in, the demon cat drew the life out of O Toyo, and in an instant it took on her shape. Of the unhappy woman herself, nothing remained but perfumed ashes upon the bedclothes. These the false O Toyo blew upon and scattered.

In the morning, the prince greeted the creature whose soft voice, loving manner, and sweet laughter were O Toyo's in every regard. They talked of plans for their wedding. Every moment, the prince's love grew deeper and deeper.

But day by day, the prince felt his strength draining away. His face grew pale, his steps uncertain. He seemed to be suffering from some terrible, wasting sickness. The physicians and herbalists summoned by his councilors prescribed one treatment after another, but nothing helped. The young man grew ever more thin and ashen.

He suffered most at night, when his sleep was troubled by hideous dreams. They seemed so real that he told his servants, "Some demon slips into my chamber at night and steals a little of my life energy."

To ease their ruler's mind, his councilors appointed one hundred guards to sit up and keep watch over the sleeping prince. But curiously, on the very first night that the watch began, the guards were seized by drowsiness. Unable to keep their eyes open, they all quickly fell asleep.

In the morning, the councilors discovered to their dismay that the guards slept like the dead, and the prince had grown weaker than ever. The guards were punished for failing in their duty, and one hundred more were assigned to keep watch the second night.

But that night, the same thing happened. The prince was troubled by horrible dreams, while his guards slept helplessly all around him.

In despair, the councilors determined to sit up themselves, and see if they could resist the drowsiness that had overcome the prince's soldiers for two nights. Yet for all their determination, they fared no better. One by one they dropped off to sleep, long before midnight.

The next morning the prince was so weak he could not rouse himself from his bed. His three chief councilors met to discuss the problem, but they could arrive at no solution.

It chanced, however, that one of the palace guards, a young man named Ito, overheard their talk. Since it was clear that even the prince's wisest advisers were helpless, Ito determined to seek the advice of the priest at the city temple.

"Your purpose is a good one," said the priest. "But surely witchcraft is involved."

"If you will give me some way of resisting the drowsiness," said the young soldier, "I will sit up with the prince's guards this very night and try to discover the cause of his suffering."

Then the priest gave him a bit of parchment with a prayer inscribed on it. He said, "Recite these words softly if you feel yourself growing drowsy." Then he painted a magical sign on each of Ito's eyelids, to help him stay awake.

That night, Ito took his place amid the circle of guards surrounding the prince's bed at the center of the room. The ninety-nine others kept themselves awake with lively conversation or other amusements.

But as the hour of midnight approached, they began to doze off where they sat, in spite of all their efforts to keep each other awake. Ito also felt a great desire to sleep creeping over him, but he steadfastly prayed the sutra— prayer—the priest had given him.

His prayer and his strong will kept him awake, while the rest of the guards slept. Then, as he watched, the sliding doors of the prince's room parted. Ito pretended to be asleep, but he kept his eyes open just enough to see. To his amazement, he saw the beautiful lady O Toyo glide into the room. Cautiously she looked all around; when she saw that the guards were asleep, she smiled an evil smile and approached the prince's bedside. She knelt down as if she would kiss the sleeping man. But when her face was near his, she breathed in, drawing some life energy out of him.

At this, Ito stood up suddenly. The false O Toyo likewise rose, and turned to face Ito, who had his hand upon the hilt of his dagger. Ignoring the threat, she drew close and said, "I am not used to seeing you here. Who are you?"

"My name is Ito," he answered. "This is the first night I have been on guard."

"The other guards are all asleep. How is it that you alone are awake?"

"Prayer and a desire to help my lord," he said.

"You are a trusty watchman," she said. "I came to see how my lord fares this night. I will depart, knowing you are protecting him."

"You will not depart, goblin!" cried Ito, drawing his dagger. "I saw you stealing the life from my lord."

With a snarl, the beautiful woman was suddenly transformed into a monstrous cat that hissed and snarled and tried to rake Ito with its claws. But the soldier fought back with his dirk. For every wound the goblin cat inflicted, the man gave two in return. The sound of the fight began to rouse the sleeping guards.

Seeing that it was no match for Ito, and fearing the newly roused soldiers who were crying out alarms and drawing their own weapons, the giant cat suddenly fled the chamber.

Ito, yelling to the others to follow him, pursued the creature until it reached the gardens. It bounded to the rooftops and escaped over the palace walls. From there it fled to the mountains from which it had come.

From that moment, the prince of Hizen began to recover from his sickness, though he mourned the loss of

the beautiful lady O Toyo. When his strength was restored, he raised Ito in rank to commander of the palace guard and richly rewarded the young man.

For a time, reports came daily of the mischief the cat was making among nearby villages. At last, the prince ordered Ito to lead a great hunt. After many days, the soldiers cornered and killed the beast. Nor did any other goblin come to trouble Hizen or its lord after that.

Windigo Island

(Canada)

Go steady wit' de oar!" shouted Cyprien Palache, leaning on the rudder. He was foreman of the crew of lumbermen paddling across Lake Manitou toward the island that would be their winter quarters.

The twelve men at their oars had been loudly singing "A-rolling My Bowl." But the cheerful refrain

A-rolly poley,
My bolie rowlie

had died away the minute the island came into view. The clouds above were motionless; there wasn't a ripple on the smooth lake. Yet it was said that even the strongest boats approaching the island were sometimes rocked by something unseen in the water.

Windigo Island was a hunters' paradise: Otters swam freely in its pools; muskrats built their mud houses and beavers their dams with little fear. The Indians never set traps there, though sometimes powerful medicine men would come to the island on secret and solitary missions.

The place was said to be haunted by a Windigo spirit. This frightful being may take many shapes—a giant with a heart of ice, a whirlwind, a demon, or a cannibal monster. Most of the men were unhappy about the choice of winter quarters, but none dared challenge the strapping, foul-tempered Cyprien Palache. So they rowed on in silence, listening for they knew not what.

They beached the boat on the rocky shore, under the spruce and pine. Bawling orders and swearing, Cyprien set the weary men to repairing the shanty built the previous year. They worked quickly, aware of the big foreman watching every move with eyes as tiny and sharp as a weasel's. If he saw a man doing something wrong or simply pausing to catch a breath, he would roar, "Hi dere, w'at you doin'?" and shake the unfortunate man until his teeth rattled.

If the men who had aroused Cyprien's displeasure were out of reach, he would sound a few shrill notes on the silver whistle that hung from a chain around his neck, and point at them in warning. The men hated the sound of the whistle. The story was whispered around that Palache had bought it in Quebec from the devil himself, who had used it to pipe orders to the sinners in Hades.

When nightfall made work impossible, the men settled into the cabin, happy to be away from the pooling dark under the trees and the sound—so like soft voices—of the rising wind in the leaves.

Their good spirits returned when, after supper, Pat Clancy drew out his fiddle and Jimmie Charbonneau unpacked his concertina. The two played, and all sang. But Palache soon put a stop to the merriment, ordering the men to bed and putting out the lamp.

Now, the youngest of the party was a Cree boy the men called Indian Johnnie. The lumber gang had found him half drowned in a river eddy the previous spring. His mother and father had drowned when their birchbark canoe had been swamped by the swollen waters that followed the thaw. Somehow the boy had managed to keep his head above water and swim free of the current. Palache treated him little better than a dog, using him as a servant and scullion. But the other men were teaching him the lumberjack's trade.

When the foreman wanted anything day or night, he would pipe three short blasts on his whistle, and Johnnie would come running. If the lad failed to appear before the whistle was sounded a second time, he would carry the bruises for days.

"How you stan' it?" asked Jimmie Charbonneau. "Why you never run away?"

But the boy just shrugged and said nothing. Jimmie knew that Johnnie would never let anyone see him cry. Still, he could see the hatred in the boy's face whenever the foreman appeared. Jimmie had the uneasy feeling that something bad was bound to happen. To his friend Pat Clancy he said, "Somebody surely die, long before de winter's over, long before we lef' dis place."

Pat only nodded grimly.

One morning after first snowfall, Jimmie noticed the boy burying something on the shore. Later, scraping away the snow, Jimmie found the body of a rabbit that the boy had caught the day before. Beside it was a little blue tobacco pouch. He didn't hear Palache come up behind him. "Hi dere, w'at you doin'?" snarled the big man, shoving Jimmie aside. "Dat's my t'bac!" he roared, snatching up the pouch.

He grabbed Jimmie by the collar, demanding, "Why you steal dis?"

Before Jimmie could say a word, the Indian boy, who had appeared from nowhere, grabbed Palache's arm. "I took dat."

"You?" the foreman said, releasing Jimmie and staring

at the Cree as though he had never really looked at him before. "Why?"

"For de *T'ing* dat's watchin', watchin' from de trees," said the boy, so softly the big man had to lean close to hear.

"What *T'ing*?" Palache snarled.

Jimmie realized then that the boy had left the rabbit and tobacco as a peace offering for the Windigo spirit. With a small shudder, he glanced right and left at the fringe of snow-dusted trees. "De boy mean de Win—"

But Johnnie suddenly reached up and stopped him from saying the word aloud.

"It ain' safe for told its name out loud," said Pat Clancy, who, with several others, had been drawn to the argument. "Dass de way it come—if it's call by its name."

At this, the foreman bellowed, "You can' all be such fools to belef' in Windigo!"

"Don' you say dat name some more!" yelled Clancy.

"Me, I say dat name all I wan'!" bellowed Palache. "Windigo! Windigo!"

Indian Johnnie groaned and clasped his hands to his ears.

"Enough dat!" The foreman dropped the boy with a blow to the side of the head. "De res' you fools get workin'. I don' wan' hear no more dis talk."

Then he stomped off toward the shanty, while the men scattered to their various tasks. Only Jimmie lingered long enough to help the dazed boy to his feet. But Johnnie just pushed his hand aside and walked away. Watching him go, Jimmie felt more sure than ever that there would be big trouble before the spring thaw.

December brought record snows. The drifts piled up so high against the cabin that sometimes only the roof and chimney could be seen. Chilling winds hammered it continually.

One evening, as Cyprien was pulling off his snowshoes and coat, he suddenly began to screech, "I los' my whissle."

Jimmie and the others saw that the devil's whistle and its chain were gone from around Palache's thick neck.

He grabbed Indian Johnnie and told him, "You mus' fin' dat silver whissle an' de chain it's hangin' by, or don' ever show yourse'f here again." Before anyone could protest, the foreman thrust the Cree through the door into the snow.

Now the wind outside grew louder. "Dat soun' lak somet'ing cryin' all aroun' us ev'ryw'ere," said Jimmie Charbonneau, shivering from more than cold.

Suddenly the fire in the stove dwindled and died.

"Charbonneau! Clancy!" yelled the foreman. "Go de woodpile before I freeze to deat'." Palache, for all his bluster, looked cold and white.

"Non!" said Jimmie. "We ain' afraid of not'ing, but we don't like takin' chance."

"I hear some wil' spirit raisin' row dere," added Pat Clancy. "You don't ketch us on no woodpile—no, siree!"

Nor would any other man budge from the circle around the cold stove, in spite of Cyprien Palache shaking his fist and threatening each in turn. Finally the big man dropped onto his bed in the corner and simply glared at his crew.

For a long time, nothing more was said. The men shivered and listened to the wind. Each one assumed that Indian Johnnie had been swallowed up by the storm—or worse.

Jimmie dozed a little. Suddenly he awoke when he heard something tap-tap-tapping at the window. He turned and, through sleep-fogged eyes, saw a face at the window. At first he thought it was Johnnie, but then he realized the face was too big: It filled the window from side to side. And the eyes were like blue-black chips of ice.

He gave a cry, waking the others. But when they looked to where he was pointing, they saw only the frosty window glass, with a crescent of snow like a half smile across the ledge.

With a shaking hand, Jimmie wiped a circle in the frost. Beyond, he could see nothing but a pine stump in the clearing, like a tombstone rising out of the snow. For a moment he thought he heard—as though across a great distance—the voice of young Johnnie.

Then the shanty began to shake as the wind slammed it with the force of a hurricane. "De shaintee, she's gon' to fall!" cried Jimmie. Wind howled down the stovepipe, scattering ashes all around.

Suddenly there was a thunderous knock on the door, followed by three whistle blasts that cut through the howling wind.

"Dat Johnnie fin' my whissle!" cried Palache. He jumped up from his bed and yanked open the door.

Some men afterward said that the wind and swirling snow sucked him right out. But Jimmie Charbonneau swore that a huge hand, made of snow and tipped with nails of ice, grabbed the man and dragged him out into the storm. Then the door slammed shut.

By the time the lumbermen pulled it open again, not a trace of the foreman could be found.

In the morning, when the storm died away completely, the men found Johnnie, nearly frozen to death, huddled under the overturned boat. In the shelter of the tallest pine, Jimmie Charbonneau discovered the imprint of a single bare foot, with clawlike toes, about the size of a double sleigh. He called the others, but the wind and fresh-falling snow soon blurred the outline, leaving only a vague hollow in the snow.

Even Pat Clancy thought Jimmie had been imagining things. But Jimmie and Johnnie's eyes met, and they nodded to each other. They knew that Cyprien Palache had been carried off by a Windigo.

The Haunted Inn

(China)

In China long ago there was a young man named Li Wei, who was traveling with three companions. Early one evening, the four found themselves in a lonely countryside, with a storm beginning to break.

Hurrying along the road that was fast becoming a sea of mud, they spotted a small inn surrounded by willow trees. Delighted at their good fortune, they splashed across to the door. The innkeeper greeted them warmly, and his wife gave them welcome cups of steaming tea. But the newcomers quickly learned that many other travelers, also caught by the storm, had arrived before them. There was not a bed to be had—or even space enough for all the guests to stretch out on the floor.

The wife whispered something to her husband. He shrugged, then said apologetically, "The only space I can offer you is in the little building that stands some distance behind our inn. But I must warn you that the corpse of my daughter-in-law is laid out there. She died suddenly, and my son has gone to fetch a priest so that we may hold a proper funeral. He has not returned, and now I do not expect him until morning. You may all sleep there if you want to."

At first, young Wei hesitated. "It is surely unlucky to sleep in the same room as a corpse," he told his friends.

"That is true," one of his fellows agreed. "But what else are we to do?"

"I am too weary to argue," said Wei's second friend.

The third companion simply said, "Listen." The sound of rain battering the window lattices, and wind rattling the roof tiles decided the matter.

"Very well," Wei said to the innkeeper, "we will accept your offer."

So the old woman gave them mats to hold over their heads, while her husband guided the four travelers to the dark outbuilding that was set some distance from the house.

Inside, the innkeeper lit a candle. There was clean straw for bedding. At the back, a heavy curtain hid the unfortunate woman's body from view.

As soon as the old man was gone, the four friends settled down onto the straw. But while the others instantly fell asleep, Wei was troubled by the sense that something was amiss. He lay listening carefully, but he could hear only the rain pattering outside. The sputtering candle cast curious shadows on the pale curtain.

Then, with a hiss, the candle went out. At the same moment, Wei was sure that he could hear a rustling from behind the curtain.

Abruptly, the cloth was pulled aside. In the faint light seeping through the lattices, Wei saw the shape of a young woman, whose ghastly skin seemed almost to glow. Her nails looked as long as daggers.

Wei tried to cry out, but he was overcome by a listlessness that left him unable to move or speak. All he could do was raise his head slightly as he watched the form of the young woman bend over his companions. At first Wei thought she was merely studying each sleeper's features. But then he saw that she was breathing a greenish-white vapor into his friends' faces.

With a tremendous effort, he forced his hand inside his robe. There he grasped a bit of parchment on which his village priest had written magical Buddhist phrases to keep him safe on his journey. Though his every muscle seemed to resist, he managed to place this on his chest, just over his heart.

When the creature approached him just as she had approached his friends, Wei closed his eyes like one asleep. Every moment he expected to feel the touch of her claw-like nails or her chill breath upon his skin.

But after a short time, he heard the whisper of her robe going away from him. Opening his eyes a bit, he saw the figure gliding toward the back curtain. When she had passed into the alcove, she let the cloth fall back into place.

For a long time, Wei listened, but he could hear no further sounds from behind the cloth. At the same time, the listlessness left him, and he was able to sit up.

Hurriedly, he tried to rouse his companions. He whispered warnings and shook each of them, but to no avail. They were dead, killed by the woman's poisonous breath.

Suddenly he heard the curtain swept aside. He spun around and saw the woman coming at him, her claws outstretched like bundles of daggers. With a cry, the young man threw open the door and fled into the night. But in his haste he dropped his magic talisman.

Wei raced toward the inn and safety, half sliding down the muddy, tree-covered slope. Behind him he could hear the woman-thing in eager pursuit.

For a time Wei was able to use the willow trees as a screen, while he zigzagged away from his pursuer. But the creature quickly caught onto the trick, turned, and sprang at him, her extended nails aiming at his throat and heart. Wei was backed up against a willow tree. In desperation he threw himself sideways, tumbling into the mud. At the same moment, the woman's clawlike nails, driven by the weight of her body and the force of her leap, embedded themselves in the willow's trunk.

Wei staggered back toward the inn to rouse the inhabitants while the imprisoned creature struggled to break free.

When he told his story, he tried to convince the others to take up weapons and destroy the creature. But the innkeeper, his wife, and all the guests refused to do anything except bar the door and huddle together. Unwilling to face the monster alone, Wei joined the others as they watched fearfully and waited for the dawn.

Toward morning, the rain ceased. When the sun had fully risen, a few of the braver souls, led by Wei, approached the willow where he had last seen the creature. There they found the corpse, still fastened to the tree, dried to a husk in the sunlight.

When the innkeeper's son arrived soon after with a priest, certain rites were performed, and the body was burned. After that, the place was never troubled again. But Wei, for the rest of his life, refused to travel the road that ran past the willow-shaded inn.

The Rolling Head

(North America—Plains Indians)

There was once a warrior whose wife had died. He lived with his young son and daughter in a lodge apart from other people, near a forest at the edge of the prairie. For a long time the hunting was poor, and the family had little to eat save roots and berries. It saddened the man to see his children growing thin and ghostlike.

Now, it happened that his daughter had a gift of powerful medicine, as her mother once had. One night she had a dream in which a voice told her where a huge spiderweb could be found. "Tell your father to hang this web across the forest path where the animals go," the voice instructed her, "and you will no longer be hungry."

As soon as she woke, the girl told her father what she had dreamed. That very morning, he did what the dream voice had said. When he returned to the web in the evening, he found deer and rabbits entangled in its thick, sticky strands. These he took back to his children for food. Soon his son and daughter grew strong.

After a while the animals learned to avoid the web trap. From time to time the man was forced to move his snare deeper and deeper into the woods.

One day, after he had hung the web in a new place far from his lodge, he chanced upon a large lake, beside which stood a huge tepee, painted all over with strange designs. Uncertain whether to approach, he remained hidden by some brush.

Suddenly a tall old woman, three times the height of a man, pushed open the door flap. She walked to the edge of the water, where she whistled. In answer, the surface of the lake began to move and shake. Soon a monstrous snake rose from the waves and crawled out upon the land. Then the warrior in hiding knew that he had come upon the lodge of Snake Old Man and his ogress wife, Hungry Old Woman. The warrior was very much afraid, and hoped they would not find out he was near.

But Hungry Old Woman began to sniff the air. "Someone is near us!" she cried. "Catch him and put him in the cooking pot. I am so hungry, hungry!"

The snake slithered so swiftly toward the hunter that the man knew there was no hope of running away. He drew his knife just as the serpent wrapped itself around his body. All the while Hungry Old Woman cried, "Kill him quickly, so we can cook him!"

But the hunter thought of his children at home, who would be all alone if he perished. He fought as hard as he could, slew Snake Old Man, and cut the monster into pieces.

Then Hungry Old Woman gave a screech and ran after the hunter. He led her down the path that ran to the spiderweb. Behind him, he heard her jaws go *clack-clack-clack* as she tried to bite his elbows and heels. Then she was caught in the spiderweb. The ogress struggled fiercely, and had almost broken free, when the hunter struck off her head with his knife.

But Hungry Old Woman's body freed itself and began to chase him. Meanwhile, the head had smelled the children. Now it rolled out of the forest toward the lone tepee on the prairie. Inside, the girl was embroidering moccasins with porcupine quills stained different colors. Her little brother, who was gathering firewood, saw Hungry Old Woman's head rolling along the ground toward him, the teeth going *clack-clack-clack*. He ran away as fast as he could, crying, "Sister, I am being chased by a head!"

"Come inside!" his sister said, grabbing his hand. "Now close the tent flap." They fastened the hide flap with wooden pegs. The head rolled against the flap and partway up the tepee; then it rolled back down. Again and again it rolled against the hide, crying, "Children, children, open the door. I am hungry, hungry." The children knew it would soon split the side of the tent.

But the girl had a plan. She grabbed her quills and her root digger, a sharp-pointed stick. Then she told her brother to stand on one side of the tent opening while she stood on the other. She unfastened the pegs and drew the flap aside. Instantly the head rolled into the lodge and all the way to the back.

Then sister and brother jumped outside while the girl let the flap fall back into place. This kept the angry head inside just long enough for them to begin running across the prairie.

But soon the boy cried out, "Sister, I am tired! I can't run anymore!" The girl looked behind them and saw that the head had gotten out of the tepee and was rolling along the ground after them. Its hair streamed out behind it while its teeth went *clack-clack-clack*.

So the girl threw a handful of yellow porcupine quills on the ground, with a prayer to the Great Spirit. Instantly a great tangle of prickly pears sprang up behind them. These grew as tall as pines and were covered with great yellow thorns. They stretched for a long way in both directions.

When the head reached the thicket, its hair kept getting caught in the thorns, and it could not get through at first. But finally it chewed free with its sharp teeth, and rolled after the boy and girl, who had now run far away.

But soon they looked behind and saw the head coming

closer. Then the frightened boy called out, "Sister, I can't run anymore! Save yourself!"

Instead, the girl threw a fistful of white quills behind her, with a second prayer to the Great Spirit. Then there sprang up a range of mountains so tall that white snow topped them.

But the head found a nest of rattlesnakes, who were the cousins of Snake Old Man, and they showed her a tunnel through the mountain. Soon she had passed to the other side, and out onto the plains again.

On and on the children ran, but when they looked back they saw that the head was almost upon them.

"Sister, I am tired!" cried the boy. "I can't run anymore!"

Then the girl flung the blue quills behind her with a prayer. Where they fell, a great canyon opened. Far below, a river of swift blue water rushed through it. But, to her dismay, she saw that her brother, who had fallen behind her, was now on the other side. The rolling head was very close to him.

"Sister, help me!" the boy cried.

All she had now was her root digger. She laid this on the edge of the ravine, and it became a wooden bridge. Her brother ran across, and right behind him came the head, its teeth going *clack-clack-clack*. But the instant her brother reached her, when the head was still on the bridge, the girl shook the end of the root digger.

With a terrible shriek, the head tumbled down, down, down into the swift-flowing water, and was swept away.

Then they heard a shout and saw their father running toward the edge of the canyon; he was still pursued by the headless body. He ran right to the edge of the cliff. When the monster was almost upon him, he jumped aside. Unable to stop, the creature fell over the edge and into the river. In a moment it was carried away, just like the head.

The girl and her brother used the root digger to cross to where their father waited. He hugged them close. Then he picked up the weary little boy and, praising his daughter for destroying the ogress, led them back to the tepee. There they continued to live in peace, enjoying the plentiful game the spiderweb provided.

The Croglin Grange Vampire

(British Isles—England)

Croglin Grange in Cumberland, England, had been owned by a family named Fisher for over a hundred years. But in the last century they moved out and rented the house to two brothers, Andrew and Gordon, and their sister, Emma.

The threesome settled in easily enough, and soon made many friends in the neighborhood.

One hot summer day, when the sultry air made any kind of work impossible, the three dined early. Afterward they sat out on the veranda, savoring the cooling air, and watching the full moon rise and bathe the lawn and gardens in silver light.

At last they grew tired, and went indoors to their separate rooms. Emma found the night still too warm for sleep. Leaving her shutters open, and mounding the pillows behind her, she sat up in her bed, watching the moon through her ground-floor window.

Gradually she became aware of two tiny lights that flickered in and out of the row of trees that separated the Grange's lawn from the village churchyard beyond. At first they seemed nothing more than fireflies to the young woman. But as she continued to stare at them, she saw them drawing nearer. To her surprise, they seemed to be embedded in a darker shadow, which had detached itself from the moon-cast shadows under the trees.

Emma's hand went to her throat as she realized that *something* was approaching the house, and growing larger the nearer it came. From time to time the dark shape was swallowed up by the shadows of trees on the lawn. But it always reemerged, larger than before, and coming closer . . . closer. . . .

Emma was filled with horror; at first she wanted to cry out, but her throat felt paralyzed. Then she dreaded making the least sound or movement, for fear that the thing outside the French doors would be drawn by it. She was sure that the pitiful barrier of glass panes and thin wooden sashes would not deter it for an instant.

Suddenly, for no reason that the terrified woman could guess, the shape turned aside. She had the impression that it was going around the house, instead of moving straight toward her. The moment the tall, dark figure was out of sight, Emma leaped from her bed and ran to the hall door.

Just as her fingers circled the knob, however, she heard a blood-chilling *scratch, scratch, scratch* at the window. Turning, she saw a hideous brown face with flaming eyes glaring in at her. The thing rattled the French windows, which were securely locked on the inside. Emma was relieved to see that the flimsy-looking panels might keep it at bay. She tried to open the bedroom door to escape into the hall beyond, but the antique latch jammed, trapping her in the room.

The creature outside scratched again at the glass; then it began to peck with its nails at the sash. Emma saw that it was scraping out the lead that held the windowpanes in place. Again she tried to scream, but only a soft moan escaped her lips.

A single, diamond-shaped pane fell inward and shattered on the floor. A long, bony finger snaked through,

found the catch on the window, and flicked it open. Emma lurched toward the bed, hoping to reach the closet beyond. But the creature burst into the room, grabbed her hair with its long fingers, and dragged her down so that her head hung over the side of the bed. Then it leaned over and bit her on the throat.

The sting released her voice, and she at last began to scream aloud. As she struggled to push the awful face away from her, she heard her brothers shouting and banging on the door. At this, the monster suddenly fled from the room.

When Andrew and Gordon found the door would not budge, they slammed themselves against it, throwing it open by sheer force.

Inside they found their sister, bleeding from a wound in the throat and unconscious. Past the open French windows, nothing moved upon the moonlit lawn at first. Then Gordon cried, "I see him!" He pointed to a tall figure that fled from the shadows under a large oak. Without hesitation, he pursued it. But the monster moved twice as fast, with long, loping strides, and quickly leaped over the wall into the churchyard.

By the time Gordon had reached the fieldstone wall, he could see nothing beyond but gravestones and vaults. His quarry had vanished. Frustrated and angry, he returned to his sister's room.

There he found that Emma had regained consciousness, while Andrew dabbed at her wound with a damp towel.

"We shall keep watch the rest of the night," Andrew was saying. "In the morning, we will take the first train back to London."

"Andrew! Here's Gordon!" the young woman said. "Did you find out who—or what—attacked me?"

"No," her brother confessed, "it escaped into the churchyard. But, whatever the devil it was, Andrew is right: We must leave here as quickly as possible."

But Emma shook her head. "I will not let this experience drive us from the house where we have been so happy!"

Though her brothers tried to persuade her to leave, Emma refused. "We have leased this house for seven years," she said, "and we have been here less than one. We cannot afford to move elsewhere, while paying rent on this place."

Her brothers uneasily agreed with the logic of her argument. The next morning the local constable helped them decide when he suggested, "It must have been a lunatic, escaped from some asylum." Then he added, with great authority, "He is not likely to return."

So they stayed at Croglin Grange. But Andrew and Emma switched rooms. Emma kept her shutters closed fast at night, and each of her brothers kept a loaded pistol in his room.

The winter passed uneventfully enough, but the following March, Emma was suddenly awakened by a dreadful scratching at the shutters. Looking up, she saw the same brown, shriveled face staring back at her through the one pane at the top of the window left uncovered by the shutters.

She screamed as loud as she could, and her brothers rushed out of the house with drawn pistols. They spotted the creature loping away across the lawn. Andrew fired and hit it in the leg, but it got away, scrambling over the graveyard wall. This time the brothers reached the wall quickly enough to see the dark form disappear into a neglected vault.

.   .   .

The next day, in the presence of the tenants of Croglin Grange, the constable, and several other local authorities, the vault was opened. Inside they discovered that all the coffins had been broken apart and their contents scattered across the floor. Only one coffin lay intact, though its lid was loose.

Andrew and Gordon, at the constable's direction, raised the coffin lid. Then Emma gasped, for there, inside, was the brown and withered figure that had twice appeared to her at the Grange. Further investigation revealed that one leg of the corpse had been damaged by a pistol shot.

Though no one said the dreaded word "vampire" aloud, by common agreement they did the only thing that can lay such a creature to rest: They burned the body to ashes.

After this there were no more disturbances at Croglin Grange.

The Yara

(Brazil)

That part of Brazil called Amazonia, where the city of Manaus now stands and that is spanned by the Manaus–Caracarai Highway, once belonged to an Indian tribe. Jaguarari, son of the chief, was handsome and lithe as the spotted jaguar. He was fearless in the face of an enemy and was a bold, skillful hunter. When he paddled his canoe upon the Amazon River, the prow, lifted like a bird's wing, hardly seemed to touch the water.

At the celebration that marked the raising of youths to the status of warriors, everyone remarked on Jaguarari's pride of bearing, keen eye, and strength. His long arrow never failed to bring down the fleeing peccary or the bounding ocelot, while his blowgun dart dropped the preying hawk to the ground.

The young women dreamed that he would one day choose them for his bride; the old men boasted of his exploits; and his comrades sang songs that foretold how Jaguarari, on some distant day when his life was over, would climb the Blue Mountains, where the greatest heroes live for eternity.

Nothing pleased the young man more than guiding his canoe through the green shade along the river shore as he went fishing for *tucunare,* the slippery soapfish. He loved the solitude, when his only companion was a white-necked heron standing on a sandbar, or a flame-red parrot calling from the shore.

Jaguarari had always returned to his village at dusk, but there came a time when he began to stay on the water until midnight.

One night, after this had been going on for some time, his worried mother sat watching until she saw her son tie up his canoe. Then she followed him to his palm-thatched hut. There she found him sitting listlessly in his hammock, his legs dangling, his elbows on his knees. His eyes, dark-circled from sleepless nights and filled with sadness, were fixed on the black waters of the river.

Gently his mother asked him, "My son, what kind of fishing keeps you out on the water so late? Only evil spirits prowl the night."

But Jaguarari just sighed, and would not take his eyes from the river's edge.

"Son," the woman persisted, "what has made you so unhappy?"

Again, she got nothing but a sigh and a shrug for an answer. In the pale moonlight she saw that he had become as thin as a man suffering from a wasting disease or stung by a scorpion.

Deeply troubled, she left him as she had found him, his dark eyes locked on the equally dark river.

Jaguarari was soon spending all his time on the river. He refused to accompany his father, the chief, on a tapir hunt; Jaguarari often abandoned his comrades when they set snares for wild birds or cast fishing nets. They would watch him paddle his canoe up the river until he was out of sight, hidden by the tall trees draped with vines. Sometimes they would call to him, asking where he was going, but he never answered.

In desperation, his mother came to him and said, "My son, evil spirits surely have poisoned the air you breathe.

Your father has decided to move the village far away from here, so that you can breathe good air and be healed."

But Jaguarari only whispered, in a voice so low that she had to bend close to him to hear his words, "Mother, I saw her, floating among the water lilies in a distant lagoon."

"Son, who have you seen?" his anxious mother asked.

"She has no name," Jaguarari said, like one speaking from a fever dream, "but she is as beautiful as the moon. Her eyes are green as the skin of the *aruana* that swims at the mouth of the creek, and her hair is as gold as the morning sun shining on the river. She sings to me in a voice that is sweeter than any bird. My ears do not understand what she is singing, but my heart knows. Once, she made the water part, and showed me where she lives below. Someday I want to go there with her. Whenever I leave her, I want to see her again. I want to hear her song once more."

At this his terrified mother cried out, "My son, that is the Yara! You must promise you will never go back to that place. Death waits in her green eyes and her song!"

But her son only turned his face away, and would not speak to her any longer.

All the next day Jaguarari remained in his hut. His mother and father visited him as he lay listlessly in his hammock. But he would not answer his father's questions, or touch the smoked fish and fruit his mother left for him.

That evening his parents were suddenly drawn to the river's edge when a group of young women, who had gone to fetch water, cried, "Come, everyone! Come and see!"

The villagers stared open-mouthed as they saw Jaguarari, his canoe aimed at the red disk of the setting sun, standing upright in the prow. His arms were outstretched like a bird about to take wing.

Beside him was the figure of a beautiful woman. Her golden hair streamed out behind her, while her arms, as pale as moonlight, were clasped about Jaguarari. She sang a haunting song in an unknown language that momentarily stilled the twilight cries of birds and howler monkeys. Her song lingered in the hearts of all who heard it, long after the sweet voice had passed out of earshot.

"The Yara!" sobbed Jaguarari's mother, turning her face to her husband's chest. And though the chief and his warriors tried to follow, and searched the river and every lagoon and tributary for days to come, they found no trace of Jaguarari or his canoe.

"Me, Myself"

(British Isles—Scotland)

Off the western coast of Scotland is a group of islands called the Hebrides, or "Western Islands." One of the largest is Islay, and near it is a smaller island, Orsay. For many years Orsay was used only for grazing cattle. These belonged to a laird, or landowner, on Islay, and were ferried across by boat, a few head at a time. The crossing was mild enough when the weather was clear and the sea was calm. Sailors knew to be careful of the fearful tides around the island, and only a foolhardy soul would attempt crossing the sound in bad weather.

Old stories said that Orsay was sometimes visited by kelpies, or water horses. These might emerge from the sea in the shape of horses or in the form of hairy, clumsy-looking men. People said that they could hear the kelpies wailing loudly near the island just before storms.

But the grass on the island was sweet and thick, and the laird would not let old stories keep him from fattening his herds. When all the cattle had been sent across, he hired a young man, Duncan MacPhee, and his new wife, Fiona, to tend his cattle. The two were very much in love, and needed only each other's company to be happy, so they got along quite well on the lonely island.

Duncan was a big, powerful man, with a handsome, weathered face dotted with freckles. Fiona was tall and fair-haired, with flashing blue eyes. At night, when the cattle were safe in the byre, or cowshed, they would close the shutters of the one-room stone cottage the laird had built them. Then they would sit by the peat fire that burned on the hearthstone in the middle of the dirt floor, talking softly, while the wind howled outside the thick stone walls and rattled the roof slates.

One afternoon, while they strolled along the rocky beach, Duncan was delighted to discover four large eider duck eggs. Fiona was far more excited when she found a handful of "fairy eggs" nestled among the seaweed and shells. These hard, light nuts, something like flat chestnuts, were gray, black, and brown.

"Ach, what are ye goin' to do with them sea nuts?" asked Duncan.

"I'll string them on a bit o' ribbon," said Fiona, "to wear 'round my neck. My granny says they keep off the evil eye and other wickedness. And cure sick cattle, too."

"Sure, they're not keepin' the kelpies away," said her husband, pointing out to sea.

"Oh!" cried Fiona, clutching the fairy eggs to her chest. As she looked out across the water, a brown head and a gray head bobbed amid the waves. Two pair of soft, curious eyes met hers.

"Shame on ye, Duncan McPhee, for givin' me such a turn!" she said. "Them's nothin' but two seals, wonderin' what we're about."

"Ach, so they are. My mistake," he said, laughing and taking her arm.

"Tease me so again," she said, with just the hint of a smile, "and ye'll not think it near as funny."

At that moment, a fulmar gave a shrill, lonely cry, and Fiona turned anxiously to look at the sea. But even the seals had gone. There was only the empty expanse of bright blue water.

"Tomorrow I must row across to Portnahaven for supplies," said Duncan as they climbed the steep path.

"Must ye?" she asked. "I feel a storm comin' on."

"There's precious few oats and barley left," he said, "and many other things we need besides. The weather will be fine, ye'll see."

Sure enough, the next day was mild, with calm and hazy sunshine over sea and land. Fiona rose early to cook barley bannocks. She wrapped the flat cakes of bread in some linen for Duncan to take with him. Standing on the bluff, she watched him rowing across the sound. Even as she gazed, she felt a wind rising, churning up waves. The little boat pitched and tossed, but Duncan was a skillful sailor, and he rowed on without mishap.

When she could no longer make out the rowboat, the young woman checked on the cattle, to be sure none was grazing too close to the cliff edge. Then she returned to the cottage, to feed the chickens and tend her little plot of turnips and potatoes. She kept busy, trying not to think of the changing weather. But when she stood up from digging in the garden, a strong, chill wind billowed her skirt and apron.

Looking toward the sound and the mainland beyond, she saw a heavy mist upon the dark blue sea. In a short time this gave way to a wind-driven rain. She prayed that Duncan would not be so foolish as to try to cross to Orsay in such foul weather.

When the cattle were secure in the byre, and the chickens in the hen coop, Fiona retreated to the cottage. She drew the shutters tight and prepared to sit out the storm, with a bowl of porridge and a cup of tea.

But while she was stirring the oatmeal with a spirtle, a wooden stick about a foot long, Fiona suddenly heard the sound of living creatures moving all around the house.

"Duncan!" she cried, thinking for a moment that her husband had returned and brought some other men with him. But the wail of the wind reminded her that the storm was too strong for Duncan to cross the sound.

"Sure now, it's the cows are out of their byre!" she exclaimed. She hurried to the nearest window and threw open the shutters. To her amazement, she found herself gazing into a pair of large, round, blazing red eyes that fastened on her own. The sight chilled her to the bone.

Gathering her wits, she pulled the shutters closed with a *bang* that set the dishes rattling on the shelf. In answer, she heard a low, whining laugh.

Too late, Fiona realized she hadn't barred the door. She reached up to drop the bar, but the door burst open. In walked an unearthly creature. He was very tall and large, and covered with rough hair everywhere except his face. This was covered with a dark, bluish skin that looked like fish scales. His long fingers were tipped with bone-white claws.

He lumbered to the fire and stared at Fiona, who stood just across from him. Between them the porridge bubbled on the hearthstone.

"What is your name?" he asked in the old language that Fiona had learned from her gran.

She answered the creature as confidently as she could, *"Mise mi Fhin,"* which means, "Me, Myself."

Suddenly the monster reached for her. But the brave young woman grabbed up the pot of boiling porridge with her apron and dashed it over him.

Yelling, the creature bounded through the door and into the rain beyond. Fiona heard a great babble of wild, growling voices asking in the old language what was wrong with their companion and who had hurt him.

"Mise mi Fihn! Mise mi Fihn!" he kept screeching. "Me, Myself! Me, Myself!"

At this, there arose a great shout of laughter. The rough voices taunted, "If you hurt yourself, then you must heal yourself."

Again there was brutish laughter. At this the girl rushed out and hid in the byre. She lay, sheltered by one of the cattle that had its back to the entrance. She touched her string of fairy eggs, hoping they might help keep her safe. Then she drew a circle around herself in the dust and prayed an "Our Father" in a whisper.

For a long time she lay shivering, hidden by the cow. Outside, the storm raged, and she heard the comings and goings of heavy footsteps. Several times she thought that one or more of the creatures had entered the cowshed, but she dared not peep around to see. She lay scarcely breathing.

As the storm grew wilder, the sounds outside turned to loud laughter, then fighting, as though the creatures had started a brawl among themselves. Fiona prayed that they would forget all about her.

Gradually the sounds of wind and rain and wild screeching began to fade. By the time that the first gray light of morning showed through chinks in the byre's rough stone wall, all was silent outside.

Making the sign of the cross, Fiona rose from her hiding place. She discovered that, though the consecrated circle had kept her safe, the cow that had protected her was dead; its back bore the marks of many claws.

The sea was calm and bright under the rising sun. Looking across the sound, she saw Duncan's rowboat on course for the island.

Her garden had been trampled by countless brutish

feet, ripping up her turnips and potatoes. Half-eaten remains were scattered all around. Inside, the spilled porridge was the only sign of the night's adventure. Shuddering, she drew on a shawl and hurried down to meet Duncan.

Though they were always on guard after this, and kept the shutters and door tightly barred after sunset, they were never again bothered by the kelpies.

Island of Fear

(North America—Seneca tribe)

There was once a young boy, Hatondas, whose parents had died. He lived with his grandparents deep in a great wood. Though they were loving and kind in many ways, they were always stern when they warned him, "When you leave our wigwam, do not go west."

Now, Hatondas was a good child, and for a long time he would explore only those forest paths that ran north and east and south. He would never venture into the dark shadows of the woods to the west.

But as he grew older, he became curious to know what might be found to the mysterious west. At last he decided to see what lay in this forbidden place. So, one morning, while his grandparents slept, he set out along the brush-choked trail that led west.

For a long time he could only advance very slowly, because the underbrush was too thick. Not even deer or other animals had worn paths through the wilderness. After a long, difficult journey, he came upon the banks of a broad, swift-flowing river.

"Is this what my grandfather and grandmother did not want me to see?" he asked himself. "Surely they have grown foolish in their old age."

He sat down very close to the water's edge to rest and to watch the shining river.

Suddenly he heard the bushes crackling behind him.

Then someone called out pleasantly, "Hai, Hai! Is this not a beautiful sight?"

Turning, Hatondas saw a handsome young warrior, his hand raised in a peaceful gesture. "Yes," Hatondas said to the newcomer, "I have never seen it before."

"Oh, then you must come with me to my canoe, not far from here," said the stranger. "I will take you to visit one of the islands nearby. We will return in a short time, and you will have seen many sights worth talking about."

Finding the young man pleasant company, Hatondas agreed. Together they walked to where a splendid birchbark canoe lay on the sandy beach of a cove. When they stepped into the canoe, the stranger gave a shove with his paddle and sent them into the current. With swift, even strokes, he quickly carried them far from shore.

Soon, a short distance ahead, Hatondas saw a small, pretty island with a dense clump of trees at the center. When they arrived on the beach of sparkling sand they both climbed out, and the stranger drew his canoe up on shore.

Beyond the beach grew masses of tall plants with blossoms as yellow as the sun. For a moment Hatondas drank in their beauty. But when he turned to look for his guide, the young man had vanished—and the canoe was no longer beached where they had left it. Amazed, Hatondas spotted the canoe far out on the river, halfway to the distant shore.

"Hai! Hai!" he shouted. "Come back! Come back!"

But the stranger would not look back. Realizing that he had been marooned, Hatondas sat down on a fallen log in the shade of some trees.

Suddenly he heard a whisper. "Boy! Boy!" The sound seemed to come up from the ground at the end of the log. There he noticed a small white spot. Scraping away at the

earth, he uncovered a skull. "Lift me into the sun for a moment," begged the skull. The whisper came from between the jaws, which never moved. "Let me feel its warmth again."

With shaking hands, Hatondas lifted the skull up to the sun. "Oh, how good! How I enjoy it! I am glad you found me!" the skull whispered. "Now I must warn you that this island is ruled by an ogre who commands powerful medicine. His son, who brings men across from the shore, only seems to be human. I was once a great medicine man myself. I came willingly to this island, thinking I would be strong enough to slay the sorcerer. But his magic was stronger than mine, and he killed me.

"He is gone away today, but he will return tomorrow with his son. Both of them eat men. They will gobble you up the way they did me and many others, unless you do as I tell you. If you heed me, you may escape and break the island's evil spell forever."

Frightened but courageous, the boy said, "I will."

"Before sunrise tomorrow, run to the beach where you landed and bury yourself in the sand so that only your eye and ear are uncovered. You must look and listen carefully, then tell me what you have learned."

The boy agreed to do this. Then he gently set the skull on a small hill, where it could enjoy the sun's warmth.

After a sleepless night, Hatondas went down to the shore at first light. He hid just as the skull had instructed him. Soon he heard the sound of singing from across the water. The song grew louder, and the boy, in hiding, guessed that the singer was approaching the island. Recognizing it as a song of power, Hatondas softly hummed it to himself, until he had learned it by heart.

Then he heard the crunch of the canoe as it touched the sandy beach. The singing stopped, but now Hatondas heard two voices: one, the voice of his young guide from the day before; the other, much older and rougher. The boy saw two ogres with horrible faces, pop eyes, and wide mouths full of sharp, yellow teeth.

"Well, where is my meal?" roared the taller of the two.

"I will fetch him," said the other. Though he no longer looked like the handsome warrior who had rowed Hatondas across to the island, his voice was the same. He vanished into the woods, while the other ogre tramped impatiently up and down the beach—often no more than a pace from where Hatondas lay hidden.

Finally the ogre son returned and said, "I cannot find him."

At this, the father stamped the ground and ordered his son to go and seek another victim. Then, grumbling, the sorcerer stormed through the woods, while his son returned to the canoe and hastened back to the mainland.

When both were out of sight, Hatondas uncovered himself and returned to tell the skull what he had seen and heard.

"You have done well. Now listen. First, go to the place where you found me, dig again in that spot, and you will find my medicine bundle. Bring it here."

The boy did as he was told, and soon uncovered a decayed medicine pouch. This he brought back to where the skull lay in a patch of sunlight. Then the skull whispered to him, "Make seven dolls from wood, and make a small bow and arrow for each. Cut the pouch into seven strips, and tie one strip around each doll. Then place them in the top of a tree near the beach. Hide yourself in the sand again at first light, and see what will happen."

The next morning the ogre son rowed across from the mainland, singing his song of power. When he reached the beach, he set down a bundle from which cries arose. Hatondas guessed that the ogre had stolen a baby. Suddenly, from the tree in which he had put the wooden dolls, came cries of "Ho-yo-ho!" When the ogre looked up to see what had made the sound, the tiny bowmen fired their arrows into the monster. From the way he cried out, Hatondas guessed that the sliverlike arrows had deadly power. Volley after volley flew from the tree. Soon the creature, bristling with arrows, fell in a heap on the sand.

Hatondas uncovered himself, grabbed the baby, and ran for the trees. When he glanced up at the dolls, he saw they were now only figures of dried wood. A moment later he heard the ogre sorcerer hurrying toward the beach. Clutching the infant, Hatondas hastened to the skull in its circle of sunlight.

Quickly, the boy told what had happened. "My magic is now finished," whispered the skull. "You must slay the sorcerer yourself."

"How can I do such a thing?" Hatondas asked.

"At the center of this island is a clearing. Within the clearing is the monster's wigwam. The creature leaves his heart inside so that he need not fear for his life. Destroy it, and you destroy the ogre."

Leaving the baby hidden beneath a bush, Hatondas hurried to find the huge wigwam deep within the woods. He thrust aside the entrance flap and saw, against the far wall, a large, beating heart. In the middle of the tent was a huge pot of boiling water.

Hatondas grabbed the heart just as the ogre came storming in. The creature snarled as he saw his intended victim holding his heart. Bellowing, the ogre grabbed for the boy, but Hatondas threw the heart into the bubbling water.

The monster gasped and screeched and then fell over backward. As his heart boiled away, so his very flesh boiled away, leaving only misshapen bones on the floor mats.

Hatondas took all the robes and blankets from the evil

wigwam, and set fire to it, so that nothing was left but ashes. Then he returned to where he had hidden the baby. The skull whispered, "When you destroyed the monster and his lodge, you broke the spell on the island. Go, take the child with you, and leave me here in the sunshine."

So Hatondas went back to the beach, took the ogre's canoe, and, singing the song of power, returned to his grandparents. They wept tears of joy to see him, because they thought he had been slain by a wild animal or drowned. Then they scolded him for going where they had told him not to go. But the boy apologized, and gave them the robes and blankets he had taken from the island, so they forgave his disobedience. Because they could not find out who the baby belonged to, he was raised as a brother to Hatondas. Now that the ogre was dead, they were free to follow any path they chose.

Three Who Sought Death

(British Isles—England—from Geoffrey Chaucer)

There were three reckless fellows in a tavern one day, who chanced to see a funeral procession passing by. They sent the tavern boy to inquire who had died. The lad returned and told them, "It is an old friend of yours, Forndronke, who was slain by the thief named Death."

"By heaven!" said the first fellow to his companions, "who is this Death that everyone is so afraid of him? Let us vow, on the spot, to go and find Death and rid the world of him before nightfall."

All three shook hands, and agreed to seek out Death and put an end to his work. When they asked the tavernkeeper where Death might be found, the man said, "Not far from here there is a village that has been ravaged by the plague. Men, women, and children, master and servant, have been claimed by Death. I am certain that you will find him there."

So off they went to find the unhappy village. But when they had gone only a little way, the three met a poor old man. They made fun of his long gray beard, his wrinkled skin, and the staff that he leaned on for support. They barred his path and would not let him pass.

"Please let me go my way," the old man begged. "For Death is following me, and I must outrun him to stay alive."

"No, old wretch, we will not let you pass," the three

said, "until you tell us where we can find Death. He has slain our friend, and now we mean to put an end to him!"

"Good sirs," said the old man, "if you want to find Death, look under that oak tree yonder."

At this, the three fellows let the old man go his way. They hurried to the tree, where they found not Death, but a chest filled with gold coins. Down they sat to count their newfound treasure, and promptly forgot their vow to seek out Death.

After a time the first man said, "We must be careful with this gold, or people will say we stole it, and hang us as thieves. Let us draw straws. Whichever of us draws the shortest will go to town and bring us food. The other two shall keep watch over the gold. Then, at night, we will each take away with us an equal part of the treasure, when no man can see us and accuse us of thievery."

This they agreed to, and accordingly drew straws. The shortest straw went to the youngest of the three. So they gave him a handful of gold coins, and off he went to town to get food.

Meanwhile, the two left guarding the remainder of the treasure decided that as soon as their fellow returned, they would kill him, eat the food, and divide up the gold two ways instead of three.

The youngest, as he walked to town, said to himself, "I could buy poison, and put it in the food, and slay my two companions. Then I would have all the treasure to my-self." So he purchased a strong and violent poison, and put it in the food and drink he bought, and carried these to his fellows.

But his companions fell upon him and slew him the minute he returned. When they had buried his body, the first wretch said, "Now let us sit and eat and make merry, for we are wealthy men."

Then they ate the food their friend had brought, and quickly died from the poison in it.

So the three men found Death, whom they had been seeking, underneath the oak tree—just as the old man had promised.

Sister Death and the Healer

(Mexico/American Southwest)

There was once a woodcutter, José, who fell asleep in the wood and did not wake until after dark. When he did, he met the skeletal figure of *Manita Muerte*, Sister Death, driving her wooden cart in which she gathers the souls of the newly departed.

"*Buenas noches, señora,*" said the woodcutter respectfully, recognizing the figure who stood before him.

"*Buenas noches, señor,*" Death replied. "Will you give me something to eat? The night is long, and I have grown hungry."

"*Sí, sí!*" said the woodcutter. He gave half of his rice and beans to her. "I am honored to share this, for I have long admired you. In a world that too much belongs to the rich and powerful, you play no favorites. All, rich or poor, will be taken into your cart sooner or later."

Now, Death was very pleased to hear him speak so. "I will give you any gift you wish for as a reward," she said.

"I have only one wish," the good-hearted man said, "that I might help those who are sick and suffering."

"Very well," said Death, "I will make you a *curandero,* a healer. All you must do is lay your hand on a sick person's brow, and he or she will be made well again. But you must *never* use your gift if you see me standing at the head of a sick person's bed. I will be there because God has decided to call the suffering one out of life. *No one* must keep me from gathering that soul into my cart."

The woodcutter readily agreed to this. With a quick nod of her head, Death sealed their bargain. Then she drove her cart away to the east, where the morning sun had begun to lighten the sky behind the mountains.

As José returned home, he wondered if he had had a waking dream. Surely, he told himself, he had not met *Manita Muerte* in fact.

Now it chanced that, on his way, he met old Luis, a friend of his. Luis was limping, because a burro had kicked him in the leg.

"Let me help you," José offered.

He started to put his arm around his friend's shoulder; but at his touch, Luis cried wonderingly, "My leg! You have healed my leg! How have you done this?"

Then José told the old man the story of his meeting with Death.

Astounded, Luis insisted on telling everyone they met about José's great gift. Soon young and old were coming to him, asking for his blessing and begging for his healing touch.

The new *curandero* used his powers carefully. Quite by accident, since his only goal was to help the sick and pain-ridden, the healer himself grew wealthy. Still, he remained a generous person, and gave away as much gold as he kept.

Then one day José fell in love with Dolores, the daughter of old Luis. They longed to spend every moment in each other's company. Often Dolores would accompany him on his healing visits. There she would comfort an anxious husband or wife, or take a tearful child onto her lap, while José prayed over the ailing person and worked

his wonderful cures through the gentle touch of his hands.

On the day before they were to be married, Dolores fell ill. When he was summoned to her bedside by her grieving father, José was distressed to see that Death was leaning upon one post at the head of the bed.

For the first and only time, José disobeyed *Manita Muerte*. He gently laid his hand upon Dolores's fevered brow and healed the young woman. At that instant, Death vanished from the room.

But as the *curandero* walked home late that night, Death's cart appeared on the road in front of him. When he dared look into the face of Death, he saw only a shadow underneath her cowl. He began to tremble.

Suddenly the moon and stars vanished. There was a moment of blinding darkness, and then he found himself in a cave filled with uncounted numbers of flickering candles. Death sat in her cart beside him. Slowly she raised a bony finger and pointed to a long and a short candle side by side on a nearby flat stone; the short one had almost guttered out.

"I warned you never to cure someone if I stood at the head of the bed, but you disobeyed me," Death said angrily. "Now you must suffer the consequences. Once you were the tall candle with a long life ahead, and the nearly extinguished one was your beloved. Your disobedience has reversed the two. Now *your* life candle is the short one."

"Have pity!" said the man, dropping to his knees and pleading with Death. "I did what I did because I couldn't live without Dolores, nor she without me."

"Then I will grant you one last mercy," said *Manita Muerte*. So saying, Sister Death leaned over and snuffed out both candles together.

In an instant, the dead man's soul was in the cart as it creaked and crept along the dusty road that leads to a distant, shadowed country. Beside him, in the silence, rode the soul of his beloved, as Death carried them out of the land of the living.

The Mouse Tower

(Germany)

In the middle of the Rhine River, near the city of Bingen, there has stood for hundreds of years a fortified rock topped by a large tower, called the *Mauseturm*, or mouse tower. Legend has long held that this was the scene of a terrible punishment sent by God upon a bishop who betrayed the faithful in his care.

In the year 970, Germany suffered from a terrible famine. In desperation, people were reduced to eating dogs and cats, and still countless numbers died of hunger. At this time, Hatto the Second was bishop of the region. Every day the starving poor would crowd around his door, begging for bread. It was widely known that he had plentiful supplies of grain set aside from the good harvest the year before.

But the bishop refused to part with the mounds of grain locked away in his bulging storehouses. His only thought was to increase his personal fortune.

From the high window of his palace, he would watch poor people fainting from hunger on the streets and storming the bread market, where they would take the bread by force. The bishop felt no pity at all for these starving people. But he soon grew weary of their cries day and night as they crowded around his palace walls, begging for a crust of bread, a handful of corn.

At last the bishop decided to quiet the mob. From his window he announced to them, "Let all you poor and needy gather in my great barn outside the city. There I shall feed you."

So it was that, from all directions, from near and far, a desperate army of hungry folk flocked to the bishop's barn. Loudly they sang the bishop's praises, while his soldiers urged them into the barn.

When the vast wooden structure could hold no more, the treacherous bishop ordered his soldiers to seal the doors. Then he had his men set fire to the barn, and burned the unfortunates, young and old, men and women. When the flames were at their highest, and the agonized cries were loudest, Hatto said, "Hear, hear, how the mice squeak! In faith, 'tis an excellent bonfire. The country is greatly obliged to me for ridding it of such mice who would only consume our precious corn."

The shouts and screams for mercy seemed to hang in the air long after the barn was reduced to nothing more than smoking embers.

Afterward, content with his day's work, the wicked man returned to his palace. There he sat down merrily to supper, and afterward slept the night like an innocent man.

But God soon saw to it that Bishop Hatto never slept again.

The very next morning, the bishop discovered his palace was infested with mice. They scurried down corridors and crawled over his feet while he took his ease or tried to read. They fouled the food in his larder and chewed his books and papers. They bit anyone who tried to drive them away. No efforts on his part could free Bishop Hatto from their torments.

When he entered his great hall, he discovered that mice had eaten his portrait out of its frame. The rectangle of splintered wood held only a few tatters of canvas. A short time later, a frightened farm servant reported to him that mice had devoured all the corn in his granaries.

Immediately thereafter, a second terrified messenger arrived and reported that a huge tide of mice was scurrying toward his palace.

Rushing to his window, the bishop could see the roads and fields dark with the advancing army. The vast horde of mice was chewing remorselessly through both hedge and wall, as the creatures made straight for the palace. The sound of their shrieking and squeaking chilled him to the heart.

Full of terror, Bishop Hatto escaped through the rear gate and commanded his men to row him out to his tower in the middle of the Rhine River. There he ordered his servants to bar every entrance.

But the mice followed him. They swam across the river, clambered up the rock, and crawled through every crack and crevice of the battlements. Swarming over the tower, they chewed their way in by the thousands, through oaken doors and plank floors and wooden ceilings.

And when they had cornered the wicked bishop, they climbed, dropped, and leaped upon him from all sides. As one old poem has it:

> *They whetted their teeth against the stones,*
> *And then they picked the bishop's bones;*
> *They gnawed the flesh from every limb,*
> *For they were sent to punish him.*

Then, as suddenly as they had appeared, the swarms of mice disappeared. Many people were convinced that the

animals were really the souls of those the bishop had so cruelly slain. The *Mauseturm* remains a place of fearful fascination. It is rumored that one can still hear the ghostly cries of the wretched bishop and the chittering of hordes of unseen mice on the anniversary of the fatal barn fire.

The Devil and Tom Walker

(United States—from a tale by Washington Irving)

A few miles from Boston, the sea has cut a deep inlet that winds several miles inland and ends in a thickly wooded swamp. On one side of the water is a dark grove of trees; on the opposite side the land rises abruptly from the shore into a high ridge, on which grow scattered oaks of immense age and size. Under one such tree, according to old stories, Captain Kidd the pirate buried a great treasure. The stories add that the devil oversaw the hiding of the money, and took it under his guardianship, as he always does with buried treasure that has been ill-gotten. Kidd never returned to claim his gold, being captured soon after at Boston, sent to England, and there hanged for piracy.

Later, in the year 1727, a miserly fellow named Tom Walker dwelled near this place. He lived in a forlorn house surrounded by a few straggling trees. One day Tom took a shortcut homeward, through the swamp. Like most shortcuts, it was an ill-chosen route.

It was dusk when Tom reached the ruins of an old fort in the middle of the swamp. He paused to rest on the trunk of a fallen hemlock. Absently, he turned up the soil with his walking staff. Suddenly his staff struck something hard, and he uncovered an ancient skull with a tomahawk buried deep in it.

"Humph!" said Tom Walker as he gave it a kick.

"Let that skull alone!" said a gruff voice. Tom looked up and saw a tall man dressed in black seated opposite him on the stump of a tree. He scowled at Tom with a pair of large red eyes. "What are you doing on my ground?"

"And pray, who are you, if I may be so bold?" said Tom.

"Oh, I go by various names. In this neighborhood I am known by the name of The Black Woodsman."

"If I mistake not," said Tom sturdily, "you are also commonly called Old Scratch."

"At your service!" replied the devil with a nod.

And so the two began a conversation as Tom returned homeward. The dark man told him of huge sums of gold and silver buried by Kidd the pirate, under the oak trees on the high ridge. This treasure was protected by his power, so that only someone who gained his favor could find it. This he offered to Tom, on certain conditions.

The conditions must have been very hard, because Tom asked for time to think about them, and he was not a man to worry about trifles when money was in view. When they reached the edge of the swamp, Tom said, "What proof have I that all you have been telling me is true?"

"Here's my signature," said Old Scratch, pressing his finger against Tom's forehead. Then he turned off into the swamp, and seemed to go down, down, down into the earth, until he totally disappeared.

When Tom reached home, he found a black fingerprint, which nothing could erase, on his forehead. This made him think even more carefully about the terms he had been offered.

Soon enough, however, greed won over caution. One evening Tom set out for the abandoned fort. Soon he met The Black Woodsman, with his ax on his shoulder, strolling through the swamp, humming a tune. By degrees Tom brought up the subject of business, and they began to haggle about the terms on which Tom was to have the pirate's treasure.

"You shall become a moneylender," the devil proposed. "You shall open a shop in Boston. You shall lend money to the desperate at ruinous rates, extort bonds, foreclose mortgages, and drive the merchants to bankruptcy—"

"I'll drive them to the devil!" cried Tom.

"Exactly," said the man in black with a grim smile. Then he extended his hand, saying, "Done!"

"Done!" said Tom Walker.

So they shook hands and struck a bargain.

Soon Tom Walker was seated behind his new desk in a countinghouse in Boston. The place was richly furnished, and had been paid for in antique gold coins to which traces of dark earth still clung.

His business was thronged by the needy who hoped to keep a roof over their heads and bread on the table; the foolhardy who dreamed of turning borrowed money into great fortunes; gamblers whose luck had run out; and merchants whose credit had dried up. In short, everyone driven to raise money by desperate means and desperate sacrifices hurried to Tom Walker.

Tom acted like a friend, but he always demanded full return and more for the money he loaned. He squeezed his customers as dry as a sponge, and sent them away destitute. In this way he became a rich and mighty man, and built himself a vast house.

As Tom grew old, however, he grew thoughtful. Having secured the good things of this world, he began to worry about the next. He regretted his deal with the devil, and tried to think of how to escape from his bargain with The Black Woodsman. All of a sudden he became a violent

churchgoer. He prayed loudly, as if he could take possession of heaven by the force of lungs. He constantly cen-
sured his neighbors, and seemed to think that every sin he
noted in them was a credit to him. Soon his zeal became as
notorious as his riches.

In spite of all this, Tom dreaded that the devil would
have his due after all and carry him off. So Tom always
kept a small Bible in his coat pocket. He also had a huge
Bible on his countinghouse desk, and was frequently
found reading the Bible when people called on business.
Then he would lay his spectacles in the book to mark the
place, while he drove some ruinous bargain.

One hot summer afternoon, as a black thunderstorm
was coming up, Tom sat in his countinghouse in his white
cap and silk robe. He was about to foreclose a mortgage,
which would ruin an unlucky man.

"My family will be driven to the poorhouse," the
wretched man pleaded.

"I must take care of myself," replied Tom.

"But you have made so much money out of me already!" the other cried.

Tom lost his patience and his piety. "The devil take me,"
said he, "if I have made a farthing!"

Just then, there were three loud knocks at the door.
Tom opened it to see who was there. A man dressed in a
black woodsman's outfit was holding a black horse, which
neighed and stamped with impatience.

"Tom, you're come for," said the fellow gruffly. Tom
shrank back, but too late. He had left his little Bible in his
coat pocket, and his big Bible on the desk, under the
mortgage he was about to foreclose. Never was a sinner
taken more unawares.

The black figure whisked him into the saddle, and the

horse galloped away down the streets. Tom Walker's white cap bobbed up and down, his robe fluttered in the wind, and the steed struck fire out of the cobblestones at every bound. The dark woodsman disappeared in a blaze of black fire.

Tom never returned to foreclose the mortgage. A man who lived on the border of the swamp reported that at the height of the thunderstorm he had heard a great clattering of hoofs and a howling along the road. He ran to the window and caught sight of a figure on a horse that raced like mad across the fields and down into the black swamp toward the old fort. Shortly thereafter, a lightning bolt fell and seemed to set the whole forest ablaze.

When neighbors searched Tom's offices they found all his bonds and mortgages burned to cinders. His huge iron chest was filled with chips and shavings of wood instead of gold and silver. The next day his house caught fire and burned to the ground.

Such was the end of Tom Walker and his ill-gotten wealth.

The Greedy Daughter

(Italy)

There once was a widow who had a daughter who was so greedy that the poor woman did not know what to do with her. She would gobble up everything in the house. When the widow came home from selling flowers in the market square, she would find nothing left to eat.

Now it happened that they had a wolf as a neighbor. The wolf had a frying pan, while the girl's mother was too poor to own one. Whenever she wanted to fry something, the mother sent her daughter, Filomena, to borrow the wolf's frying pan.

The wolf was very glad to loan the skillet to the widow. And he always sent a nice omelette in it so it would not be empty. The wolf intended this omelette for both mother and daughter. But Filomena was so greedy and so selfish that she always ate the omelette on the way home. Her poor mother never had so much as a taste.

When the good woman was finished with her frying, she would say to her daughter, "Filomena, in the morning scour the pan clean and return it to our neighbor. Take with you a loaf of the bread I baked today to thank him."

Filomena was lazy as well as greedy. She refused to clean the greasy frying pan. She waited until her mother had gone to the market square. Then she ate the loaf of bread meant for the wolf. After this, she took some mud, baked it in the fireplace, and put it in the frying pan. "Our neighbor is only a wolf, after all," she said to herself. "He will not know baked dirt from good bread."

The wolf was hurt when he saw the earthen loaf, but he was too good-hearted to say anything. After Filomena was gone, he said to himself, "Well, well! Perhaps things are going so badly for the widow that she can offer me no more than a bit of baked mud and ash. Next time they borrow the frying pan, I will make them an even finer omelette."

Soon enough, the old woman asked Filomena to visit the wolf and beg for the loan of his skillet. This time the wolf gave the girl the pan with an omelette so light and filled with fine herbs and cheese and ham that the greedy girl got only a short distance from the wolf's house before she gobbled up every bit of it. Not a speck was left for her mother that evening.

When the widow had finished her frying, she said to Filomena, "In the morning, scrub out the skillet and return it. And take with you this pitcher of cream to thank our neighbor."

As soon as her mother had left the next morning, greedy Filomena drank down every drop of the cream. Then she took the empty pitcher and the greasy frying pan with her and walked to the wolf's house. She paused on the way to dip up a pitcherful of ditch water, muttering, "Why waste sweet cream on a wolf? This will serve quite as well."

Again the wolf was offended by the sight of the greasy pan and the pitcher of ditch water. But he thanked the unkind girl anyway. To himself, he said, "Now things must really be desperate in the poor woman's house, that she can only send common ditch water by way of thanks."

Then he set to scouring the pan himself.

It chanced soon after this that the wolf met the widow in the market square. "How are things with you?" he asked.

"Well enough," she said.

"How do you like my omelettes?" asked the wolf.

"I am sure you make delicious omelettes," replied the confused woman. "But I have never had the pleasure of tasting so much as a mouthful."

"Never tasted them!" exclaimed the wolf. "How many times have you sent Filomena to borrow my frying pan?"

"I am ashamed to say how many times," said the flustered woman. "A great many, certainly."

"And every time I sent you an omelette in it," the wolf said.

"Never a bit of one reached me," the woman confessed.

"Then that greedy girl of yours must have eaten them on the way home every time."

Now the poor mother, anxious to keep the wolf from being angry at her daughter, made all manner of excuses for Filomena's greediness. But the wolf had grown even more suspicious, so he said, "The omelettes would have been better had the frying pan been properly cleaned before it was sent back to me."

"Surely you are mistaken!" cried the widow. "Filomena told me herself that she always cleaned it inside and out, until it sparkled as bright as new silver." Then, worried because the wolf was growing angrier by the minute, the good woman said, "I hope you enjoyed the little gifts of bread and cream I sent to you."

"Dirty ash and ditch water are all your wretched child brought to me!" cried the wolf.

"Dear neighbor, surely you are joking!" said the worried woman. "Perhaps I burned the bread myself. If there was water in the cream, then the farmer I bought it from was a cheat."

"Oh, I know who has been the cheat," said the wolf. "Now I must be on my way. Farewell."

So saying, he hurried away.

But he did not return to his own home. Instead he raced to the woman's house.

When Filomena saw the angry wolf approaching, she slammed shut the door. Then she called out, "Why have you come here?"

"I'm here to punish you for your unkind gifts of dirt and ditch water," he roared, "and your greedy way with the omelettes entrusted to you and the bread and cream that were meant for me!"

"Surely," the wicked girl cried out, "if anything is amiss, it was my mother's doing. She is in the market square. Go and gobble up that good-for-nothing if you must."

The wolf just growled and broke down the door. The frightened girl scrambled under the bed to hide herself, but it was as easy for the wolf to go under the bed as to get anywhere else. So under he went, and dragged her out, and gobbled her down on the spot.

And that was the end of the greedy daughter.

The Pirate

(United States—adapted from a poem by Richard H. Dana)

Near the close of the eighteenth century, a ship lay in a Spanish port, being outfitted for a voyage to America. One day, a Spanish doña, a widow, came to the dock, seeking passage to America. The unfortunate woman had no way of knowing that Captain Lee, grown weary of the poverty that dogged his life, had turned pirate.

Eyeing her fine dress, her golden rings, and her jewels, Lee offered her false sympathy for the loss of her husband and falser promises of a swift, safe passage across the ocean. Charmed by the captain's manner, the woman put herself, her servants, and all her wealth in the buccaneer's grasp.

At the very last moment—just before the ship set sail—the *señora* had her most prized possession brought on board: a milk-white Arabian horse. The stallion was tethered on deck. But from the first it stamped and reared and whinnied as though it sensed the danger hiding behind the captain's polite words and gracious manner.

As soon as the ship was out of sight of land, the crew, at a signal from Lee, slew all the lady's attendants as they slept. Then he and his men forced the door of her cabin open. It fell inward with a crash, but the lady fought the pirate with all her strength. She managed to break free of Lee's grasp and fled to the deck of the ship.

There, she tried to untie the Arabian as it raged against the ropes that kept it captive. Realizing that she could not free the horse in time, the brave woman drew her dagger and climbed onto the railing. Calling down the vengeance of heaven on the pirate who had betrayed her, she swore to battle to the end. Lee, tiring of the game, signaled one of his men to stun the frantic woman with a belaying pin, and take her prisoner. But in the confusion, the stricken woman fell backward, into the sea, with a dreadful shriek.

At the sound, the horse snapped its bonds and charged around the deck, trampling many of the pirate's men underhoof. Firing twice with his long-barreled pistols, Lee dropped the Arabian to its knees. Then he had his men throw the still-living horse into the sea.

For a time the stallion seemed almost to ride the swelling waves. Then it gave a cry unlike any heard by mortal men before. It rang out over the wide waters, causing even the fiercest pirate to shiver. Lee clasped his hands to the sides of his head and prayed he would never hear such a sound again.

For a time the cries continued, but they grew fainter as the milk-white steed was carried farther and farther away by the waves. After a while they blended with the cries of the ever-present gulls, and the pirate captain's moment of fear passed.

Then Lee divided up the *señora's* gold. Several fights broke out over the division of the booty. "Avast!" Lee roared. "I'll have no more fighting on my ship!" He pitched one of his men overboard as a warning to the others. An uneasy quiet followed, for the men knew their captain would toss anyone who defied his orders to the sharks.

When they neared Block Island, off the coast of Rhode Island, Lee decided that his ship was too well known in the coastal waters of America. With the *señora*'s gold loaded into a lifeboat, he ordered the ship abandoned and set on fire. Then he and his surviving cutthroats rowed to shore. There they silenced any suspicious locals with a little extra gold.

Soon all but Lee drifted away to other ports and pursuits. With his stolen fortune, Lee no longer felt he needed the life of a pirate. He became a wealthy merchant, and began to woo the daughter of the town judge.

Exactly one year from the night when he had hurled a torch into the rigging of his pirate ship and rowed toward a new life with his stolen gold, Lee was walking along the shore toward his lady's house on the edge of town. Suddenly a glare lit up the sea, and he froze in midstride. Even more chilling was the unearthly cry that issued from the brightness—a cry Lee had heard only once before and had hoped he would never hear again.

The light on the horizon rapidly grew until it was the size of a rising moon, shooting streamers of milk-white and blood-red light across the waves. Now the man could see that it came from a ship, all on fire. Her hull was ablaze; each mast was a pillar of fire; her sails were sheets of flame. She raced shoreward with uncanny speed.

But faster yet came a ghastly white shape: a spectral horse's head rising from the depths. In an instant, the milk-white stallion had emerged from the water. It galloped from wave to wave as though it were crossing land. A moment later it reached the shore, and sped like the wind across the sand to where the hapless Lee stood watching in horror. Never once did the burning eyes—like twin coals in the beast's head—leave Lee's own.

When it was only a few paces from him, the horse stopped, snorting and stamping the ground impatiently. A power he could not resist forced Lee to mount the dreadful steed. The moment he was astride the devil horse, the creature carried him to the highest cliff of the island.

From here Lee could clearly see not only the burning ship, but also, in the water tinted white and red by the ghostly blaze, he could make out the bodies of all those he had slain. They rose from the depths, their arms outstretched to him, beckoning him into their midst. Clearest of all was the image of the wretched *señora,* whose pale, waterlogged skirts seemed to melt into the waves upon which she walked. She pointed her finger at him and smiled a grim smile that turned his insides to ice.

"Have mercy, I beg you!" cried the former pirate.

But the horse shook its head as if it understood his plea. To his horror, Lee saw there was no mercy in the faces of his ghostly victims. With a shudder, he remembered that he had not shown any one of them mercy. All around, the night was filled with their calls: "Join us, join us, join us."

But more terrifying yet was the *señora.* As if his fright were some vast joke, she threw back her head and laughed. At first the sound was as shrill as a seagull's call—but it quickly deepened until it became as loud as the howl of gale winds that would tear a ship apart on the open sea.

Then the ghostly woman made a single gesture with her hand and vanished in a spout of flame.

Suddenly the specter horse leaped into the air and plunged down through the night air as if it were a steep slope. Across the sand it galloped while Lee twisted and cried out in wild despair.

But he was bound to the horse by some fearful spell. Soon the steed was racing across the water lit by the burning ship. All around Lee, half-submerged figures clawed at his boots and clutched at the tails of his coat.

On and on the demon horse rode, until the fiery hull

rose before Lee like a curtain of flame. With an anguished cry, he flung his arms over his eyes.

There was a final burst of twining red and white flame that lit the sea from one end of the island to the other. Then horse and rider, ship and ghosts vanished—extinguished as suddenly as a candle flame.

There was only an expanse of shadow-dark waves rolling endlessly, endlessly shoreward.

The Golden Arm

(British Isles—England)

There was once a handsome but miserly man who traveled far and wide in search of a wife. He cared little that a woman was young or old, pretty or plain, sweet-tempered or shrewish—he only insisted that she be rich, not poor.

At last he found a beautiful woman who was raven-haired, blue-eyed, and rosy-cheeked, with lips as full and ripe as cherries. She had been born without a right arm; but her father was so rich, he had had the finest goldsmith in England fashion her an arm of gold. It was this and her own fortune that made the miser decide to marry her. In truth, he was fonder of her golden arm than of all his wife's other gifts combined.

At first the young woman was in love with her husband, and dreamed that her good nature would sweeten his sour disposition. But his greed and miserliness soon turned her as sharp and bitter as himself. They spent long days and longer nights arguing. Whenever it seemed that she might go away and leave him, he would stroke her cheek, pat her golden arm, and promise to mend his pinchpenny ways.

But he never did. Again and again she would threaten to leave, but she never did. As time went on, the man grew even more tightfisted with their money.

In the depth of winter, his shivering wife said,

We have no wood,
We lack for coals:
Outside the winds howl like lost souls.
Husband, dear, I beg you, please,
Let me buy fuel before we freeze.

But he answered,

Wood and coal cost more each day.
I will not pay and pay and pay,
And so throw all my wealth away.
Not one penny will you get today.

When their underfed horse no longer had the strength
to pull their ancient carriage, his wife pleaded,

Our starving horse
Is skin and bone.
Our greaseless carriage wheels groan.
Husband, dear, I beg you, please,
Let me buy some oats and grease.

But all he would say was,

Oats and grease cost more each day.
I will not pay and pay and pay,
And so throw all my wealth away.
Not one penny will you get today.

They had no food in the larder, and hunger made the
poor woman frantic. She begged,

Our tea is weak,
Our soup is thin,

We live on crusts and turnip skins.
Husband, dear, I beg you, please,
Let me buy some meat and cheese.

But his answer was always the same,

Meat and cheese cost more each day.
I will not pay and pay and pay,
And so throw all my wealth away.
Not one penny will you get today.

Soon his wife grew sickly from lack of food and from loneliness. She would sit by the cold hearth, the fingers of her hand of flesh twined around the fingers of her golden hand, listening to the wind whistle up and down the chimney.

Her husband often sat beside her, just as silent, his eyes drawn always to the golden arm, which seemed to grow more beautiful every day, while her other arm wasted away.

Finally she took to her bed, knowing she would not rise from it again. Her husband sat beside her, stroking the golden arm, while she said:

Husband, as my last request,
I charge you: See that I shall rest
For all eternity
In the gown I wore as bride
With my golden arm beside,
Then shall I slumber peacefully.

He nodded and patted her golden arm. Then she sighed and closed her eyes a final time.

·　　·　　·

After she was dead, her husband put on his tall black hat and long black coat, and even managed to have a few tears in his eyes when he met his wife's family at her funeral. When she was laid to rest in the churchyard, he wept as though his heart were broken.

But as soon as the other mourners were gone, in the dead of night, he returned to the churchyard. There he dug up his wife's coffin and took her golden arm. Then he hurried home with his ghastly treasure, certain that no one would ever know what he had done.

To keep the golden arm safe from thieves, he hid it under his bed pillows. For two nights he fell asleep, dreaming dreams of golden kingdoms.

But on the third night, just as he was drifting into sleep, he suddenly woke up, thinking he had heard footsteps on the staircase.

> *I locked the door with special care,*
> *Surely there is no one there,*

he told himself as he drew the covers up to his chest.
He heard the sound again, a step or two higher.

> *That's just a mouse upon the stair,*
> *Surely there is no one there.*

But he drew the bedclothes up to his chin all the same.
A third time he heard the sound.

> *A drape was moved by restless air—*
> *Surely there is no one there,*

he whispered. Then he drew the blankets up to his nose.

One more time he heard the faint sound of a footstep; now it was just outside the door to his room.

Mustering all his courage, he said aloud,

> *I have no reason to beware:*
> *And yet I must know,* Who is there?

At these words, the ghost of his dead wife glided into the room. She stood at the foot of the bed and stared at him reproachfully.

Pretending not to be afraid, he spoke to the ghost, saying, "Your raven hair's grown lank and gray."

She answered, "The grave has stolen its sheen away."

"Your hollow eyes brim with dismay."

"The grave has stolen my joy away."

"Your cheeks are marked by sad decay."

"The grave has stolen their bloom away."

"Your gown is stained with moss and clay."

"The grave has stolen its beauty away."

"Why have you left your grave this day?"

"To fetch my arm you stole away!"

At this, the man cried out, and backed away from the ghost, as deep into the pillows on his bed as he could. But before he could deny the theft, he felt fingers—hard as steel, cold as the grave—wrap around his throat.

In a moment there was only silence.

In another moment,

> *There was a footfall on the stair,*
> *A gleam of gold,*
> *Then nothing there.*

The Serpent Woman

(Spain)

Long ago, in Spain, near the city of Cordova, there dwelled a man named Don Juan de Amarillo. Though he was far from young himself, he had a handsome young wife, Doña Pepa. No one knew where she came from: All anyone knew was that Don Juan had gone traveling for many years, and had returned with a new wife.

There was something uncanny about her perfect features, dark eyes, and skin as pale as marble and as cool to the touch. Her tall, thin form was strangely flexible and lithe. Though all Don Juan's friends were charmed by her beauty and elegant manners at first, they soon went out of their way to avoid the lady.

There was a *strangeness* about her. When pleased, she swayed her body to and fro with delight. If she was displeased, her head seemed to flatten out, and the touch of her hand was like a bite. She delighted in spreading gossip about her neighbors, whether they had offended her or not.

To all appearances, Don Juan adored his wife. But the servants whispered that they argued from morning to night, and that Don Juan seemed deathly afraid of Doña Pepa—especially when her head flattened in anger. Stories circulated that she was a sorceress who had bewitched the unhappy Don Juan.

.   .   .

Because Don Juan and his wife had no children, the old man decided to leave his wealth to his poor nephew, Don Luis, of whom he was very fond. He invited the young man to come from Aragon for a visit.

Don Luis was an honest, open-hearted young man who quickly became popular with his uncle's servants and friends. Only Doña Pepa disliked him. She seemed disgusted that people should discover that Don Juan had such poor relations.

Whenever she saw the young man, she would smile politely if anyone was watching. But when only he could see, she would shoot him a look of such scorn and hatred that he shuddered. At such moments her head flattened, her eyes grew long and narrow, and she moistened her lips (white with rage) with a hissing sound.

Don Luis lived in constant fear of her, and kept out of her way by every polite means. But she would not let him escape, and always revealed a little more of her hatred to him. He was sure that she hoped to drive him away from his uncle's house and his inheritance. Yet, for love of the kind Don Juan, the young man said nothing.

One night, returning from a visit to a friend, Don Luis lit a candle and headed toward his room. As he walked down the hall, he stumbled over what he thought was a coil of rope. To his horror, the rope uncoiled itself, and a large black snake glided upstairs and disappeared under his uncle's door.

Fearing for Don Juan, he pounded on the door until his uncle opened it and demanded crossly, "Why do you disturb my sleep in the middle of the night?"

"I saw a large black snake creep under your door, my dear uncle," the young man hastily explained.

"Nonsense!" exclaimed Don Juan, turning pale. "There is no serpent here."

"I insist on searching your room," said Don Luis.

"Very well," said his uncle, "but be quick about it."

Don Luis searched everywhere but found nothing. He was so quiet that he did not awaken Doña Pepa, who slept on until the moment he was leaving. Then she suddenly opened her eyes; her head flattened, and her eyes grew long and narrow. The young man quickly left the room with many apologies, but his dreams that night were filled with loathsome snakes.

The next morning, Don Luis found only his aunt when he went down to breakfast.

Doña Pepa stared at him coldly. "I warn you, nephew, you do not belong here," she said. "If you stay, I will teach you the true meaning of fear."

As she said this, she seized him by the wrist. He felt a stinging pain. He threw her hand aside and hurried out. But by the afternoon his arm had begun to swell and throb, until he had to go to the doctor in town.

The doctor examined his arm, noted a wound on his wrist, and said, "That is a serpent's bite."

"No," said Don Luis, "my aunt grabbed my arm in anger."

"I can give you medicine for the bite," said the doctor, who had met Doña Pepa many times. "For the rest, you will have to decide your own course of action."

The two men shared a glance of deep understanding.

That night, as Don Luis climbed into bed, he found the black snake coiled by his feet. Instantly he drew his sword and struck the reptile, cutting off a piece of its tail. The snake reared its head and bared its fangs, preparing to strike. But Don Luis slashed another piece off the tail. Hissing, the snake flowed to the door, then under it.

Don Luis followed it upstairs and saw it disappear under Don Juan's door. Don Luis did not alarm his uncle this time. He decided that the snake had a hiding hole in the wall or floor of the room and would remain hidden from any searchers.

The next morning, Doña Pepa did not appear. "Your aunt has a habit of sleepwalking," Don Juan explained to his nephew. "Last night she stepped on something sharp."

For days, Don Luis did not see his aunt. When she reappeared, she greeted him politely enough, but he noticed that she walked with a limp.

That night, Don Luis was surprised by the snake, which had hidden in a corner of his room. Only his quick reflexes saved him. He spun away from the deadly jaws, grabbed his sword, and struck the creature a few inches below its head. The wounded snake escaped before he could strike it again. When he looked down the hallway, he could see no trace of the thing. But he was sure that it had fled to its secret hiding place in his uncle's room.

For a month afterward, Doña Pepa kept to her darkened room. His uncle explained that she had fallen victim to a fever that required her to rest and avoid all company. At last, looking paler than ever, she appeared and accompanied Don Juan on an errand to Cordova. As she passed Don Luis, her dark eyes flashed with such hatred that he felt it like a blow.

When they were gone, he began a search of their room, determined to find out the secret of the black snake. He looked everywhere, but found nothing. Then, in a chest under a window, he discovered a skin striped like a serpent's. He guessed that the snake had hidden in the chest long enough to shed its skin.

Don Luis was taking the unwholesome thing downstairs when he heard his uncle's carriage returning. Since it was evening, the great fire in the main hall was burning. Without a thought, the young man threw the skin on the fire. It blazed, then quickly crisped and curled into nothing.

Suddenly there was a great commotion at the front door. Servants ran to and fro as Don Juan came in, carrying Doña Pepa, who had fainted. They set her on a couch, where she lay looking very pale and ill. A man was sent to fetch the doctor.

"What happened, dear uncle?" asked Don Luis.

"I don't know, I don't know," his uncle answered. "We had just stepped from the carriage when your aunt suddenly screamed that her skin was on fire. She began to twist about and beat her hands upon her skirt as though it were in flames. A moment later, she fell into my arms."

Don Luis glanced at the fireplace, where not a trace of the snakeskin remained. He remembered his mother telling him, when he was a child, "God sometimes punishes an evil woman by making her become a snake every night for a number of years equal to her crimes."

His thoughts were interrupted when the doctor arrived. He rushed to Doña Pepa's side, took up her hand, and felt for her pulse.

"What is the matter with her?" asked Don Luis.

"She is dead," replied the doctor.

Though Don Juan was genuinely saddened by his wife's untimely death, it seemed to his nephew that a burden of worries had dropped from him. His uncle's friends, arriving to offer comfort, commented that they had not seen the old man looking so well in years.

For a time, Don Luis concerned himself with setting his uncle's affairs in order. He began to think that his aunt's death at the moment he burned the snakeskin was merely an unhappy coincidence.

Then one morning the old woman who was his uncle's most trusted servant confided in Don Luis. "You know, *señor,* I prepared Doña Pepa for burial. While I was busy at my sad work, I saw the figure of a large snake traced upon the length of her body. Was that not strange?"

"Indeed," said Don Luis. "My aunt, God give her rest, took many secrets with her to the grave. And that, I think, is best for all of us."

Loft the Enchanter

(Iceland)

In the Middle Ages there was a boy named Loft, who chose to study magic, learning certain small spells and charms from a hermit who lived in the wilderness a distance from the village. It was rumored that the man had once been a great sorcerer but had lost most of his skill—and his senses—when he probed too deeply into the shadowy world of magic.

"Have a care, Loft," his neighbors warned, "or thou wilt suffer the same fate. Or a worse one!"

But the young man only laughed at them. "I will become the greatest wizard of all," he boasted. "I will hold the most powerful spirits in my hands."

When the good pastor of the village urged him to change his ways, Loft grew angry. He caused a monstrous shape to appear and frighten the pastor's horse while he was crossing a stream swollen with snowmelt. The pastor was tumbled into the raging water and barely escaped with his life. Thereafter, the clergyman offered prayers for Loft's soul but stayed out of his path.

In time, Loft traveled far to the north, where the most powerful sorcerers in the region kept a school for the study of the black arts. There he increased his skills and learned the dangerous secrets of the terrible book called *Greyskin*. In this, the greatest wizards and warlocks of the past had written down many of their most potent spells.

His unceasing pursuit of dark secrets turned his mind to wickedness. While he was still a student he punished a fellow student, a bully who had beaten him. Using magic, Loft created a doorway in a solid wall. From within came elfin music and sweet singing. When the curious boy stepped through it, the wall flowed back together, trapping him forever in the stone. The mystery of his disappearance caused great puzzlement, and more than a little suspicion was cast on Loft. But the young man denied any knowledge of the missing pupil's whereabouts.

Greedy for even more knowledge and power, Loft vowed to conjure up the ghost of the mightiest sorcerer of old, Gottskalk the Cruel. He hoped to compel that spirit to hand over the legendary book *Redskin,* which had been buried with the magician in his secret grave. In this book Gottskalk had gathered the most fearsome spells of old.

On a moonlit night, Loft barred the door to his tower room and began the conjuring spell. But as soon as he started, a voice moaned, "Cease, while there is still time."

"I will not," Loft answered boldly. He continued about his evil business.

A second time the voice warned, "Cease! There is but a little time to save yourself."

"Silence!" Loft commanded.

When Loft had fully cast his spell, the ghost of Gottskalk appeared. The figure was tall and lean, with burning eyes and skin as gray as the grave.

"Thou hast chanted well enough," said the spirit, "for all that thou didst stumble over certain words."

"I command thee, hand over the book *Redskin,*" ordered Loft.

"Upstart," growled the specter. "Dost thou dare to treat me like some mere apprentice? Though thou study for a hundred times a hundred years, thou shalt never force me to surrender *Redskin* to thee."

"Give it here," Loft persisted, extending his hand. "As I have summoned thee, thou must do my bidding."

By the flickering candlelight, the ghost began to grow huge until it bent double at the ceiling. "Arrogant fool," the monstrous shape said with a laugh, "thy doom is sealed, because thou hast tampered with power thou cannot begin to understand."

Then the ghost began to laugh again. The sound was so loud that Loft pressed his hands to his ears. All the while, the vast gray figure continued to grow and swell, until it filled the room and forced Loft out onto the stairway landing.

Standing upright, the ghastly giant pressed its shoulders against the ceiling beams. The wood snapped and masonry rained down as it lifted the roof off the tower.

Loft fled, but the booming laughter followed him down the winding stairs. Suddenly a great foot thrust down through the overhead wreckage and tried to smash him like a bug. Loft threw himself out of the way, tumbling down the remaining steps and landing, bruised and dazed, at the bottom.

He forced himself to his feet, while the whole tower around him heaved and shook as in an earthquake. Walls cracked and falling dust nearly blinded him. From outside he could hear alarms and the cries of masters and students.

Loft stumbled to the stable, saddled his horse, and fled the sorcerers' school. Behind him a voice roared, "Run to the ends of the earth or cross the seven seas, thou shalt *never* escape my vengeance." Then came peals of titanic laughter.

Loft lashed his horse and sped away until the thunderous laughter dwindled to an echo in his ears. The night grew silent.

He rode west for several days and nights. Finally he took refuge in a small hamlet called Stadastadur, where green hills sloped down to the sea. The simple houses built of rough blocks of lava with roofs of turf were a far cry from the grand halls of the school.

Here he found the pastor kindly disposed toward him. The old man charged Loft with the upkeep of the church and grounds; in return, he promised to help Loft study Scripture.

For a long while, Loft refused to leave the blessed grounds of the church. At night he stayed indoors and would only read his Bible and pray.

But in time his fear subsided, as one day became the next and there was no sign of punishment from beyond the grave. At first Loft only dared to venture into the village on errands. Later he would sometimes stroll the outskirts of the town, or go for longer walks in the countryside.

"I have escaped the doom that Gottskalk pronounced on me," he decided. "Whatever power I gave him that night must have faded with the dawn. He cannot reach me in my new life here."

One sunny day not long after this, when the sea was calm and the sky was clear, Loft decided to row out into the cove to do some fishing. Several locals who happened to be gazing seaward later reported to the pastor that they had seen his boat bobbing on gentle waves in the windless afternoon. And they had recognized the figure of the assistant pastor fishing.

Then, to their horror, they saw a huge arm, gray as the

grave and covered with dripping seaweed, rise up out of the sea. It grabbed the boat by the stern and, in a trice, pulled it under the water.

No bit of wreckage—not so much as an oarblade—floated back to shore. Nor was Loft ever seen on earth again.

The Accursed House

(United States—Ohio)

An old farmhouse belonging to a man named Herman Deluse once stood near Gallipolis, Ohio. Though he paid scant attention to his fields or livestock, and the house was little better than a ruin, the old man never lacked for anything. He kept to himself, and discouraged his neighbors from visiting.

Many people suspected that Deluse had been a pirate. He called his place the Isle of Pines, after a notorious gathering place for buccaneers in the West Indies. On those rare occasions when the Reverend Henry Galbraith and his son William visited—the only two callers Deluse would tolerate—the man made no attempt to conceal the strange objects from distant lands and curious weapons that filled his house.

As William grew older, he asked more and more questions about the old man's source of wealth. The boy was sure that Deluse had pirate treasure hidden in the house. Though the old man never appeared to have much money at one time, he always had enough to meet his needs. And he always paid for things with old Spanish gold pieces. This convinced the people of Gallipolis—and young William in particular—that he was a former pirate. Some even suggested that he had moved so far away from the ocean because there was a price on his head.

But all William's efforts to get the old man to reveal the

source of his gold failed. Deluse remained tight-lipped, never providing any clue as to the whereabouts of his treasure—if, indeed, it existed.

When it came time for Deluse to die, he passed away alone, and was buried quietly in the nearby cemetery. Isle of Pines was locked up, while inquiries were made to determine if there were any relatives to claim the estate.

Now, it chanced that while this was going on, the Reverend Galbraith was away for a month-long visit to Cincinnati. He did not know that Herman Deluse had died. One night he returned home in the middle of a terrible storm. The snow was so deep and the road so blocked with drifts and fallen branches that he looked around for shelter.

To his relief, he saw a light. He followed it through the driving snow and recognized the Isle of Pines. As he neared the place, he noted that the light was moving about the house, brightening one darkened room after another. Whatever could old Deluse be up to? he wondered as he knocked. When no one came to the door, he rapped again even more loudly.

But still he was ignored, as the light moved from chamber to chamber. Finally, afraid of freezing to death, the reverend put his shoulder to the door and forced it open.

"Hello, Herman!" he called. "I apologize for my rude entry."

But when the old man at last appeared, carrying a candle, he paid no attention to the clergyman. Instead, he wandered about like a sleepwalker, muttering to himself, searching for something. His visitor tried to strike up a conversation, but Herman persisted in running his hands over each wall, then dropping to his knees and searching the floor.

"What have you lost?" asked the concerned Reverend Galbraith. "Can I help you search?"

Still the old man would not look at him; rather, he carried his candle to a room at the end of the passageway. In the chilly darkness, the reverend could hear him muttering over and over again. The sound made the reverend as uncomfortable as the cold. To ease his mind and body, he set about building a fire in the fireplace. Then, spreading his coat before it, he lay down, intending but a few moments' rest.

Instead, he fell into a deep sleep that lasted the better part of the night. The first light of dawn was just visible through the thinning snow when Reverend Galbraith was roused by Deluse's triumphant cry, " 'Tis here! 'Tis found!"

Pulling his coat around him, the clergyman hurried down the hall to the little room at its end. He was sure that was where the cry had come from.

But when he entered the room, he found no trace of Herman Deluse. Against the northern wall was an unlit candle stub in the curious holder that the old man had carried during his midnight search. In the dust that coated the wall, he could just make out the impression of two hands, as though someone—old Deluse, surely—had pressed his palms against the surface.

More puzzled than ever, Reverend Galbraith called out his friend's name. But though he searched from cellar to attic, he could find no trace of the man. The doors and windows were all shut tight. Nor, as he peered through the early morning dimness, could he see any footsteps in the newfallen snow.

Daunted by this mystery, Reverend Galbraith took his horse from its shelter in the tumbledown barn and continued the rest of the way home, the storm having fully abated.

·   ·   ·

He was welcomed by his wife and son and a good friend —a lawyer named Maren—who had come by on some bit of business that morning. But when he told his story, his wife and son merely glanced at each other, while the lawyer remarked, "Didn't you know that Deluse was dead and buried?"

The clergyman, speechless, merely shook his head.

"You must have been dreaming," said his son. But William's eyes shone with a curious light.

Reverend Galbraith insisted, "I tell you, it happened just as I said."

"If you like," said the lawyer good-naturedly, "we will go there tonight and investigate. Perhaps the ghost will appear again after dark."

"Play the fools if you want!" exclaimed William, adding, "I have business on the other side of town. I won't be back until supper."

By nine o'clock, when the lawyer came by to accompany Reverend Galbraith to Isle of Pines, William had not returned. "I'm relieved he isn't here," the clergyman confessed to Maren. "He seems to have no patience with talk of ghosts."

Together they rode out to the farm. Just as the clergyman had reported, the two men saw a light appearing first at one window, then the next. But when they drew near, the place went suddenly dark.

The front door stood open. "I know that I locked it securely when I left," said Reverend Galbraith.

Inside, all was darkness and silence. The men had brought candles, which they now lighted. In the thick dust on the floor they saw the marks of the clergyman's stay and his footprints. A second set of footprints led purposefully from the front door down the hall to the little room at its end. The door, which had been open that morning, was now shut. Flickering candlelight shone beneath it.

"Someone else has been here since you left," said the lawyer. "And I believe he is still here."

Suddenly from behind the door came a scream, then the sound of a heavy body hitting the floor, then silence.

Trembling, the two men hurried down the passage. Inside the little room they found the northern wall broken open. From the hollow space behind it several pouches had spilled their golden contents, while just below, William Galbraith lay sprawled on the floor, covered with antique Spanish coins.

With a cry, his father stooped to pick him up, then staggered back in horror, for the young man was cold and dead.

A postmortem examination revealed no cause of death, and a jury issued a verdict of death due to a "visitation of God." But Reverend Galbraith remained convinced to the end of his days that his son had been frightened to death by something quite *un*godly in that accursed farmhouse.

Escape up the Tree

(Nigeria)

There was a young man, a hunter, who had some power with charms and magic. Each day, when he set out into the forest, he would place a bowl of water in the sun. Then he would tell his mother, "If this water turns the color of blood, you will know I am in danger. Then you must unchain my three dogs and send them to rescue me."

The old woman always promised that she would do as he asked.

Now it happened that, one day while he was hunting, the young man came to a nearby village. There he found a crowd of people watching as all the unmarried young men tried to toss *ege*, tree seeds, into a hollow calabash shell. Behind the gourd knelt the most beautiful woman the hunter had ever seen.

When the young man asked what was going on, he was told that the woman had promised to marry whichever man could toss the most *ege* into the calabash.

Thinking to try his luck, the hunter took his place at the proper distance from the gourd. The woman glanced up at him and smiled. Now he was more determined than ever to win the contest. Carefully he tossed the seeds one after another into the calabash. Every seed hit its mark, a feat no one else was able to match.

At last the headman of the village declared that the

hunter had won the contest and earned the woman's hand.

She came to him shyly, but when he asked where she lived, she only said, "A great distance from here."

"Then I will take you with me to my home," the man said, "where my mother will welcome you like a daughter."

Now, despite the hunter's skills with magic, he did not realize that the young woman was really a she-devil. She had come to town seeking to lure away a man so that she could satisfy her hunger for human flesh.

After they had walked for a time, the young woman said, "Let us stop in this clearing and rest awhile. I have grown very tired."

Indeed, the young man was feeling weary himself, so he was quite willing to sit down with his back to a tree. Across from him, his bride-to-be sat watching him, smiling and licking her lips.

His eyes closed. He slept. Then an insect stung him on the shoulder, waking him. The woman across from him was no longer a woman. She was changing into a big mass of red eyes and sharp teeth.

Instantly the young man jumped up and climbed into the lower branches of the tree, just as the horror rolled across the clearing toward him. Dozens of sets of teeth snapped at his heels as he scrambled higher and higher.

Now, the she-demon could not climb the tree, but she set to work chewing the trunk, determined to topple it. The hunter recited one of the magical chants he knew, and ordered the tree to grow higher while the trunk grew thicker.

At this, the monster roared in anger. "Whatever power you have," the many mouths said together, "it will not be enough to escape me. You are going to die. I will pick your bones clean and then grind them to dust!"

So saying, the she-devil redoubled her efforts to topple the tree. Again and again the hunter used his chant, but each time he found his magic had grown weaker. The tree would grow only a tiny bit higher; the trunk would thicken only a little more.

"Why have my dogs not come to rescue me?" he wondered.

Now, his mother had taken some clothes to the stream to wash them, so she had not seen the water in the bowl turn blood red. The dogs, sensing something was amiss, were howling and trying to burst their chains. Finally the old woman at the riverbank heard them barking. Gathering up her washing, she ran to the hut.

The moment she saw the blood-red water bubbling in the pot, she gave a frightened cry. Then she unchained her son's three dogs. Instantly they raced into the woods. They reached the clearing just as the mass of teeth, busy at the base of the tree, had bitten almost all the way through the trunk.

The three huge hounds attacked the monstrous thing from all sides. As they worried it, and chased it away from the tree, the hunter slipped down and recovered his spear, which he had left lying on the ground. The dogs had already badly wounded the demon, so the hunter was able to kill it with a single thrust of his spear.

The rolling eyes grew dark; the snapping teeth were stilled; the thing shuddered and died.

Then the hunter returned home with his three dogs. There his mother, overjoyed to see him safe, prepared a great meal, to which she invited all their friends. And the hunter's three faithful dogs ate as well as any of the guests.

The Headrest

(Papua New Guinea)

In the old days, it happened that Inay, a man
from the hills, came to a certain village, leading his little
son by the hand. He spent the day trading with the villagers and talking with them. His boy, Mimau, sat beside
him, silent and smiling shyly. People remarked what a
well-behaved child he was—a blessing to his father and
mother. The women kindly gave father and son taro, bananas, plantains, and sugarcane to eat.

When darkness fell, the stranger went into the *potuma*,
the common house, where the men slept, to spend the
night. He took his son with him. But in the *potuma* was
Kakak, a man of the village who was short-tempered and
violent. When he saw the hill man's child about to fall
asleep beside his father, Kakak raised a great cry. While
two of Kakak's friends held the hill man in check, the
angry villager shook Mimau. "What are you doing here,
boy?" he cried. "Don't you know that this is a house for
men? Go away at once!" Then Kakak beat the little child
and shoved him out of the door into the dirt beyond. The
boy lay still; his spirit had fled his body.

Inay also was expelled from the *potuma*. When he saw
the lifeless form of his son, he gave a cry that echoed from
the distant hills. Then wordlessly, he gathered the body of
his little Mimau in his arms and walked away into the
night. At this Kakak boasted, "That is how I will deal with

all strangers who do not respect our customs." Then, contented, he lay down to sleep.

Only a few days after this it happened that all the people of the village were fishing at the river, so no one noticed Inay creep into the empty *potuma*. When the hill man entered, he carried something in his hands; but when he left, his hands were empty. Still unseen, Inay hurried back to the hills.

At evening, the men of the village returned. After they had eaten, they went into the *potuma* and made ready to sleep, for they were weary after a day spent fishing. In the center of the sleeping place, Kakak saw a headrest carved of wood. Instantly, he claimed it for his own, saying, "This is my pillow. If any of you wish it, you must take it from me in a wrestling match—if you dare."

But the other men, knowing his fierceness and strength, refused to wrestle with him. They just shrugged and let him be. Then Kakak lay down, rested his neck on the carved wooden headrest, and was soon asleep.

In the morning, the men awoke, stretched, and one by one came out of the *potuma* into the village. But Kakak was not among them. It surprised the others that he was still sleeping, for he was usually the first to arise. After a time, one man went in and tried to rouse the fierce man. But when he looked closely, he saw that Kakak was dead. Then he made a great outcry, calling to the other men. When they saw the body, the men were very much afraid. "How could he have died so quickly and quietly?" they asked each other. "Surely he was bewitched."

Kakak was buried, and his name was no longer spoken aloud, as was the custom when someone died. But the man who had first tried to wake him took the headrest for himself. It chanced that he was one of the two who had held back the hill man while Kakak beat his child. That night he lay down to sleep. And in the morning he also was found dead.

"What evil comes into the *potuma* at night that kills men so swiftly?" the villagers wondered fearfully. "Let us watch all through the night to see what shape our enemy takes."

So the men sat up all through the night, but they saw nothing. In the morning they went wearily about their business, unsure whether the evil had truly gone away, or was merely waiting to strike again when they might be less watchful.

In the warmth of the afternoon, one man crept back to the *potuma* to sleep, while all his fellows were fishing. As it happened, this was the second of the two men who had held the hill man while his child was beaten. Seeing the headrest in a corner, he placed it under his neck, sighed contentedly, and was soon fast asleep.

Now his fellows, noticing that he was gone from the riverbank, sent a boy to fetch him. The child had just reached the entrance of the *potuma* when he saw the headrest slide out from under the sleeping man, fly into the air, then fall with great force on the sleeper's head. The man lay dead upon the ground, with the headrest beside him, before the child could so much as cry out a warning.

Fearful that the thing might fall on his own head, the boy ran back to the river, shouting to tell everyone what he had seen.

For a long time the men remained outside the common house, staring at the slain man's body and the headrest beside it. After much discussion, they gathered as much wood as possible and built a great fire in the open space outside the *potuma*. Then the strongest and bravest man went inside and picked up the headrest. To the touch, it seemed nothing more than ordinary wood. But when he neared the bonfire, the headrest began to twist about in his grip, as though it would break free.

With a cry partly of fear and partly of disgust, the man cast the headrest into the hottest part of the flames. Instantly, the wood caught fire. Then, as the villagers watched aghast, it writhed and crawled about the pyre as if it were truly alive. All the while it groaned, "A-ge-ge-ge-ge-ge!" and screamed, "A-ke-ke-ke-ke-ke!" until it was burned to ashes.

Then, from the heart of the dying fire arose a whirlwind. It carried the ashes of the headrest high into the air. There other winds caught them and carried them across the river and over the trees toward the distant hills and a village high in the mountains. They would be a sign to Inay, watching silently from the door of his hut, that vengeance had been exacted for the violence done to his little son.

The Thing in the Woods

(United States—Louisiana)

Once, in the Louisiana backwoods, there was a Cajun woman, Odette, who wanted nothing more than to have a child. But God had not granted her and her husband that gift. Sometimes she would be going about her housework when she would pause and gaze into the yard, imagining a child playing there. Her husband, Alcide, would often say, "I wish I had a son, me. That boy, when he grow up he would be best hunter in whole bayou country and Unite' States, him!"

Poor Odette spent most of her days in church, praying to the Virgin Mary. "Please let me have a *bebe* for Alcide," she would plead. "I promise I would love that child so."

But no child was sent to them.

Now, there was a stretch of woods haunted by the evil one, the devil himself. People were safe as long as they stayed on the path that ran through the forest, but they risked their lives and very souls if they strayed into the trees on either side.

When Odette was a little girl, her mother had often warned her, as she set out to school, "You be careful, Odette! You keep your feets on the road, yes. Don't you go wandering off after a flower or nothing. You walk straight to the schoolhouse and don't pay no mind to nothing else!"

But now, one spring day, as Odette was walking to church along that very road, she spied a beautiful flower growing right beside the path. It had long white petals surrounding a center as red as the finest ruby. So perfect was it that it might have been fashioned by an artist instead of growing wild. A little ways beyond it, she saw another such blossom and another.

"I will take these to church and give them to the Virgin Mary," she said. "Maybe then she will give me a *bebe*, yes?"

So she began to gather a bouquet, and didn't notice that each flower she picked led her deeper into the woods.

Suddenly she heard a sound like a child crying. Looking around anxiously, she spotted something blue under a tree. It was a bundle wrapped in blankets, from which came the child's cries. Instantly Odette dropped her flowers and ran toward it.

Swaddled in the sky-blue cloth was a handsome little baby boy, with skin as white as milk. As she reached down and gently lifted the infant in her arms, he laughed and gurgled in a way that went straight to her heart.

"Has your careless mother left you all alone here?" she asked the child. But the *bebe* only laughed and cooed even louder. Then Odette said to herself, "Maybe the Virgin has answered my prayers by sending me to find this child. I will take him home, yes. He will be a son for Alcide."

With the child gathered in her arms, the young woman hurried out of the woods. But as she neared the road, she remembered she had not thanked the Virgin for giving her this son. She carefully spread out her shawl in the shade of a tree. Upon this she gently set her blue-wrapped bundle. Then she knelt to pray.

But as soon as she had uttered the first words of her prayer, the infant began to yell and shriek. At first she tried to pray in spite of his cries. But he screamed louder and louder, almost as if her prayers were causing him pain.

At last Odette whispered to the Virgin that she would say her prayer of thanksgiving when she got home. "Let me get this *bebe* some milk and put him to bed. Then I'll pray some more, me," she promised.

So she started to pick the little one up. She raised the corner of the blanket that covered his face to speak a soothing word to the squirming baby. But when she did, her heart turned to ice.

No perfect infant with milk-white skin was in her arms. Instead she was holding something that was all black and shiny and ugly—like some beetle. And even as she watched, the thing began to grow, getting bigger and bigger by the minute. Poor Odette was so frightened that she nearly died on the spot.

She dropped the writhing bundle on the ground. To her horror she found she couldn't move: Her legs felt like they were rooted to the spot. Not knowing what else to do, she made the sign of the cross in the air over the tangled blanket, from which two shiny black claws had emerged.

To her everlasting relief, she found that she had done the right thing. The evil one hates the mark of the cross. The creature that was still half hidden gave a yell like forty devils. Then Odette saw something that looked partly like a giant beetle, and partly like a little hunched-up man with shiny insect skin, run off into the woods.

As soon as its cries had died away, Odette found that she could move again.

Still shaking, she hastened directly to the church, where she thanked God and the Virgin for her escape.

The very next day, Alcide and Odette moved far away to Bayou Barataria. There they made a new life for them-

selves, and in time they were blessed with a family of five sons and four daughters. Odette was careful to see that each child said his or her prayers day and night, went to church faithfully, and never went picking flowers in the woods.

King of the Cats

(British Isles—England)

On a chilly winter's evening, a gravedigger's wife sat by the fireside, waiting for her husband to come home. Across from her sat her big black cat, Old Tom, who was half asleep, like his mistress.

"Wherever can the man be?" the woman asked.

"Meow," said Old Tom, stretching his legs.

So they waited and waited.

Suddenly both jumped to hear footsteps pounding up the path. A minute later, the gravedigger, all out of breath, came rushing into the room.

"Who's Tom Tildrum?" he shouted in such a wild way that both his wife and his cat stared at him in surprise.

"Why, what's the matter?" asked his wife. "And why do you want to know who Tom Tildrum is?"

The gravedigger caught his breath and pulled a chair up to the fire. "What an adventure I've had! There I was, digging away at old Mr. Fordyce's grave. Hard work it was, so I paused for a rest, sitting in the hole itself, where the wind couldn't reach me. Then I suppose I dropped off to sleep. How long I remained so, I can't say. But I woke up when I heard a cat's *meow.*"

"Meow," said Old Tom in answer.

"Yes, just like that! So I peeped over the edge of the grave, and what do you think I saw?"

"Now, how could I know that?" his wife said. "Get on with the telling."

"Indeed, I saw nine black cats that looked for all the world like our own Tom here," said her husband. "Each had a white spot on its chest, just like him. And what do you think they were carrying?" he asked his wife.

"You might as well ask Old Tom as ask me," said his wife, who was growing impatient, "since we were both of us sitting by the fire."

"Well, those cats were walking upright, and eight of them were carrying a little coffin on their shoulders. It was covered with a black velvet cloth, and the cloth was all bordered in little gold crowns. The ninth cat—bigger than the others—walked in front. At every third step, he would call out, '*Meow!*' Then the others would all answer together, '*Meow!*' "

"*Meow!*" wailed Old Tom again.

"Yes, just like that!" exclaimed the gravedigger. "And as they came nearer and nearer to me, I could see them even more clearly, because their eyes seemed to shine with a strange green light. Well, they all came toward me, and the leader looked for all the world like—but look at our Tom!" the man said, pointing a finger at the cat on the hearth. "See how he's staring at me! You'd think he understood every word I was saying."

"Go on, go on," said his wife. "Never mind Old Tom."

"Well, as I was saying," the gravedigger continued, "those cats came slowly toward me, marching as solemnly as proper mourners, and every third step crying out, '*Meow!*' in answer to the leader's own '*Meow!*' "

"*Meow!*" bawled Old Tom again.

"Yes, just like that," the man said with a nod. "On they came, until they stood alongside Mr. Fordyce's grave. There they stood still and stared right at me. It made me feel odd, that it did! Those nine pair of glowing green eyes peering at me." Then the man looked at his own cat and

said, "But look at Old Tom. He's staring at me just the way they did. And—bless me!—but there seems to be more green in his eyes than I've ever seen before."

"Go on, go on," said his wife, "finish the story and never mind Old Tom!"

"Where was I?" said the man. "Oh, yes, I recall now. Those nine big cats just stood still, looking at me. Then the one that wasn't carrying the coffin came forward, stood on the edge of the grave gazing down at me, and said—"

"Are you saying that the cat *spoke* to you?" his wife asked, shaking her head in disbelief.

Now it was her husband's turn to grow impatient. "*Yes,* I swear to you, he said to me, in a squeaky voice, 'Tell Tom Tildrum that Tim Toldrum is dead.' I was so unnerved, I ran from the churchyard that very minute. And that's why, when I first came in here, I asked you if you know who Tom Tildrum is. How can I tell Tom Tildrum that Tim Toldrum is dead, if I don't for the life of me know who Tom Tildrum is?"

But his wife suddenly shouted, "Look at Old Tom! *Look at Old Tom!*"

Then the both of them gaped, for Old Tom seemed to grow to twice his normal size, while his eyes blazed with a terrible green light. He shrieked out, "What? Old Tim dead? Then *I'm* King of the Cats!"

With a howl of triumph he rushed up the chimney and was nevermore seen by the gravedigger or his wife.

The Dead Mother

(Russia)

Long, long ago, in the days when the czars ruled Russia, a husband and wife lived in a small village. Though they were poor, and their life from day to day was always hard, they remained happy and loving. The mere sight of Ivan and Anya walking hand-in-hand gave pleasure to their neighbors; their shared joy lightened the labors of farmhand and housewife alike.

When the couple found out that they were to have a child, they were delighted. This was the miracle they had been praying for for years. Now their dearest dream would be fulfilled.

But a dark cloud cast its shadow over their happiness. Shortly after Anya bore a son, she died with the infant resting in her arms. To the last, the poor woman's eyes were fixed on the sweet, tiny face of her sleeping child. The sadness and longing in her eyes shattered the already breaking heart of her husband. A moment later, she sighed her last. Then poor Ivan dropped to his knees beside the bed, holding his wife's cold hand, and moaned and wept until his cries woke the child.

Gently he gathered his son into his arms. How was he to bring up his motherless child alone? he wondered. He determined to do the best that he could. So he hired an old woman named Tatiana to look after the baby while he worked in the fields.

But a strange thing happened. All day long the infant would cry endlessly, refusing all food, refusing to be comforted. Yet, during the deepest hours of the night, he remained so quiet that neither Ivan nor old Tatiana sleeping beside the child's cradle was ever disturbed. One might have thought the baby wasn't there at all.

The old woman grew increasingly worried about why a child so fretful by day should remain strangely silent throughout the night. It seemed to her unnatural. Finally, determined to get to the bottom of the mystery, she decided to stay awake and watch until dawn.

The next night, having settled the baby (who had fussed the whole day) as best she could in his cradle, Tatiana sat on the bench near the hearth. By the fire's glow she mended one of Ivan's shirts. From the room behind the curtain she could hear the man's soft snoring.

As the hour grew late, the baby stopped crying. When Tatiana leaned over the cradle to see if he was asleep, she was surprised to find the baby wide-eyed, with a look on his tiny face that suggested he was watching and listening for something. When the infant first saw her, he smiled and stretched his little arms up to her. Then he seemed to recognize her, and screwed up his face as though he would burst into tears. Startled, the old woman stepped back. Instantly the child sighed, and became as quiet and watchful as before.

Puzzled, Tatiana retreated to her corner by the fireplace. She took up her mending, but kept her eyes on the cradle, hardly daring to breathe. An expectant hush had fallen on the room.

Suddenly, just at midnight, she heard someone softly open the door. Looking up, she saw the figure of a woman, shrouded in veils, tiptoe to the cradle. Tatiana tried to call out, but her voice was frozen in her throat as surely as she herself was frozen to the bench.

The stranger's veils were draped over the cradle. From beneath came the sound of the infant's contented gurgling and occasional chuckles of pleasure.

After what seemed like hours, the veiled figure abandoned the cradle and once again tiptoed to the door. When the door was opened, Tatiana could see streaks of dawn light to the east.

The moment the door shut behind the figure, the old woman was able to rise. She ran to the cradle and looked in, but the baby was sleeping peacefully. Yanking the cottage door wide, she gazed across the yard, which was lightly powdered with the first snow of winter. But she saw no trace of the mysterious woman. Not so much as a single footprint marred the smooth expanse of snow.

Uncertain whether she had really seen anything, or had merely fallen asleep beside the fireplace and dreamed it, the old woman decided to say nothing to Ivan. She would keep watch a second night to see what happened.

But the next night, the same thing happened.

When it happened the third night, she told Ivan what she had seen. Deeply troubled, he called together his kinsfolk to ask their advice on what to do.

After much discussion, they decided to stay with Ivan that same night, to see who came to visit the infant in the dead of night. As soon as the sun set, they all lay down on the floor. Ivan rested with them, with a lighted candle hidden beneath an old earthen pot beside his head. The baby, as though troubled by so many people around his cradle, seemed more restless than ever.

At midnight, the door of the cottage slowly opened, just as Tatiana had said. A silken rustling and the sounds of someone tiptoeing toward the cradle could be heard by all. At that instant, the baby ceased his crying and began to gurgle happily. But the watchers felt their limbs growing heavy and their voices catching in their throats. Only Ivan

was able to resist the weariness long enough to reach over and uncover the candle.

In the light, the spell was broken. Ivan scrambled to his feet and held out the taper toward the veiled figure. His eyes grew wide with astonishment and fear when he recognized his beloved Anya, clad in the very same clothes in which she had been buried. She was on her knees beside the cradle, clutching the child to her heart.

Ivan whispered her name as he took a step closer. But the candle suddenly blazed up. At the same instant, she set the infant down in the crib and gazed mournfully at her tiny son. Then she turned and left the room without a sound, with never a word to Ivan or any of his kinsfolk who stood around the chamber, terror-struck.

Ivan stared as the door closed gently behind Anya. Then, with a soft moan, he stooped and picked up the baby. But his moan quickly turned to cries of anguish when he realized that the child he held in his arms was dead.

Knock . . . Knock . . . Knock . . .

(United States/Canada—urban folklore)

You're wearing *that* to a costume party?" exclaimed Nicole. "That's not a *costume*."

"I'm going as a jogger," said Mark.

"You jog every day. That's only your old gray running suit!"

"So, it's authentic," Mark said. "Anyhow, I didn't have time to come up with a real costume."

"You could have rented one," Nicole pointed out.

"I'm not wasting my hard-earned college money on a giant bunny outfit," he said. "Besides, you're dressed up enough for both of us."

"I'm Queen Guinevere," she explained. "You know, she married King Arthur."

"Yeah, I saw the movie on TV," Mark said. "Um, Nic. Just to put you on yellow alert, my car's been giving me a little trouble."

Nicole sighed. "Will it get us there?"

"Ninety-eight percent certainty."

"And back?" she wondered, then added quickly, "Don't give me the odds: Just get us there. We'll work the rest out later."

"You got it!" Mark said, offering her his arm. "Queen Guinevere, your Toyota awaits."

"Lancelot you're not," she said, laughing. "But you do look pretty good—even in a grungy jogging suit." •

. . .

However, Nicole's high spirits soon evaporated. Mark's car managed nearly to stall out at every stop sign or intersection.

"Are you sure we'll get to the country club?" she asked anxiously.

"Yeah, I'm sure," Mark snapped as the engine sputtered and the car shuddered.

Nicole held her breath, but the problem seemed to correct itself. It wasn't just the car that made her jittery; a heavy fog had settled over the lonely, twisting country road.

"Relax, put on some music," Mark suggested, adding quickly, "—um, on the radio. The cassette player is broken."

Nicole almost said something about what bad shape everything was in, but she decided not to risk an argument. As the hills grew higher, the music stations faded into static. All she could get was a news station.

"Great," she said, making a face. Then she paused, listening intently, as the radio announced:

". . . warning everyone in the Norris Valley area that convicted killer Owen Helms—the so-called Hangman— has escaped from the criminal asylum at Pinecrest . . ."

"That's just at the other end of the valley!" cried Nicole. She was going to *insist* that Mark turn the car around, when two things happened. The radio program dissolved into crackling static, and the car bucked twice and died. Mark used what momentum was left to steer the Toyota to the side of the road. They came to a stop under a tree. Condensed fog dripped from an overhanging branch, *thunk, thunk, thunk.*

Mark turned the ignition key several times, but all the engine would do was gurgle and chuff. Soon even these noises grew weaker. The car refused to start.

Finally Nicole said, "Give it a rest; you're just draining the battery."

Mark slammed his fist against the steering wheel. Then he climbed out, lifted the hood, and fiddled with the engine.

"Try it now!" he'd call every few minutes. But when Nicole turned the key, all she got were clicks. In between, she tried to get some more news on the escaped killer. But the radio just gave off creepy sounds like whispers, so she snapped it off.

"I'm going to have to go and get help. Lucky I wore my jog togs and Nikes after all. I think we're just a few miles from the country club. I'll call a tow truck from there, then have someone bring me back here. I shouldn't be gone more than a half hour or so."

"No way am I staying out here by myself," said Nicole. "Not with the Happy Hangman on the loose."

"Be reasonable, Nic! How are you gonna jog in that costume of yours? And I'm not about to go for a stroll through this freezing fog."

"No, Mark, *please!*"

"If you're really worried, crouch down on the floor in back under the old blanket. If anyone comes along, they'll think the car is empty. But no one will bother you, I promise."

"You also promised to get us to the party," she said. But she was more scared than angry. "Oh, all right—but I *swear* I'm not coming out from under that blanket until I'm sure it's you."

"I'm gonna leave you the keys for safekeeping. When I get back, I'll knock three times, like this." He went *knock . . . knock . . . knock . . .* on the roof of the car, just above the door on the driver's side. "Don't come out until you hear that signal."

"I won't," she said, "believe me."

He kissed her good-bye, watched while she locked and tested both doors, then waved as he jogged away into the fog. The minute he was out of sight, she climbed into the backseat, bunched up in the narrow space, and arranged the musty old blanket over herself.

How long she remained there Nicole wasn't sure. When her legs began to cramp, she brought her watch up to her face without disturbing the blanket and read the illuminated dial. Less than half an hour had passed, but it felt more like years.

Suddenly she heard a *knock* on the roof of the car.

"Mark," she whispered. She was about to throw off the blanket, when she remembered he'd promised to knock *three* times. She had a sudden, sickening feeling that someone else was outside—maybe trying to find a way into the locked car.

"Please, please, knock again," she whispered. "Make it be Mark!"

Knock.

"Once more—please; just once more."

Knock.

She almost laughed out loud with relief . . .

Knock.

Her blood turned to ice water.

Knock . . . knock . . . knock . . .

She froze, hardly daring to breathe, as the knocks continued on and on, spaced just about the same. Each one was like a fist in her stomach.

At first she was sure that the Hangman was trying to get in. Then she imagined that he was so wacko that he was just beating on the car like a child pounding endlessly on a toy drum. Finally she wondered if he *knew* she was inside, and was tormenting her until he smashed a window.

Knock . . . knock . . . knock . . .

"Please, someone, come help me!" she prayed.

Knock . . . knock . . .

Then she heard the sound of heavy boots crunching on the gravel. Voices. And a radio, with a dispatcher's voice giving instructions that she couldn't make out.

Knock.

Then, mercifully, it stopped. Mark must have come. Or the tow truck. Nicole sat up and looked out the window— and screamed!

Two men were staring in at her. After a terrifying, confused moment, she realized that they were police. Behind them she saw the spinning blue and red lights on top of their police car.

"It's okay, young lady," the first officer said. "You can come out now."

Her shaking hand found the lock release. She climbed unsteadily out.

"Where's Mark?" she asked, looking around. "Didn't he come with you?"

"Come to the patrol car," said the second officer. "*Don't look back*—just keep your eyes on the patrol car."

"Why can't I look?" Nicole asked. She turned suddenly and saw Mark's body, still in the gray jogging outfit, hanging from the tree limb above the car.

"Hey!" yelled the officer. "You don't want to see this, miss!" As he reached out to grab her the body started swinging. Nicole watched in horror as one Nike-clad foot began to beat against the roof of the car:

Knock . . . knock . . . knock . . .

Twice Surprised

(*Japan*)

Late one winter night, a schoolteacher was walking along a road that ran beside a rice field. To his surprise, he discovered a lovely young woman seated on a large, white stone at the edge of the field. Her face was hidden from him as she read, by moonlight, a book spread open on her lap.

Surprised to find anyone else on the lonely road so late, the man greeted her politely. She nodded, but did not look up from her book.

"What text are you studying so carefully?" he asked.

Still, she did not answer him or look up.

Finally the teacher said lightly, "Is it wise for you to be alone out here so late at night? This is the hour when ghosts are prowling about, you know. Perhaps I am a ghost myself."

She did not respond to his little joke, but she looked up at him. The top half of her face was a mass of ghastly, glittering eyes all different sizes and colors. The lower half of her face split wide open from side to side, revealing a serpent's jaws with bared fangs. From deep within her throat came a warning growl.

One look at her horrible face, and the teacher fled in terror, his coat thrown over his head for fear he might see that ghastly face again.

The unfortunate man was gasping for breath and still trembling when he reached his home. Though the house

was quite warm, he felt as cold as if he were lost in the heart of a blizzard.

His wife, without looking up from the letter she was writing, asked him, "Why are you so out of breath and distressed?"

"I saw something horrible on my way home," her husband answered. "It must have been a ghost or a demon."

"What did it look like?" she asked.

"It appeared, in the moonlight, to be a beautiful young woman," he said.

"If she was beautiful," his wife asked, her inkbrush gracefully shaping characters on the page in front of her, "why were you frightened?"

"When she looked up at me, her face was horrible! *Horrible!*" said the man, beginning to shake again.

"What did it look like?" his wife asked.

"I cannot describe it," the poor man said, "it was so terrible. One cannot capture in words how frightful that face was."

"But what did it look like?" his wife persisted.

"I cannot tell you what it looked like," the teacher answered helplessly.

"Was it this kind of face?" his wife asked. So saying, she turned away from her letter, toward her husband. Before him was the horrible face he had seen in the moonlight. But now it seemed to grow until it filled the room with dreadful eyes and teeth.

Scared out of his wits, the man gave a cry of terror, then sank senseless to the floor.

When he awoke the next morning, the sun was shining brightly on him as he lay facedown beside a large white stone at the edge of the road.

Notes on Sources

"HOLD HIM, TABB!" This African-American ghost story from Virginia was originally published in the *Southern Workman and Hampton School Record* (Vol. 26, No. 6, June 1897, Hampton, Va.: Hampton Normal & Agricultural Institute). It was reprinted in the *Journal of American Folk-Lore* and in B. A. Botkin's *A Treasury of Southern Folklore: Stories, Ballads, Traditions, and Folkways of the People of the South* (New York: Crown Publishers, 1949). I have closely followed the original narrative, adding only some details and dialogue.

THE WITCHES' EYES. I have retold this story, familiar throughout the southwestern United States and Mexico, from many variant readings, including versions in José Manuel Espinosa's *Spanish Folk-Tales from New Mexico* (Memoirs of the American Folk-Lore Society, Vol. XXX, 1937, New York: Kraus Reprint Company, 1976), Riley Aiken's *Mexican Tales from the Borderland: From the Publications of the Texas Folklore Society* (Dallas: Southern Methodist University Press, 1980), and John O. West's *Mexican-American Folklore: Legends, Songs, Festivals, Proverbs, Crafts, Tales of Saints, of Revolutionaries, and More* (Little Rock: August House, Inc., 1988). Additional details came from numerous sources, including Aurora Lucero-White Lea's *Literary Folklore of the Hispanic Southwest* (San Antonio, Tex.: The Naylor Company, 1953).

THE DUPPY. This original tale incorporates Caribbean folklore from a variety of sources, including Zora Neale Hurston's groundbreaking study of Haitian folklore, *Tell My Horse* (New York: Lippincott & Crowell Publishers, 1938; reprint, New York: HarperCollins, 1989). See also the excellent article "Parallels in West African, West Indian, and North Carolina Folklore" in *North Carolina Folklore* (Vol. XVII, No. 2, November 1969, Raleigh: North Carolina Folklore Society) by David K. Evans, Don Stephen Rice, and Joanne Kline Partin. They note that "duppy" may come from "doorpeep," suggesting something peeping through a keyhole, or from the West African Ashanti *dupon*, referring to the thick roots of certain trees in which duppies may live. In Sierra Leone in West Africa, the word refers to ancestors who watch over villages. In Jamaica it can mean a ghost or other supernatural being. See also *Funk & Wagnalls Standard Dictionary of Folklore, Mythology, and Legend: An Unabridged*

Edition of the Original Work with a Key to Place Names, Cultures, and People, edited by Maria Leach (New York: Harper & Row, Publishers, Inc., 1949, 1950, 1972; paperback reprint, Harper San Francisco, 1982).

TWO SNAKES. Retold from a tale that appears under the title "Two Snakes" in *100 Chinese Myths and Fantasies,* selected and translated by Ding Wangdao (Beijing: Foreign Language Teaching and Research Press; published and printed in Hong Kong, n.d.). The same tale, under the title "The Hunter," appears in *The Man Who Sold a Ghost: Chinese Tales of the 3rd–6th Centuries,* translated by Yang Hsien-Yi and Gladys Yang (Hong Kong: The Commercial Press, 1958, 1977).

THE DRAUG. Retold from various accounts in *Phantoms and Fairies from Norwegian Folklore,* Tor Age Bringsvaerd, translated by Pat Shaw Iversen (Oslo, Norway: Johan Grundt Tanum Forlag, n.d.). Published in cooperation with the Department of Cultural Relations, Ministry of Foreign Affairs. Other accounts are found in Reider Christiansen's *Folktales of Norway* (Chicago: The University of Chicago Press, 1964). Christiansen comments, "The *Draug* . . . is a sinister, malevolent being, and his appearance is an omen of impending disaster. In the tradition his name is identical with Old Norse *draugr,* i.e., ghost, or more precisely, 'a living dead person.' "

THE VAMPIRE CAT. Retold from an account in A. B. Mitford (Lord Redesdale), *Tales of Old Japan* (first published in London in 1871; reprinted, Boston: Charles E. Tuttle, 1966). The tale is also available in many other collections. Additional details were incorporated from Lafcadio Hearn, *Kwaidan: Stories and Studies of Strange Things* (Boston: Houghton, Mifflin, and Company, 1904; reprinted, Boston: Charles E. Tuttle Company, 1971).

WINDIGO ISLAND. This story is a prose retelling, somewhat amplified, of a poem by William Henry Drummond (1854–1907), "The Windigo," originally published in *Johnny Corteau and Other Poems* (1901), and reprinted in *Windigo: An Anthology of Fact and Fantastic Fiction,* edited by John Robert Colombo (Saskatoon, Sask.: Western Prairie Books, 1982; distributed by The University of Nebraska Press). I incorporated details from E. W. Thomson's "Red-Headed Windego" (1895), also reprinted in the Colombo anthology. The lyrics to *"En Roulant Ma Boule"* ("A-rolling My Bowl") come from the chapter titled "Songs of the Voyageurs" in *Were-Wolves and Will-o-the-Wisps: French Tales of Mackinac Retold,* written and illustrated by Dirk Gringhuis (Mackinac Island, Mich.: Mackinac Island State Park Commission, 1974). Additional information and gruesomely fascinating accounts can be found in *Where the Chill Came From: Cree Windigo Tales and Journeys,* gathered and translated by Howard Norman (San Francisco: North Point Press, 1982).

THE HAUNTED INN. This story from classical China has been retold in many versions. Readers might want to consult Bernhardt J. Hurwood's *Passport to the Supernatural* (New York: Taplinger Publishing Company, 1972) and Bernhardt J. Hurwood's *Monsters Galore* (New York: Fawcett Publications, 1965), or

Classical Chinese Tales of the Supernatural and Fantastic: Selections from the Third to the Tenth Century, edited by Karl S. Y. Kao (Bloomington: Indiana University Press, 1985).

THE ROLLING HEAD. I based this tale on accounts by plains people, enhancing the descriptions of Hungry Old Woman and Snake Old Man from parallel texts. Key sources include a Blackfeet account in Lewis Spence, *North American Indians: Myths and Legends* (London: George G. Harrap & Company, 1914; reprinted, London: Bracken Books, 1986) and a Cheyenne narrative in *Indian Tales of North America: An Anthology for the Adult Reader,* edited by Tristram P. Coffin (Philadelphia: American Folklore Society, 1961).

Coffin notes that "the motif of the rolling head is worldwide, being known to Europeans, Indonesians, and Africans, as well as to the North American Indians." The Cheyenne version has the young girl use quills and a root digger to escape the head and save her brother. The Blackfeet tale has two boys use a stick, a stone, and water squeezed from moss. The Modocs of northern California and southern Oregon tell of a monstrous, man-eating head that is disposed of by two old women, who promise to ferry the head across a stream, but push it into the water instead (Jeremiah Curtain, *Myths of the Modocs,* published in 1912; reissued, New York: Benjamin Blom, 1971).

THE CROGLIN GRANGE VAMPIRE. This account first appeared in a book called *In My Solitary Life* by Augustus Hare (4 volumes; London: Allen, 1896–1901), and has been reprinted in *Aidan Chambers' Book of Ghosts and Hauntings* (originally published, London: Longman Young Books, 1973; reissued, Hammondsworth, England: Kestrel Books/Penguin Books, 1981); Raymond T. McNally, *A Clutch of Vampires* (New York: Bell Publishing Company, 1974); and, somewhat recast, in Nancy Garden, *Vampires* (New York: J. B. Lippincott Company, 1973). Charles Harper, in his book *Haunted Houses* (1924), said there was no place called Croglin Grange. Others pointed out that part of Hare's report resembled the novel *Varney the Vampire* (London: 1847).

But in the Spring 1963 issue of *Tomorrow* magazine, F. Clive Ross claimed he visited the area in Britain where the events Hare reported took place. Ross said he met a woman who had known a Mr. Fisher, a member of the family that, according to the story, owned Croglin Grange. Born in the 1860s, Mr. Fisher said he had heard the tale from his grandparents who told him these events happened between 1680 and 1690, rather than 1875, as Hare reported.

THE YARA. This legend is adapted from "The Yara," by Brazilian journalist and historian Affonso Arinhos de Melo Franco (1868–1916), reprinted in *The Golden Land: An Anthology of Latin American Folklore in Literature,* selected, edited, and translated by Harriet de Onis (New York: Alfred A. Knopf, 1948); and from Frances Carpenter, "Mario and the Yara," *South American Wonder Tales* (Chicago and New York: Follett Publishing Company, 1969). Details of Indian life and culture, as well as natural history, came from such sources as Alex Shoumatoff, *The Rivers Amazon* (San Francisco: Sierra Club Books, 1978, revised 1986), and F. Bruce Lamb, *Wizard of the Upper Amazon: The Story of Manuel Cordova-Rios* (Boston: Houghton Mifflin Company, 1971, revised 1974).

Affonso Arinhos de Melo Franco calls the people "the Manaus," but it is unclear whether that names a tribe or merely a village. He might refer to ancestors of the reclusive Waimiri-Atroari tribe, whom Alex Shoumatoff describes in 1978 as living in nine villages 150 miles north of the present-day town of Manaus.

"ME, MYSELF". Adapted from J. F. Campbell, *Popular Tales of the West Highlands, Orally Collected: New Edition* (London: Alexander Gardner Publisher, 1890). Campbell notes that this "is a story which is all over the [Scottish] Highlands in various shapes."

Added facts about the Hebrides Islands come from John McPhee, *The Crofter & the Laird* (New York: Farrar, Straus & Giroux, 1969), which explains: "The large seeds of a treelike West Indian plant called *Entada scandens* have drifted to the shores of [the islands] for thousands of years, and they have always been called fairy eggs. People once wore them around their necks, believing that this protected them from the evil moods of fairies." Other references include Ronald Macdonald Douglas, *Scottish Lore and Folklore* (New York: Beekman House, 1982), and Lillian Beckwith, *The Hills Is Lonely* (New York: E. P. Dutton & Company, 1963), an account of the author's stay in the Hebrides.

ISLAND OF FEAR. Retold from "The Island of the Cannibal" in Arthur C. Parker, *Seneca Myths & Folk Tales* (originally published, Buffalo, New York: Buffalo Historical Society, 1923; reissued, Lincoln: University of Nebraska/ Bison Books, 1989), and "The Friendly Skeleton" in Lewis Spence, *North American Indians: Myths & Legends* (original publication: London: George G. Harrap & Company, 1914; reprinted, London: Bracken Books, 1985). Many other versions have been recorded from Native American storytellers throughout the Northeast region.

THREE WHO SOUGHT DEATH. Adapted from "The Pardoner's Tale" in Geoffrey Chaucer's *The Canterbury Tales,* from *The Works of Geoffrey Chaucer,* edited by F. N. Robinson, second edition (Boston: Houghton Mifflin Company, 1933, 1957). Versions of this moral tale turn up in the literature of ancient India, Arabia, Italy, and central Asia.

SISTER DEATH AND THE HEALER. This widely known Hispanic tale from the Mexican-American border region is rooted in an older story from Spain. Among many versions consulted were those in John O. West, *Mexican-American Folklore: Legends, Songs, Festivals, Proverbs, Crafts, Tales of Saints, of Revolutionaries, and More* (Little Rock: August House, 1988); José Griego y Maestas and Rudolfo A. Anaya, *Cuentos: Tales from the Hispanic Southwest: Bilingual Stories in Spanish and English* (Santa Fe: Museum of New Mexico Press, 1980); and the Editors of Time-Life Books, *The Enchanted World: Tales of Terror* (Chicago:

Time-Life Books, 1987). For my retelling, I borrowed a few details from Spanish counterparts.

THE MOUSE TOWER. Adapted from accounts in *Curious Myths of the Middle Ages* by Reverend Sabine Baring-Gould (London: Rivingtons, 1866), and an account in *The German Legends of the Brothers Grimm, Volume I,* edited and translated by Donald Ward (Philadelphia, Penn.: Institute for the Study of Human Issues Incorporated, 1981). The Grimms' work was originally published in 1816. See also *The Finest Legends of the Rhine* by Wilhelm Ruland (Bonn, Germany: Stollfuss Verlag, 1969).

Baring-Gould argues that the real-life Bishop Hatto was not "hard-hearted and wicked" and that "the [mouse] tower was erected as a station for collecting tolls on vessels passing up and down the river." Maria Leach, editor of *Funk & Wagnalls Standard Dictionary of Folklore, Mythology, and Legend,* notes that stories of a miser devoured by mice or rats in a tower are widespread throughout Germany, Austria, Switzerland, Poland, and Scandinavia.

THE DEVIL AND TOM WALKER. This account was first published in Washington Irving, *Tales of a Traveller* (New York: 1825; reprinted in *The Works of Washington Irving, Volume I,* New York: P. F. Collier, n.d.). Folklorist Richard M. Dorson, in his *Jonathan Draws the Long Bow: New England Popular Tales and Legends* (Cambridge, Mass.: Harvard University Press, 1946), comments that it is a literary tale that has evolved into regional folklore, noting that the story was included in Charles M. Skinner's *Myths and Legends of Our Own Land, Volume I* (Philadelphia: J. B. Lippincott Company, 1896).

I have omitted many of Irving's satirical jabs at business, politics, and social custom, and the subtext about Tom Walker's wife. But the text remains substantially Irving's, with only minimal additions for the sake of continuity or clarity.

THE GREEDY DAUGHTER. Adapted from the story of the same title originally published in R. H. Busk, *The Folk-Lore of Rome* (n.d.), reprinted in *Folk Tales of All Nations,* edited by F. H. Lee (New York: Tudor Publishing Company, 1930). I also consulted the more extended and earthier version titled "Uncle Wolf" in *Italian Folktales,* selected and retold by Italo Calvino, published in Italy in 1956; English translation by George Martin (New York: Harcourt Brace Jovanovich, 1980); available in paperback in *The Pantheon Fairy Tale and Folklore Library* (New York: Random House, 1981).

THE PIRATE. Adapted from Richard H. Dana's eighteenth-century poem "The Buccaneer," reprinted with commentary in Samuel Adams Drake, *A Book of New England Legends and Folk Lore: In Prose and Poetry* (first edition, 1884; revised, 1906; reprinted, Boston: Charles E. Tuttle, 1971). I have also consulted the prose version by Charles M. Skinner in his *Myths and Legends of Our Own Land* (Philadelphia: J. B. Lippincott Company, 1896). These accounts are loosely based on the actual burning of the ship *Palantine* in the winter of 1750–51, which gave rise to many tales about a blazing ghostly vessel.

THE GOLDEN ARM. Adapted and expanded from Joseph Jacobs, *English Fairy Tales* (London, 1890), this tale is akin to such formula stories as the English "Teeny Tiny," in which a teeny-tiny woman takes a teeny-tiny bone from a churchyard to make some teeny-tiny soup, and "Tailypo," from the American South, retold in the first volume of *Short & Shivery* (New York: Bantam Doubleday Dell, 1986).

Folklorist Maria Leach comments in her *The Thing at the Foot of the Bed: And Other Scary Tales* (Cleveland, Ohio: William Collins & World Publishing Company, 1959; reprinted by New York: Bantam Doubleday Dell, 1977), "This is one of the most famous scary stories told. It is said to have been told around every Boy and Girl Scout campfire ever kindled . . . the story Mark Twain used to tell to scare whole audiences."

THE SERPENT WOMAN. This tale has been condensed and rewritten from the story of the same title originally published in Mrs. Middlemore, *Spanish Legendary Tales* (n.d.), reprinted in *Folk Tales of All Nations* edited by F. H. Lee (New York: Tudor Publishing Company, 1930). The story uses the familiar element of the witch transformed into another form (black cat, raven, serpent) and discovered when a wound inflicted on the animal is revealed in its human form. For a parallel, one might look at "The Witch Cat" in my first *Short & Shivery* collection.

There is also an echo of the swan-maiden or seal-maiden motif in which magical beings put aside a coat of feathers or a fishskin to become beautiful, seemingly human women.

LOFT THE ENCHANTER. Adapted from accounts in *Ghosts, Witchcraft, and the Other World: Icelandic Folktales I,* translated by Alan Boucher (Reykjavik, Iceland: Iceland Review Library, 1977) and *Legends of Icelandic Magicians,* translated by Jacqueline Simpson (Cambridge, England: D. S. Brewer, Ltd.; Totowa, N.J.: Rowan and Littlefield, 1975). Additional background details are from *Nagel's Encyclopedia-Guide: Iceland, Third Edition, Completely Revised* (Geneva, Paris, Munich: Nagel Publishers, 1984), and *A Family in Iceland: Families Around the World Series* (New York: The Bookwright Press, 1985).

THE ACCURSED HOUSE. Adapted and expanded from an account in Charles M. Skinner, *Myths & Legends of Our Own Land: Volume II* (Philadelphia: J. B. Lippincott Company, 1896). This story picks up the classic folkloric theme of the ghost who guards a hidden treasure.

ESCAPE UP THE TREE. I based this story on a Nigerian version of a well-known African tale because of the unique form the pursuing creature takes. I have added details from Caribbean versions—clearly from African roots—from the islands of Trinidad, Martinique, Dominica, Guadeloupe, Les Saintes, and Haiti. In these stories, a witch, a female demon, or the devil himself forces a boy/young man to escape up the tree. The tale has similarities to "Brother and Sister" in the first *Short & Shivery* collection. In the United States, a variant story is widely known as "Wiley and the Hairy Man." Here a young boy is eventually trapped by the hairy man or the devil, and is rescued by his three (or four) dogs.

For the originals, see "The Hunter and the Witch" in *Nigerian Folk Tales*, as told by Olawale Idewu and Omotayo Adu (New Brunswick, N.J.: Rutgers University Press, 1961). See also variants grouped under the heading "Escape up the Tree" in *Folk-Lore of the Antilles, French and English, Part III*, by Elsie Clews Parsons (first published by the American Folk-Lore Society in 1943; reprinted, New York: Kraus Reprint Company, 1969). Maria Leach discusses the tale in *God Had a Dog: Folklore of the Dog* (New Brunswick, N.J.: Rutgers University Press, 1961).

THE HEADREST. Retold from Annie Ker's *Papuan Fairy Tales* (c. 1912), a collection of folktales from the northeastern coast of New Guinea, reprinted in F. H. Lee, *Folk Tales of All Nations* (New York: Tudor Publishing Company, 1930). Mrs. Ker lived at a mission compound in New Guinea in 1910.

THE THING IN THE WOODS. Adapted from an account in *Gumbo Ya-Ya: A Collection of Louisiana Folk Tales* by Lyle Saxon, Robert Tallant, and Edward Dryer (first published in 1945 by Louisiana Writers Project Publications; reprinted, New York: Bonanza Books, n.d.). Details of Cajun life and language came from William Faulkner Rushton, *The Cajuns: From Acadia to Louisiana* (New York: Farrar, Straus & Giroux, 1970), and other sources.

The Cajuns live mainly in rural southern Louisiana, are largely Roman Catholic, and are the largest French-speaking group in the United States. "Cajun" comes from "Acadian," referring to the part of Canada to which their ancestors came from France. Those early French settlers immigrated to Louisiana after their farms were seized and burned by the English governor of Nova Scotia in 1755. Henry Wadsworth Longfellow tells the story of their exile in his poem *Evangeline*.

KING OF THE CATS. Adapted from Joseph Jacobs's classic *More English Fairy Tales* (London, 1894). Jacobs's version, which is widely anthologized, was put together by that author from several earlier narratives. He cites five variants of the legend, commenting, "An interesting example of the spread and development of a single anecdote throughout England . . . a tale which is, in its way, as weird and fantastic as E[dgar] A[llan] Poe."

THE DEAD MOTHER. Retold from *Russian Folk Tales* by William R. Shedden-Ralston (London, 1873); reprinted in Bernhardt J. Hurwood, *Passport to the Supernatural: An Occult Compendium from All Ages and Many Lands* (New York: Taplinger Publishing Company, 1972).

KNOCK . . . KNOCK . . . KNOCK . . . A retelling of one of the most popular examples of urban folklore. In *The Vanishing Hitchhiker: American Urban Legends & Their Meanings* (New York: W. W. Norton & Company, 1981), Jan Harold Brunvand offers an extended discussion of this "well-known urban legend that folklorists have named 'The Boyfriend's Death' . . . a story that has traveled rapidly to reach nationwide oral circulation." In *Folklore of Can-*

ada (Canada: McClelland and Stewart, 1976), Edith Fowke refers to "The Boyfriend's Death" as being "widely known today. . . . Such legends are particularly rife among teen-agers, who sometimes call them 'scary stories.' These tales, which are always sworn to be true, are told at social get-togethers such as pajama parties, nights at summer camps, canoe trips, or camp reunions."

TWICE SURPRISED. This is one of the most widely repeated ghost stories in Japan. It is known variously under such titles as "Surprised Twice," "The Terrible Face," "The Ghost Covered with Eyes," "The Face That Grew Long," "The Eyeless Demon in Monjuroku," and "Was It This Kind of Face?"

I have based this retelling on a version in *Ancient Tales in Modern Japan: An Anthology of Japanese Folk Tales,* selected and translated by Fanny Hagin Mayer (Bloomington: Indiana University Press, copublished with *Asian Folklore Studies,* 1984), and on a study of the story and its variants found in *The Yanagita Kunio Guide to the Japanese Folk Tale* by Yanagita Kunio, translated and edited by Fanny Hagin Mayer (Bloomington: Indiana University Press, copublished with *Asian Folklore Studies,* 1986). The latter volume is a translation of *Nihon Mukashibanashi Meii,* originally published in Tokyo in 1948.

About the Author

Robert D. San Souci is the award-winning author of many books for young readers, including *Larger Than Life, Young Merlin, Young Guinevere, Feathertop, The Legend of Sleepy Hollow, Sootface,* and *The Hobyahs.* Widely traveled and a popular speaker, he has lectured in schools, libraries, universities, and conferences in more than thirty states. A native Californian, Robert San Souci lives in the San Francisco Bay Area.